D0757836

PORK CITY

PORK CITY

HOWARD BROWNE

A
JOan
Kahn
BOOK

ST. MARTIN'S PRESS
New York

Copyedited by Daniel Otis
Design by Janet Tingey

Library of Congress Cataloging-in-Publication Data

Browne , Howard, 1908–
Pork city/by Howard Browne.
p.   cm.
"A Joan Kahn Book"
ISBN 0-312-01493-7 : $16.95
I. Title.
PS3503.R8436P6 1988   87-27486
813'.54—dc 19

First Edition

10 9 8 7 6 5 4 3 2 1

FOR DORIS

*Who somehow was able to retain both
her patience and her sanity while
this book was being written*

DEATH OF A LEGMAN

There's two kinds of guys you don't lay a
finger on—men of the cloth and newspaper
slobs.

—Dion O'Banion,
Chicago's North Side gang leader,
1924

1

MONDAY, JUNE 9, 1930

On the last morning of his life, Jake awoke at 9:33. With a second effort he swung his feet to the floor and sat slumped on the edge of the bed, his mind a gray fog in which nothing moved. Finally he groped for the bedside phone and asked the hotel operator to ring the security chief.

A crisp voice said, "Moore speaking."

"This is Jake, Ernie. Any calls?"

"Good morning, Mister Lingle," Moore said. "If you don't mind holding on a second, I'll see."

Waiting, Jake fumbled open the cover of the cedarwood humidor next to the phone and took out one of the three remaining cigars. About to bite off the tip, he hesitated, shrugged resignedly, and dropped the cigar back into the box.

"Mister Lingle?"

"Yeah, Ernie."

"Police Commissioner Russell's office called to remind you you're having dinner tonight with the commissioner; eight-thirty at Henrici's. And Miss Terrell called at eight-forty-five. Said to make sure you telephoned her before one." Moore cleared his throat, added apologetically: "She was quite . . . emphatic about it, Mister Lingle."

Jake grunted sourly. "I'll just bet she was. Anything else?"

"That's about the size of it, sir."

"How's the weather out?"

"Fella couldn't ask for a better day, Mister Lingle. If you know what I mean."

"I'll figure it out. Thanks, Ernie. You get those Cub tickets I sent over?"

"Yes, *sir!* And I certainly thank you, Mister Lingle."

"Forget it," Jake said. He put back the receiver, shucked off his pajamas and padded into the white-tiled bathroom. Adjusting the water temperature to tepid, he stepped under the circular tin showerhead and let the cascading spray cut away the last cobwebs of a mild hangover.

After toweling himself dry, he moved close to the sink and stared analytically at his reflection in the medicine cabinet mirror. The whites of his eyes were undeniably bloodshot, but probably not more than for anyone with his habits and the hours he kept. The patches of gray at his temples seemed larger than before, but the network of fine lines at the outer corners of his seal-brown eyes appeared to be holding their own. He peered closer: no sign of a double chin. Backing off a step, he ran a hand over his bare belly: soft—but reasonably flat. Not all that bad, he told himself smugly, for a bozo pushing thirty-eight.

If he could just get rid of that fucking ulcer. . . .

He brushed his teeth vigorously (ignoring a stab from a neglected molar), shaved, then doused his face and underarms liberally with bay rum. A touch of Stacomb controlled the tendency of his thick black hair to curl at the edges.

Returning to the bedroom, Jake picked out a lightweight suit in blue serge with a thin gray stripe, a belt with an eighteen-carat gold buckle monogrammed AJL in tiny diamonds, a dark blue silk tie, a white Madras shirt, and a new pair of wing-tipped black-and-white oxfords. A display handkerchief, edged in blue, went into the jacket's breast pocket with the points meticulously adjusted. A black billfold with gold corners came off the dresser top and into a hip pocket. The pearl-gray fedora was on the bedroom chair where he'd tossed it shortly after three that morning. He slipped it on, cocked it slightly to the right.

The dresser mirror nodded its approval.

One item missing. Jake briefly reviewed Dr. Gilchrist's warning, dismissed it with a shrug, transferred the cigars from the humidor to a black pigskin case, which he slipped into the inner pocket of his coat.

The tall narrow windows of Suite 2706 faced the east, overlooking Grant Park and, beyond that, the leaden swells of Lake Michigan. The two rooms made up one of the Stevens Hotel's prestigious "permanent" suites, furnished throughout in a kind of Grand Rapids Modern that did nothing for the eye and very little for comfort. Russet drapes in both rooms matched the short-piled carpeting and, for a touch of culture, a three-colored reproduction of the Parthenon, slightly off register, graced the gray wall behind a couch upholstered in a reddish-brown tweed with the texture of armor plate.

While the going rate for all this was three hundred a month, Jake was charged a flat one-fifty with the tacit understanding that he would use his newspaper connection to keep out of print any publicity unfavorable to the hotel. Meanwhile, the bed was comfortable, the bathroom facilities in working order, the floor maids picked up after him, and the valet service took unobtrusive care of his dry cleaning and laundry.

He was across the living room and about to open the corridor door when a sudden sharp spasm of abdominal pain brought him up short, gasping. He turned, staggered back to the couch, collapsed onto the edge and doubled over, pressing both hands against his stomach while taking deep shuddering breaths.

Finally, grudgingly, the cutting edge of pain receded . . . was gone. Jake straightened cautiously, waited to be sure, then dug out a handkerchief and mopped the cold beads of sweat from his face and hands. Such attacks had happened before, but never this severe nor as close together as the last two.

Dr. Gilchrist, not noted for his bedside manner, had made it clear six weeks earlier that he had no patience with idiots. "Any son-vabitch," he'd roared at Jake, "who smokes fifteen cigars a day, swills bathtub gin, sleeps six hours a night and spends the other eighteen stewing over the goddamn stock market is gonna end up with an ulcer. Duodenal. You hear what I'm sayin', asshole?"

But there was more on Jake's mind than the state of his health. He realized now that the con job he'd pulled on Jack Zuta could be a mistake—a big mistake. Not that Jack would try any rough stuff, he was quick to assure himself. Dion O'Banion, dead these past six years, rest his black soul, had put it into words: "Two kinds of guys you don't lay a finger on—men of the cloth and newspaper slobs."

Jake glanced at his wristwatch, started to rise from the couch, then sank back again. Angela Terrell. She'd be sitting by her phone, tight-lipped, sore as a scalded skunk over being stood up last night. He spent a moment or two trying to think of a story plausible enough to placate her, gave up and placed the call from the end-table extension.

The receiver at the other end was lifted in the middle of the first ring. Then silence. Jake hesitated, said, "Angel? That you?"

Those who knew her socially, if not intimately, always spoke glowingly of Angela Terrell's voice: melodic, the purity of a crystal bell, La Scala should have grabbed her years ago. Now, dulcet as ever, the voice spoke. Calmly, quietly, without heat.

"About time, you miserable son of a bitch. Two fucking hours you leave me sitting on my ass in that shitty speakeasy, waiting—"

Jake lowered the receiver. Gutter language from the lips of a woman had long since ceased to be a novelty, but it never failed to embarrass him. Gingerly, he brought the receiver back to his ear. "Angel, will you for Christ's—"

"—looking to get laid, you can go—"

He hung up. Get Angela mad, she talked dirty; that simple. In a day or two she'd call again, soft-spoken, accepting his apologies. End of quarrel . . . till the next time.

He went on sitting there, toying with the thought of breaking off with Angela altogether. It annoyed him that, although the day of the flapper was over and done with, Angela went right on wearing dresses halfway up to her ass, getting blotto on the rotgut she swilled down, and flourishing a silly foot-long cigarette holder like it was a fucking orchestra leader's baton.

They had met four years ago. Jake was at the far end of the bar of a speakeasy on the fifth floor of the Garrick Building, having a quiet drink with a detective from the Warren Avenue station, when a slim girl in her early twenties with shining black hair worn in a shingle bob had climbed onto a table, whipped a pearl-handled .22 revolver out of her bag and began shooting bottles off the back bar. The detective had knocked the gun out of her hand, slapped her twice across the face to get her attention, and was to the point of calling in for a paddy wagon before Jake was able to talk him into giving the girl a pass. By the time he managed to get her out onto Randolph Street and into a cab, Angela Terrell had passed out.

Under the suspicious eye of the cabby, Jake went through the girl's purse, turning up a thick wad of currency and an identification card with the bearer's name and a North Lake Shore Drive address. That last bit of information took her out of the secretary-out-on-a-spree category, since, as Jake was aware, yearly rentals for apartments in that particular building could run as high as ten thousand dollars.

While the cab waited, Jake had turned the befuddled young lady over to the building doorman and given him a look at his press card before leaving.

Two days later, Angela Terrell reached Jake through the paper. She thanked him warmly for keeping her off the police blotter, then invited him to her apartment for a drink. The four rooms turned out to be tastefully and expensively furnished, a superior grade of gin went into the gin rickies, and the bedroom windows gave a spectacular view of the lakefront—something Jake didn't discover till he was out of her bed, out of the shower and fully dressed.

The affair that followed was heated—so much so, in fact, that it was almost two weeks before Jake made any real effort to find out just who Angela actually was. She had vaguely mentioned being from back East, that she was in Chicago to study at the Art Institute, and that her family "had money." "Back East" proved to be Brooklyn, and her father was one Guiliano Torenello, a close associate of a high-ranking figure in New York's branch of the *Unione Siciliana.*

Jake's first reaction was to end the affair. But it would be just like Angela, he decided, to turn her old man loose on him. Most fathers didn't take kindly to somebody screwing their young daughters— virgins or not. Not that Angela had been a virgin at the time, but Jake was reasonably sure that bringing something like that out wouldn't go far in getting him off the hook.

So, Jake fell back on a hoary axiom: in case of doubt, do nothing. In the four years since then, he'd had no reason to regret the decision.

WEDNESDAY, SEPTEMBER 5, 1912

It was more cubbyhole than office, with one grimy window looking out on Madison Street one floor below. The pudgy, balding man in the soiled white shirt put down a newspaper and looked at the young man across the desk from him. "What's on your mind, kid?"

In the bowels of the building, two floors below street level, giant presses were running off the afternoon edition of the Tribune, *the vibrations sending small, rhythmic tremors through the young man's wiry frame. Outside the cubicle, typewriters clattered, pneumatic tubes slammed small brass cylinders into wire baskets, telephones rang impatiently, and male voices overrode the bedlam.*

"Sergeant Russell said I could maybe get a job here, sir," *the young man said.* "If I was to talk to you about it."

"How do you come to know Bill Russell?" *the man asked.*

"His beat's in my neighborhood," *the young man said.* "Jackson and Western. Around there."

"What's your name?"

"Alfred Lingle, sir."

"How old are you, Al?"

"Nineteen, sir."

"How far'd you get in school?"

"I graduated Calhoun High, sir."

"Where'd you work last?"

"At Schoeling's, sir. They sell surgical stuff."

"Why'd you leave?"

"I . . . still work there, sir."

"Then what're you doing here?"

"I guess I'd like to work on a newspaper, sir."

"You guess, huh? Want to be a hot-shot reporter."

"I . . . don't know, sir. I'd just like to work here."

"What're they paying you? At Schoeling's?"

"Fifteen dollars a week, sir."

"Here, you'd start at twelve. Still want a job?"

"Yes, sir."

The balding man eyed the youth appraisingly. Clothes threadbare but neat, took his cap off the minute he walked in, looked you straight in the eye, polite as a Horatio Alger hero, answered your questions straight out and to the point. No wonder Russell had sent him over.

The balding man opened a desk drawer, took out a job application form and tossed it over to the young man. "Fill it out. If you've done nothing worse than second-degree manslaughter, report for work this Sunday. Six A.M. sharp."

After four months as copy boy, Alfred J. Lingle was moved up to cub reporter. Not because a latent talent had suddenly blossomed; it was simply the Tribune's policy.

MONDAY, JUNE 9, 1930

At the lobby newsstand, Jake picked up the early edition of the *Tribune*, slid onto a counter stool at the hotel's coffee shop. Over coffee and toast, he read *Gasoline Alley* and *Moon Mullins* before skimming through the sports section. Finishing, he thought of having Red bring around the car, decided against it. The sky was cloudless, the sun pleasantly warm, and a slight breeze off the lake made the morning just right for a leisurely stroll through Chicago's Loop.

Walking north along Michigan Avenue, Jake paused four times in as many blocks to greet by name and handshake the alderman of the Eighteenth Ward, the current mistress of the city's leading architect, a minor West Side hoodlum who had been useful to Jake in the past, and a detective attached to the state's attorney's staff. Each responded warmly, two asked about his family, the hoodlum "borrowed" a ten-spot and gave Jake a sure-fire tip on a long shot in the fifth at Washington Park.

A block north of Madison, Jake noticed a display of straw hats in a shop window and was reminded that he still wore last winter's gray fedora. Nobody with any claim to class should be caught dead in a felt hat after Decoration Day—especially a snappy dresser like Alfred J. Lingle! He drew open the heavy glass door and went in.

Evidently he was the only customer. A pale slender young man wrapped in faultless blue twill put aside the morning edition of the *Herald-Examiner*, said, "Good morning, sir," and joined him. "May I be of service?"

"Like to see a hat," Jake told him. "A straw hat."

"Certainly, sir." The clerk gestured gracefully at the well-stocked shelves behind him. "Did you have a boater in mind? Or perhaps something in a Panama. Very popular this year."

Jake shrugged. "Might as well have a look at both. Long as I'm at it."

"Of course." The clerk put out a hand. "May I have the one you're wearing?"

Jake complied. The clerk ran a finger under the sweatband, glanced at the underside. "Seven and an eighth."

"Sounds about right."

Two hats came off the shelves and were placed gently on the counter in front of Jake. Each was the top-of-the-line selection; whenever a customer shows up in a custom-tailored suit, a Sulka necktie, and bench-made oxfords, you don't start him off with loss leaders.

Jake took up the Panama and slipped it on as the clerk set a pedestaled mirror in front of him. Self-consciously, Jake peered at his reflection, tilted the hat a little to the right.

"Very becoming," the clerk murmured.

The mirrored image stared back at Jake without approval. Makes me look like a fucking gangster, he thought. Stick a couple of scars on my puss and I could pass for the Big Fella himself.

"Imported from Panama," the clerk said impressively. "Actually woven under water. The way they make them down there."

"That case, I better take the other one," Jake said, straight-faced. "They might've forgot to wring this one out."

The clerk gave him a quarter-inch smile in tribute to his wit. Jake slapped on the stiff-brimmed sailor, set it at a jaunty angle, tried the mirror again, nodded, and got out his wallet. "What's she gonna set me back?"

"That will be twenty-seven fifty, sir."

Jake blinked. Fifteen more than he'd paid for last year's skimmer. He dropped a hundred-dollar bill on the counter. "Swell-looking lid like this, guess it's worth it, huh?"

The clerk moved off, came back with the correct change, and placed the fedora in a paper bag. Jake said, "Mind sticking that away somewhere? I'll pick it up later."

"Glad to oblige, sir," the clerk said. He watched as Jake went out the door and turned left into the avenue. A hundred bucks in one piece. First he'd seen since the stock market hit the skids last October. And judging by the brief gander he'd had at the wallet's contents, there had to be a good twelve or fifteen more just like it in there.

Which meant, the clerk concluded with the normal amount of Chicago-born cynicism, that the chap was either a politician or a bootlegger.

Or both.

The Parkway, a large apartment hotel, stood at the southwest corner of Lincoln Park West and Garfield Avenue on the city's near North Side. It dated back before the turn of the century and, in earlier days, society-page columnists had referred to it as fashionable. A short block to the west was a distinctly unfashionable area of rundown rooming houses, sleazy shops, and the garage where, on a snowy St. Valentine's day a year earlier, five members of the Moran gang, an auto mechanic and a young optometrist had been machine-gunned to death.

By ten o'clock the occupant of an undersized apartment on the Parkway's sixth floor had finished a substantial meal sent up from the hotel coffee shop and smoked his fourth Murad of the morning. Now, wearing only BVDs, he was in front of his bathroom mirror, carefully applying a coat of off-white cosmetic powder to his freshly shaven face. His strong spatulate fingers worked the fine granules into the skin from hairline to the base of his throat, giving his normally sallow complexion an almost ghostly cast.

Finishing, he lit a cigarette and bent close to the glass. His deep-set hazel eyes seemed to have sunk even deeper into their sockets, while his dark-brown hair now looked coal black.

"Jesus!" he muttered. "I look two months dead!"

From the mirror shelf he took a short-haired blond wig, slipped it on and adjusted it with meticulous care. Although this seemed to bring back the normal color to his eyes, the unnatural pallor of his skin, he decided, still left him looking like something out of a fucking cemetery.

He scrubbed his face clean and started over.

By eleven-twenty he was fully dressed: a lightweight gray suit, white shirt, a patternless blue tie and black shoes. Nothing to get him noticed, alone or in a crowd. He went back to the bathroom mirror for a final inspection, made certain the blond wig was firmly in place, then stepped back into the bedroom.

A chifforobe drawer yielded a snub-nosed .38-caliber Colt revolver and a pair of thin black silk dress gloves. The right glove went back into the drawer, the other into the suit jacket's left-hand pocket along with the gun.

Once his stiff-brimmed straw hat was in place and tilted at exactly the right angle, Frankie Foster left the hotel, walked a block west to Clark Street and boarded a southbound trolley to the Loop.

TUESDAY, APRIL 17, 1917

An hour or so before midnight, a deep fog bank had rolled in along San Francisco's waterfront, cutting visibility almost to zero and transforming street lights into pale areolae.

Ferdinand Bruna, eighteen, the collar of his pea coat drawn up to mask most of his face, caught up with the man at the mouth of an alley two blocks from Bixby's Saloon. Slipping softly from the shadows, he slammed the muzzle of a gun into the small of his victim's back.

"Stick 'em up!" he growled . . . and screamed in agony as the heel of a sea boot slammed down on his right foot. He reeled back, caught a subliminal glimpse of a fury-distorted face as his finger closed convulsively on the gun's trigger.

In the heavy fog the sound of the single shot seemed oddly muted. The bullet shattered the victim's heart, killing him instantly.

An hour before dawn that same morning, Bruna climbed into a boxcar attached to a slow-moving eastbound freight train. Pinned to the lining of his heavy coat were four ten-dollar bills and three singles: the profit from his first murder.

Nine days later, Ferdinand Bruna was loading produce trucks for a wholesale grocery firm at Randolph and Halsted on Chicago's West Side.

Company payroll records listed him as Frank Foster.

MONDAY, JUNE 9, 1930

It was shortly before noon when Jake reached the intersection of Clark and Randolph. Sidewalks were multicolored rivers of surging humanity, and, at the moment, vehicular traffic, horns cursing, had ground to a halt while a Checker cab and a bell-clanging streetcar fought over a left turn. At the southwest corner the hulking thirteen-story combined City Hall and Cook County building—not unaffectionately dubbed "the old gray whore" (commonly pronounced "hoor")—wore a shabbily dissolute air under the revealing glare of the midday sun.

Inching past car bumpers and running boards, Jake crossed Clark Street against the lights and was almost at the entrance to the Hotel Sherman when a finger tapped him lightly on the shoulder.

The man behind the finger proved to be Milt Kavanaugh, a North Side precinct captain and a silent partner in a Rogers Park handbook operation. He shook Jake's hand effusively, said, "Figured I'd find you around here. How they hangin', pal?"

Forcing a cordial smile, Jake told him how they were hanging, aware that he'd probably be stuck with this asshole till train time. But while precinct captains normally didn't carry any real clout, Kavanaugh had enough of it to make him somebody you didn't go out of your way to high-hat.

"Listen, Jake," Kavanaugh said, his expression sobering. "I gotta have a talk with you. How's about us tying on the feed bag? I haven't even had breakfast yet."

"A cupa java, maybe," Jake said. "I'm catching the one-thirty to Washington Park."

"Shit, you got plenty time."

They were shown to a corner table in the Sherman's Celtic Grill just off the lobby. A middle-aged waiter in a green jacket and black trousers ignored several already seated patrons to rush over with billboard-sized menus. "Certainly nice to see you again, Mister Lingle."

"How are you, Charlie? And, say, how's the missus doing?"

"Coming out of the hospital end of this week."

"That's swell news, Charlie. Be sure and give her my love."

They ordered and the waiter hurried off. Kavanaugh said, "That's one way to get service: be chummy with the help."

"That's not it," Jake told him. "Waiters, doormen, cabbies—anybody like that—they hear things. Like maybe something that might interest a good friend that works for a newspaper. Otherwise," he added casually, "piss on 'em."

Kavanaugh, his earlier tension back, wasn't listening. He drew his chair closer to the table and leaned toward the man across from him. "Listen, Jake. I just didn't run into you by accident, see? It's about

. . . well, they got this new police captain out at Rogers Park. Fella name of Kelsey? Big guy, big beer belly on 'im?"

Jake nodded. "Yeah, sure. Frank Kelsey. Got transferred outta Hyde Park here couple months back."

"Well anyway," Kavanaugh said, "the point is he's been coming at me. Either I up the present ante, he tells me, or he's gonna close my place of business down on me. I told him, I said to him, 'Christ a'mighty, Captain, I'm just about breaking even, what with the way the economy is and all.' Jake, I'm telling you this fat cocksucker wouldn't even give me the courtesy to finish. Said he's got his own problems, and if I expect—"

He stopped short as a nattily dressed man in his early twenties sauntered up to the table. Cement-gray eyes set close to a blackhead-haunted nose looked at Jake with chronic insolence. With no attempt to keep his voice down, he said, "Got somethin' I'm supposed to tell ya, Jake."

An aura of latent violence seemed to settle in over the three men. At nearby tables diners began to stir uneasily. Jake's expression had gone slowly blank and his hands were motionless on the tabletop. He said softly, "Back off, Arnie. You know better'n to—"

Arnie's rasping voice overrode him. "It's kinda private." He flicked an edged glance at Kavanaugh. "Beat it, you."

The precinct captain started to rise. Jake put a hand on his arm, stopping him. "Sit down, Milt." Nothing in his voice or face betrayed the rage boiling up in him. "Arnie. Don't tell me you coming in here was *Joe's* idea."

"Who else? Joe's kinda sore at yuh, Jake. He says to tell—"

In a carefully controlled voice, Jake said, "I don't give a shit *what* he told you. You go back and tell that Polack prick he ever—*ever*—pulls a stunt like this again, I'll have his balls shoved up his fucking ass for him. Now, you think you can remember that? Or you want to hear it again?"

In the seething silence that followed, two men at the next table stood up quickly and hurried off. Arnie stood rooted. Twice he opened and closed his mouth but no sound came out. Kavanaugh, ashen-faced, sat frozen. Then Arnie took two shuffling steps backward, wheeled, and careened blindly across the room, barely avoiding a collision with a busboy's cart before plunging through the restaurant doors.

Kavanaugh said shakily, "My *God*, Jake! A guy like that? He coulda plugged you! Right here in front of ever'body."

Jake showed him a lopsided grin. "C'mon, Milt. A nice guy like me? Never happen."

The middle-aged waiter wheeled a service cart up to the table, set out their orders, said, "Enjoy your lunch, gentlemen," and vanished. Jake helped himself to a slice of Kavanaugh's toast and began mangling it between sips of coffee.

His earlier euphoria was gone, swept away by his brush with Joe Saltis's messenger. The same sense of uneasiness that had plagued him these past few days was back again. Here lately he seemed to be picking up enemies. That pimp Jack Zuta. Spike O'Donnell. Joe Aiello. Potatoes Kaufman, who he'd palled around with for years. Even the Big Fella, he suddenly realized, had been kind of standoffish here the last couple months.

He took a cigar from the pigskin case, used a kitchen match to ignite the rich golden Cuban tobacco, blew out a plume of oily smoke. So, a couple of pricks were sore at him. Fuck 'em. With what he had on the bastards, he could have them behind bars tomorrow. A couple of them even in the hot squat, if it came down to that. Nobody fucks around with a *Tribune* man.

". . . Milt."

The precinct captain looked up from his ham and eggs. Jake said, "This police captain. Kelsey. How much of a boost has he got you down for?"

"Another eight hundred," Kavanaugh said sourly. "A month. Jake, you got any idea what that'd—"

Jake put up a restraining hand. "It's gonna have to cost you something, Milt. Let's say three hundred. Only, that's for me. For it you get my personal guarantee that Kelsey'll stick with what you're paying him as of now. Okay by you?"

Their eyes met, held briefly, then Kavanaugh nodded. "Okay, Jake. Least it beats the hell outta paying eight hundred."

"Maybe you know Red Kissane?" Jake said. "Big red-headed fella that drives me around?"

"Can't say's I do; no."

"Well anyway, Red'll be dropping in on you around the first of every month. And, Milt . . . it'll have to be cash. No checks."

"Sounds fine," Kavanaugh said dully, then added quickly: "And incident'ly, I sure do appreciate your help in my behalf."

Jake gestured disparagingly. "Glad to do it for you, Milt. This way, both of us end up with a little extra do-re-mi, right?"

He glanced at his watch, drained his coffee cup, got to his feet. "Hate running out on you like this, pal, but I gotta train to catch." He set the new boater at a jaunty angle, said, "See you around," and strode briskly off.

Scowling, Kavanaugh watched Jake enter the hotel lobby, stop to shake hands with one man, slap another on the back, and move on. For three hundred a month, he thought ruefully, the cheap bastard could've at least picked up the fucking check.

A narrow band of black fabric encircled the left sleeve of Bob McLaughlin's tweed suit jacket. He was seated alongside a golden oak desk in a small private office on the third floor of the new Cook County Criminal Courts building. He sat relaxed, legs crossed, arms casually folded across his chest. His expression was placid.

"You called me up, Pat," he said, "and you said to come on over. Okay; you're a cop; you gotta right to ask that, so here I am. This about Gene?"

" 'Tis about Gene," Roche said. Nothing showed in his face.

McLaughlin sighed heavily. "My kid brother's dead, Pat. Dead and buried and his immortal soul in the care of a merciful God. Anyway, that's what Father McBride assures me. So, what's there left to talk about?"

"About who killed him," Roche said flatly. "I'm after finding the man that put two bullets through your brother's head there, hung forty pounds of scrap iron around his neck and dumped him in the Drainage Canal."

McLaughlin flinched visibly. "Jesus, Pat! I *know* how Gene died.

But on the phone I could've told you I got no idea who wanta do a thing like that. Listen: okay, the kid was a little wild—that I give you. But—"

" 'A little wild.' " Roche's narrow lips curled mockingly. "I guess you *could* be saying as much. Seeing as how he bumped off four men that I know of, was mixed in with a couple of jewelry store stickups, and raped a sixteen-year-old high school kid out in Melrose Park not three months ago."

McLaughlin stiffened as a rush of angry blood flooded his already ruddy cheeks. "That, my friend, is a fucking lie! Gene was never one to take a woman against her wishes."

"Horseshit," Roche said contemptuously. "The lass picked your brother outta the mug book. She fingered him in a lineup—as did two witnesses that saw him drag her into the car."

"Gene had an alibi."

"That he did. Four poolroom bums."

They sat unmoving, glowering at each other from across the desk. Traffic sounds from Twenty-sixth Street three floors below floated in through the open window behind Roche's chair.

Normal color began to seep back into McLaughlin's cheeks and he settled slowly back into his seat. ". . . Whatta you want from me, Pat?"

"A lead to who killed your brother. And why."

"C'mon, will ya. Even if I *was* to know, what good's it gonna do? Suppose I said, okay, it was one'a . . . Bugs Moran's boom-boom boys. Or Al Capone's. No matter how much you got on him, no jury's gonna put him away. Not a mob guy, not in this man's town, it wouldn't. And who's to know that better than you?"

McLaughlin pushed his chair back, stood, picked his straw hat off a corner of the desk. "It'll come out, Pat. One'a these days it's gonna come out. And when it does, there'll be no lawyers, no judge, no jury. And I'll tell you why, Pat. Because that louse won't live long enough to blow his fucking nose. That, *I'm* going to see to. Personally."

Roche said wearily, "Go away, boyo. 'Tis no more breath I have to waste on the likes of you."

McLaughlin gave him an empty smile, turned, went to the door and out.

A few moments later, Walter Wendt put his head in. "Pat?"

"C'mon in."

Wendt entered, closed the door and approached the desk. He was a tall sinewy man in his late thirties, with thick black hair, a long, lantern-jawed face pitted with smallpox scars, and deep-set vivid blue eyes that would overlook anything smaller than a virus of the common cold.

He took the chair McLaughlin had vacated, crossed his legs, and lit a Sano cigarette from a crumpled pack. "What'd you get from your loud-mouth friend?"

"Two bits' worth of nothing," Roche said. "But I'm not to be worrying my pretty head; himself has promised to take care of the matter. By personally shooting the arse offa the first hood comes in sight there."

Wendt said, "Everybody's Billy the Kid here lately, you know? Only nine days into the month and we already got eleven of 'em either in the county morgue or fresh in the cemetery. Dodge City. That's what they oughta call this burg."

Roche rose to the bait. "Nothing's wrong with this town that can't be cured, Walter. Go back ten years and there was not one better in the whole U.S. of A. Soon as folks wise up and get rid of the Prohibition, it'll be the end of the Capones, the Morans, the bullets and the bootleg booze. I tell you—"

"Patrick." Grinning, Wendt lifted both palms. "I've heard it all before, remember? Ten times—or are we up to twenty?"

"All right, then." Absently, Roche picked up a surveillance report, eyed it blankly, dropped it back on the desk. "Anything fresh on George Druggan and that what's-her-name McGinnis woman?"

"Talked to the hospital no more'n a half hour ago. Druggan's hanging on by a hair. The dame they expect to pull through."

"Anything on the vine as to who or why?"

"On who, not a peep. The why—that's easy. Happens the Druggans were all set to move Capone beer into some of them borderline joints out on the North Shore. Except that's still Moran territory and

I guess he didn't exactly cotton to the idea, you know? So—triggers got pulled." His lips quirked. "Like I been telling you, Patrick: Dodge City."

"Be taking your kraut arse outta here," Roche said.

THURSDAY, MARCH 11, 1909

They buried Terence Liam Roche on the day following his forty-sixth birthday, while a raw wind whipped off Galway Bay and sullen storm clouds scudded overhead. Nine mourners had gathered at the graveside; of those nine, five were the dead man's tippling cronies from the Rose and Pike public house in Kinvara, four kilometers to the north.

No tears chilled the cheeks of young Patrick Roche, the first born of Terence's two sons. As far back as he could recall he had hated his father, hated him as a whisky-sodden, foul-mouthed tyrant whose vicious temper and drunken cruelties over the years had scarred his sons and hastened the death of his wife only two months before. To Patrick's way of thinking, the man was in no manner deserving of a Christian burial; better he should be dumped into a roadside ditch and covered over with six feet of cowshit.

Father O'Beirn, ignoring the strident screams of atheistic seagulls, intoned the final Latin exhortations, and frozen clods of Lough Neagh clay began thudding against the crude pine coffin. Patrick, now four months past his seventeenth birthday, prodded the shoulder of his brother Tom, sixteen. "We'll be goin' now."

Tom Roche's face was pale and drawn, and fear of the future flickered in his dark eyes. "And where is it we're to be goin'?" he demanded, his voice close to breaking. "You know damned well old man Delaney will be after taking the farm from us before the week is out."

"And welcome to it he is," Patrick said firmly. His brooding expression softened under a sudden smile. "There's a place for us, lad. After the evening Mass I'll be telling you what's in me mind."

Aware that Father O'Beirn was walking slowly toward them, Pat-

rick turned away. "Come along now," he told his brother. "In this one day 'tis enough I've heard of God's infinite wisdom and mercy to do me a lifetime."

The freighter Bonnie M., *bound for New York with a cargo of wool and Scotch, was two days out of Cork Harbor when the second mate found the two teenaged stowaways in the bow chain locker.*

MONDAY, JUNE 9, 1930

After leaving the Sherman Hotel, Jake crossed to the south side of Randolph and walked east. Reminding himself that he was running short of cigars, he stopped off at the smokeshop next to the Triangle restaurant to pick up a handful of Perfecto Garcias, chatted briefly with the man behind the counter, and was on his way out when sight of the shop's phone booth brought him up short.

He really ought to call Helen, he thought guiltily. At least find out how the kids were doing. He liked to think they missed him, but at their ages how could you know.

For a nickel he could find out.

At the door to the booth he hesitated. Say he did call. Before he could get two words out Helen would be all over him for shelling out all that dough for living at a hotel when he had a perfectly good home with his own family. Not that she'd *dream* of expecting him to stick around on *her* account, but Buddy and Lori had every right to have their father there while they were growing up.

She had a reason to beef; he'd be the first to admit it. But after nine years they'd begun to get on each other's nerves. Only natural, seeing as how she expected him to hang around the house in his spare time. Not with all the irons he had in the fire. So, one thing had led to another and he'd pulled out. At least she didn't have any money worries. Even with what the fucking stock market was doing to him here lately.

He'd call her tomorrow, Jake told himself firmly. Absolutely. Or maybe even drive out to the house, talk things over, try to work out something. Then spend some time with the kids, take 'em to River-view Park for hot dogs and the rides. Let 'em know they had a father that by God loved them. A father they could look up to!

With his momentary guilt thus assuaged, Jake lit up a cigar and continued east on Randolph, crossed State Street, gave a quick glance or two at the Marshall Field window displays, then ducked across Wabash Avenue between lights.

Pausing, he looked at his watch. 1:14. No big rush; the special to Washington Park wouldn't be pulling out for another sixteen min-utes—if then. A bare-headed man in a tweed suit yelled, "How ya doin' there, Jake?" from across the street, but the words were drowned out by the clatter of an El train directly overhead.

After Walter Wendt left the office, Roche drifted over to the tall win-dow. Hands clasped behind his back, he stood there looking out to the north at a checkerboard of narrow streets and alleys lined with high-shouldered, peak-roofed houses, most of them one-story clap-board structures behind picket fences or knee-high box-elder hedges. A Bohunk neighborhood. Four churches and nine beer flats inside of two square miles. And one whorehouse, on South Oakley, run by the sister-in-law of Captain Norris at the Nineteenth Precinct.

Still and all, Roche reflected, a good neighborhood. A few local toughs but not much in the way of gang action. Which was one hell of a lot more than could be said for some other sections of town. The wops over around Taylor Street, for instance. Or out around Milton and Oak. You think they'd be satisfied swinging a pickax for the Sanitary District instead of cooking up batches of alky in the family bathroom or using the streets for shooting galleries.

Not just the Italians, either. You had your kikes like that pimp Jack Zuta and the Davey Miller mob out around Kedzie and Roose-velt. And the mackerel-snappers like bullet-proof Spike O'Donnell and that turd Frankie McErlane, who'd as soon shoot your balls off as look at you. And the Polacks. Like Joe Saltis and that crew of his from out back of the stockyards.

Scum from the devil's slop jar, every stinking one of them. Living in high-toned flats, dolled up in three-hundred-buck suits, riding around in fancy Hupmobiles and Packards, giving the whole entire city a bad name. And all because a flock of tight-pussied old maids had sneaked the Prohibition through when nobody was looking. Turning decent God-fearing folks into lawbreakers and making millionaires out of a bunch of murdering bums.

Hell, he had any sense he'd go on the take himself. Like the pols and the judges and ninety percent of the fucking police force. Along with the few bad apples in his own department. With his job he could stick enough under the mattress to be set for life. Take him a year—two at the most. Then travel around, see the world, maybe go back to Ireland and piss on the old man's grave. Or how about Hollywood out there in California? Take the wife and kid there, see the movie stars. Maybe he'd even end up crawling in bed with somebody like Clara Bow. Or that Joan Crawford, her with them swell legs there.

So, how's about it, Pat? All it'd take was a word with the right fella. Like that fat guy with the scars on his face. Okay?

Sure. You bet. He'd get right on it. Hollywood, here we come.

At Michigan Avenue the operator of a newsstand in the shadow of the public library's main branch thrust a *Racing Form* at Jake, gave him change from a pocket in a blue canvas apron with the *Tribune* logo stenciled across the bib. Jake leafed rapidly through the pages to the Washington Park entries, then walked on while scanning the fine print.

"Hey, Jake! Over here!"

He glanced up quickly, startled. Two men he failed to recognize were in the front seat of a dark Willys-Knight sedan standing at the curb. The man on the passenger side called out, "Get down on Hy Schneider in the third. A shoo-in!"

"Already got him," Jake called back. "But thanks just the same."

Teeth clamped firmly on his cigar, his eyes riveted to the tipsheet, Jake went through an arched opening and on down a wide flight of cement steps to a pedestrian tunnel that passed under the avenue and eventually debouched into the Illinois Central suburban train station. Foot traffic was heavy in both directions; Jake was jostled several times but his concentration on the paper remained unbroken. He was disappointed at the odds quoted on two of his earlier picks, but Hy Schneider was listed at seven to one. Five hundred on the nose, he thought, and this could turn out to be one of his lucky days. Here lately the lucky days were coming up farther and farther apart.

He was halfway along the brightly lighted stretch of tunnel when a blond, pale-faced man wearing a gray suit and a straw boater moved briskly up behind him. A snub-nosed revolver seemed to blossom suddenly in his left hand. He placed the muzzle close to the back of Jake's head and fired a single shot into the base of his brain.

Alfred J. Lingle, thirty-eight, veteran crime-beat legman for the *Chicago Tribune*, was already dead when his body crashed face down against the subway floor.

AFTERSHOCKS

Chicago ain't no sissy town.

—*Michael "Hinky Dink" McKenna,*
alderman, First Ward,
1908

2

The signal light changed. Officer Anthony Ruthy blew his whistle and held up a white-gloved palm. Eastbound traffic entering Michigan Avenue from Randolph Street obediently ground to a halt. Before Ruthy could wave on the opposite lines of cars, a new Ford station wagon raced through the red light and made a tire-squealing left turn into the avenue.

A furious burst of shrill notes from Ruthy's whistle shocked the station wagon's driver into slamming on his brakes and pulling hastily over to the curb as northbound traffic bore down on him.

The two men in the front seat sat frozen as Ruthy strode up to the open window on the driver's side. "Fuck's the matter with you guys?" he roared, reaching for his citation pad. "Yuh blind or somethin'?"

"Honest to God, Officer," the driver said contritely, "I swear I didn't even—"

From somewhere off to Ruthy's left a man's voice yelled hoarsely, "Stop him! Stop that guy!"

Ruthy turned quickly, reaching for his gun. A slender man in a gray suit and straw hat had dashed out into the avenue, racing toward the Randolph Street intersection with two men in hot pursuit some twenty yards behind him.

Instinctively Ruthy leveled his gun at the fleeing figure, lowered it (you don't shoot a man for maybe just grabbing some dame's pocketbook), and joined in the chase.

Reaching the far corner, the gunman sprinted west along Raldolph, plowing a path through pedestrians while maintaining a precarious lead over his pursuers. Halfway down the block the mouth of an alleyway yawned. The killer veered sharply left into it and disappeared.

Ruthy entered the alley at a run, then after a few steps slowed to a halt, his breathing labored. No one in sight. A few yards farther along, the passageway angled sharply to the left and, Ruthy knew, opened onto busy Wabash Avenue.

The chase was over.

The other two members of the posse joined him, panting. Ruthy gave them a frustrated scowl. "Somebody wanta tell me what he done?"

"Shot some fella," a stocky, heavily tanned man told him. "Back in that I. C. underpass."

"Hell you say. Killed him?"

"Sure looked like it to me," the second man said.

A teenaged boy in a broken-billed cap and tan coveralls came hesitantly up to Ruthy. "That guy you was chasin' after there?"

"So what about him?"

The young man said, "Well, I seen him trun this away," and put a black silk glove in Ruthy's hand.

At the turn of the century, the Lexington Hotel, at Michigan Avenue and East Twenty-second Street, had been a fashionable address. Now it was a moldering relic, its neighbors automobile agencies, small manufacturing plants and—through the courtesy of Alderman "Bathhouse John" Coughlin—four gin mills masquerading as run-down cafés.

In a four-room suite on the Lexington's sixth floor, Alphonse Capone, in a silk lounging robe, dark trousers and a white silk shirt, was having lunch at his office desk. The three telephones were pushed aside to make room for a mammoth plate of pasta drowned in meat sauce. And as he shoveled in the dripping strands of spaghetti, he talked.

"Me—I'm a businessman. Just like Henry Ford or the guy runs General Motors. Only the way the newspapers and the cops talk you'd think I go around with a big black machine gun shooting people. Listen to them, I killed more guys got bumped off in the war. That's a lotta bull. How you think my wife and ten-year-old boy feels reading something like that, huh?

"Ever'body says I'm in the beer business. They say that about a lotta men all over this great country of ours. Sure, we got a law against beer and whiskey. Only, law or not, you notice the swells up on the Gold Coast and Lake Shore serve the stuff at their fancy parties. Now I ask you: how come it's okay for them to drink it but wrong to make it?"

He paused there, used an Irish linen napkin to wipe sauce off his chin. His audience—not including the two unobtrusive young bodyguards at the far end of the large room—was a Miss Rosemary Evans, twenty-two, a reporter in town from Omaha, Nebraska, to visit her uncle, a municipal court judge. Rosemary had wistfully mentioned to him her dream of actually interviewing a real gangster: "It would be such a divine *scoop*, Uncle Harry!"

What the Omaha relatives didn't know was that Uncle Harry had been on the Capone payroll for the past five years.

"Lemme tell you something else, young lady," Capone was saying. "People keep calling me Italian. Well, they're all wet, see? I'm an American, not some fu—, some goombah from the Old Country. Born back in Brooklyn—on Navy Street if you wanta know. Okay, so my fadder—*father*—and mother come over on the boat. From Naples, you know?"

Rosemary, the notebook on her knee forgotten, couldn't take her eyes off the man. He seemed so—so *average*—not at all like the stories she'd heard about him. And he wasn't a short man at all; at least six feet. Maybe because he was so . . . well, fat . . . made him seem shorter. The truth was, he looked almost exactly like Mr. Rossini who owned the hardware store back home. She tried to imagine Mr. Rossini killing people with a machine gun. It was to laugh! Why, Mr. Capone even had pictures of George Washington and Abraham Lincoln on one of the walls, along with some other man she wasn't able to place at the moment. You couldn't tell her a really *evil* person would do something like that!

Alphonse Capone pushed aside the empty plate, gulped from his wineglass and took a cigar from an ornately carved teak humidor. "Something else I'm gonna tell you a lot of people don't know." He paused to light the cigar, using a kitchen match from a pocket of his robe. "I fought in the war for my country. Seventy-ninth Division, over in France." He ran a hand over the two parallel three-inch scars on his left cheek. "That's how I got these. Load of shrapnel right in the kisser. Put me in the hospital over there for—"

One of the telephones rang. Capone, annoyed, gestured an apology and scooped up the receiver. "Yeah?"

The receiver diaphragm rattled under the caller's excited response. Fascinated, Miss Evans watched the gang leader's pudgy frame stiffen with shock and the soft brown eyes chill over.

"*Jake* Lingle?" he bellowed. "You shittin' me, Danny?" The diaphragm rattled again. "What kinda stupid prick'd do a—"

Catching a glimpse of Rosemary Evans's disapproving expression, Capone stopped short, snapped, "Get over here, Danny," slammed down the receiver, slumped back in the leather swivel chair and glared at the reporter.

"Wanta know somethin', lady?" he snapped. "I don't like bobbed hair on a dame."

Taken aback by the non sequitur, the girl flushed to the roots of her shingle cut. "Really, sir," she said icily. "I fail to see what—"

An annoyed gesture cut her short. "G'wan, kid. Get your ass outta here."

Rosemary Evans had had her scoop.

THURSDAY, JULY 25, 1918

A chill, intermittent rain had made this a slow night at the Harvard Inn (Francesco Uale, prop.). Three longshoremen were drinking beer and matching quarters at the bar, a lone diner picked listlessly at a fish dinner, while at a rear table Emilia Portola, seventeen, sat waiting for her boyfriend to show up.

Lounging at the far end of the bar, the Inn's nineteen-year-old bouncer and second-string bartender was eyeing Emilia with mildly erotic interest. Close to six feet, lithe and powerfully built, his iron fists and ruthless handling of troublemakers made this particular saloon one of the more problem-free joints on Brooklyn's Coney Island waterfront.

Another ten minutes passed. Outside, the rain was beginning to let up. The bouncer straightened casually and sauntered over to Emilia's table.

The slender dark-haired girl looked up and smiled tentatively as he drew out the chair next to her and sat down, his back to the street door. He gave her a moment to take an appreciative gander at his striped silk shirt and bright green sleeve garters before he spoke.

"Galooch still givin' yuh the run-around, huh, Emmy?" His voice was soft, deep, oddly hypnotic. "When yuh gonna wise up, he's just stringin' yuh along?"

Her smile faded. "Don't be a pill," she said crossly. "Frankie's okay."

"For some girls, maybe." He reached over, put a hand on her arm. "Not you, babe. Yuh got too much class to go wastin' it on a mug like him."

She glanced briefly at the hand on her arm, then up at him. Her smile was faintly mocking. "Maybe somebody like you, huh? Just asking."

He shrugged, gestured expansively. "Lemme tell yuh somethin', kiddo. Yuh sure could do a lot worse."

Neither of them noticed as the street door opened and a lean, wiry young man wearing a raincoat came in. He glanced quickly about, saw the couple at the far end of the room, and walked toward them as the bouncer transferred his hand smoothly from Emilia Portola's arm to her left knee.

Before the girl could react, a hand closed on the back of the *bouncer's chair and yanked it from under him, dropping him heavily to the floor.*

By the time Alphonse Caponi had scrambled catlike to his feet, Frank Galluccio, a twenty-two-year-old steamfitter, was already closing in. A knife blade glinted in the saloon's dim light, lashed out at the young bouncer's throat.

Caponi, his reflexes honed by a life in Brooklyn's meaner streets, was able to keep the blade from its intended target. Still it managed to carve three quick, deep slashes along his left cheek and jawline before a granite fist exploded against the steamfitter's chin, knocking him across three nearby tables and, unconscious, to the floor.

Only the quick intervention of the bartender and the three longshoremen kept Frank Galluccio from death by his own knife.

MONDAY, JUNE 9, 1930

"I'm sure I don't have to tell you, Millie," Jack Zuta said, "that the house rule is two towels each trick. No exceptions. That's understood, right?"

"Yessir." Millie Koslak fought to keep her voice steady. She'd known all along she'd never get away with it. This guy was no chump; he'd been mixed up in the life before she was even born. It was just that Larry had been so damned desperate for money. . . .

"Now," Zuta went on, "last night you were on from midnight to eight. In the schoolroom. That correct?"

"Yessir."

They were in a room on the third floor of what was once a small hotel in the heart of the city's skid row on the near West Side. Zuta's golden oak swivel chair was sandwiched between a battered rolltop desk and a cheap pine table holding an ancient adding machine, an untidy pile of ledgers, and an ashtray loaded with the butts of Omar cigarettes. A wall calendar above the desk advertised the virtues of the Edward Hines Lumber Company.

Zuta reached out a flabby hand and picked the top ledger off the pile, thumbed to one of the pages, and looked up at the woman seated across the table from him.

"The towel count," he said, "for last night's midnight-to-eight shift is two hundred fourteen. Dividing that by two means a hundred and seven johns climbed those stairs. Ten dollars a trick: one thousand seventy dollars."

He flipped the ledger shut and leaned back. "But you turned in nine hundred and ten dollars, Millie. One-sixty short. Why?"

He knows why, she thought bitterly. This is a game to him; cat-and-mouse shit. She was aware of her sweating palms, of the tiny tremors in her knees. "Sometimes," she ventured in a voice she knew would convince nobody, "mistakes get made. Like in the towel count. You know?"

"*I* made that count, Millie. Twice. Twice I went through two hundred and fourteen whore-stinking towels." His voice took on a wintry edge. "When Lou gets a short count three nights in a row, he calls me. But you wouldn't know that."

He lunged to his feet, came quickly around the table to loom over her. "It's the customers supposed to get fucked, sister. Not me. Not by some stupid cunt thinks she can short the till on me." She shrank back, terrified, as he brought his face inches from hers. "Four hundred and eighty bucks, honey." He slapped a palm savagely against the tabletop. "Get it here! By noon tomorrow. And I mean—every—fucking—penny of it!"

She was suddenly aware of a warm wetness on the inner sides of her thighs ("My God, I'm pissing my pants!"), and began to shake uncontrollably. "Y-y-yessir! I'll get— Please believe— Tomorrow! I'll—"

The rush of broken words ended in a spate of tears. The man straightened and went back to his chair. Silence folded in around them, broken only by the woman's sobs and the mutter of traffic three floors below the open window.

". . . Millie."

Her head came up slowly.

"Beat it."

She rose woodenly and went to the door. As she opened it, the man at the table said, "Four hundred and eighty dollars. By noon."

The door closed softly behind her.

Zuta sat back and considered. There was no way she could come up with that kind of dough—least not in one piece. Which meant he had a decision to make: keep her on and take a bite out of her paychecks or hand her over to one of the South Side nigger cribs. She'd been around for years, but there was still a lot of miles left between her and the ashcan. Either way, an example had to be set. Give the rest of the help something to think twice about. Case they got any funny ideas of their own.

He picked up the phone, pushed a button set in its base.

". . . Albert? . . . Sol around? . . . Put him on. . . . It's Jack, Sol. You know this bimbo we got on nights in the schoolroom? Millie somebody? . . . Yeah, that's the one. Well, it just so happens she went and stepped outta line on us. What I want you to do for me is sic a couple of the boys on her. . . . No-no; nothing like that. Some sore ribs and a maybe a shiner or two. . . . Good."

He hung up the receiver, leaned back in the chair, and looked at his wristwatch. 2:17. Where *is* the son of a bitch? Should've been here easy twenty minutes ago. He bent to fumble an Omar out of the pack next to the phone, got it burning, emptied the ashtray into the wastebasket and slumped back again.

Nerve of that dumb broad trying to pull a stunt like that! Not that he was much surprised; he'd been up to his ass in whores since he put together a stable of his classmates while still in high school back in Middlesboro. Eight (come to think of it, nine) of the horniest quiffs in that end of Kentucky—and even back then, damn near thirty years ago, kids or not, he'd had to get tough with them.

He remembered something Willie Bioff told him a few years back. "Any time one'a your bags gets too far outta line on you, take a handful of powdered ice and shove it right up her twat. Christ, way they yell, it's like you shoved a fucking blowtorch up there on 'em!" Then Willie had turned on that lopsided grin of his and added: "And the nice thing about it, Jack, it don't damage the merchandise any."

He pushed the chair back sharply, got to his feet and moved over near the window to turn on the radio: a Stromberg-Carlson super-heterodyne console set. Two years earlier, when he'd thrown in with the Aiello-Moran outfit out on the North Side, Joe Aiello had sent the machine over as a token of appreciation. Not a bad guy—Joe. At least not for a wop.

He pinched out the cigarette, stepped to the window and stood staring blankly down at the light flow of traffic along Monroe Street. From the radio came the strains of "Singin' in the Rain," featuring a barrel-house piano and a wailing clarinet. A patrol car out of the Desplaines station stopped at the curb across from the hotel. Two harness cops got out, crossed the sidewalk leisurely, ignored a sleeping wino, and went into a blind pig masquerading as a confectionery store. . . .

Two-thirty-three. At the back of his mind a small pustule of worry was beginning to balloon into outright panic. His man should have been here by this time. It was going to turn out to have been a shitty idea all along; he knew that now. Letting some prick make him look like a fucking idiot had made him *act* like one. And here he'd always thought of himself as a guy who played things close to the vest, who didn't go off half-cocked!

Behind him the door opened and Frankie Foster came in.

3

"Where the hell you been?"

Foster stared open-mouthed at the furious pander. "Whadda yuh mean, where've I been? I was hungry, for chrissake. So I stopped to eat somethin'. Okay?"

"You could've *called* me!"

Foster spread his hands and shrugged an apology. "Yeah. You're right. I shoulda called you."

"So? What happened?"

Slowly Foster brought up his left hand, put the forefinger behind his ear. "Bang," he said softly. Then he grinned.

Zuta was aware of a heady surge of satisfaction. ("I want that fifty grand back, Jake." "Go fuck yourself, pimp.") He said, "Nice clean getaway, huh?"

"Nothin' else but. Some traffic cop tried to be a hero. Except he couldn't run all that good."

Zuta turned off the radio, went back to the desk and sank into the swivel chair. Foster lit a cigarette, dropped into the chair used by Zuta's earlier visitor . . . and bounded to his feet.

"This fuckin' thing's wet!" he sputtered, brushing angrily at his buttocks.

Zuta managed to suppress a smile. He drew open a desk drawer, took out a dustcloth and tossed it to Foster. "I had to chew out one of the girls from downstairs and she musta got a little excited."

"Swell!" Foster snapped, fuming. "So she goes and pisses her pants and I have to go and *set* in it!" He sniffed cautiously at his fingers, made a face, and, after using the cloth to scrub the chair seat dry, sat down across from the pander.

Zuta's earlier nervousness was beginning to seep back. "Frank. Listen to me. You're positive you got the right man? I have to be sure."

"Aw c'mon, Jack," Foster said, insulted. "Whadda yuh take me for—some greener? A'course I got the right guy. Seen him I don't know how many times out around Diversey and Clark. Hell, Ted Newberry gave me a knock-down to him one night at the Rienzi. Shook his fucking hand, you wanta know the truth."

Zuta nodded, satisfied. "Long as you're sure." He bent to open a bottom drawer of the rolltop desk and lift out a metal cash box. Placing it on the table, he fished a key from the watch pocket of his pants, unlocked the box and turned back the lid. The interior was crammed with banded packets of currency.

"Five thousand. Right?"

Foster wet his lips, nodded shortly. "Right."

The man across from him removed two of the bundles and handed them over. As they disappeared into an inner pocket of Foster's jacket, Zuta freed two bills from one of the remaining packets and dropped them on the table in front of Foster. "A little traveling money. They tell me Los Angeles is a great place to be this time'a year."

Foster stared at him, confused. "What's wrong with right here? Cubs got a home stand comin' up, for chrissake."

"Think about it a minute," Zuta said patiently. "A newspaper re-porter—a *Tribune* reporter—just got handed his wings. That's big time, Frank; if I know anything, this town's got to be burning up for the next month—maybe two. And I don't think it's smart for you to be around. Get me?"

Scowling, Foster got out his wallet and tucked the two bills away. "Los Angeles," he muttered. "I don't know anybody out there."

"Look up a friend of mine," Zuta said. "Joe Ross at the Hollywood Hotel. Joe's usually got something on the fire he can cut you in on."

Shrugging in surrender, Foster stood up, put his wallet away. "They don't even have a ball club, you know that? Palm trees is all. A buncha fuckin' palm trees!"

"Call me in a couple weeks," Zuta said. "But no mail."

At the door, Foster paused to look back at the man behind the table. "Just for the hell of it, Jack, lemme ask you what you had against the guy."

His expression impassive, Zuta said, "A double cross, Frank. I can't afford to be played for a sucker. Bad for business."

They had stripped him to the skin, wired a five-inch yellow name tag to the big toe of his left foot, covered him with a threadbare white muslin sheet, and left him on a zinc-coated wooden table near the far wall of the large subterranean chamber. The room's temperature, a notch or two above the freezing point, had formed patches of condensation on the rough cement walls.

He was not alone. Four of the remaining seven tables were occupied by other draped figures. His nearest neighbor, the late Elmer Washington, twenty-four and ebon-skinned, had been shot dead while trying to run a pair of shaved dice into a South Side alley crap game.

In the morgue office at the north end of the big room, detectives Schuler and Moriarity sat at an unpainted deal table and sorted through the contents of the dead reporter's pockets. On the wall behind them a campaign poster, long out of date, yelled:

THE GANGS MUST GO!
RE-ELECT
ANTON J. CERMAK
President Cook County Board of Commissioners

Schuler pulled the black wallet from the pile of effects and removed the thin sheaf of currency. He glanced up quickly. The morgue attendant, back turned, was at his desk using a pencil and the point of his tongue to fill out a report.

Moriarity, bemused, was running the ball of his thumb lightly over the small diamonds encrusting the gold belt buckle. Still eyeing the morgue attendant, Schuler put a hand on his partner's arm.

Moriarity looked up. His eyes widened as Schuler silently fanned out sixteen hundred-dollar bills.

Among the items officially listed as having been found on the body of Alfred J. Lingle, deceased, was a wallet containing fourteen hundred dollars in currency.

Statement made by Mrs. Abigail Wilson, 8126 Vernon Avenue, Chicago, Ill., to Commissioner of Detectives John Stege, Chicago Police Department, June 10, 1930.

Q: Now, Mrs. Wilson, can you tell us please where you were about one-thirty on the afternoon of June 9 of this year?

A: Yes, sir. I was downstairs in that tunnel that goes under Michigan Avenue where Randolph Street comes in.

Q: By "tunnel," I take it you are referring to the underpass leading to the Illinois Central railway station?

A: Yes, sir. I am.

Q: And what direction were you going? By that I mean were you going away from or toward the station itself?

A: Away from the station. I had had lunch with my daughter at the junior high school over near Cottage Grove and Seventy-eighth, then came downtown on the I.C. to do some shopping at the Boston Store.

Q: After leaving the train and while walking through the underpass previously referred to, did you observe anything that seemed out of the ordinary?

A: I should say I certainly did, yes, sir.

Q: Would you please tell us in your own words, Mrs. Wilson, and as best you can, what it was that struck you as unusual, out of the ordinary?

A: Well, I saw a shooting. Right in front of me, not ten feet away, if that much. I saw the man that fired the shot very well. The man that fell down, I didn't see him all that good.

Q: Would you describe to us, to the best of your ability, the man who did this shooting you speak of?

A: Well, I can certainly try, Mr. Stege. I'd say he was about maybe five-seven or -eight tall, I'd guess around a hundred and fifty pounds or about that. His face looked awfully white to me, I'd say. Like he didn't get outdoors much, you see. And he had all this blond hair. You see, I got a good look at what the color of his hair was when he took his hat off there for a minute.

Q: What he was wearing? Could you describe that?

A: Well, it looked like a gray suit, I think. A straw hat; I'm sure of that. Had a stiff brim. With a ribbon, but for the life of me I couldn't tell you what color ribbon.

Q: I do hope we're not tiring you out, Mrs. Wilson. Would you like some coffee to drink?

A: I'm not a coffee drinker, Mr. Stege. But I do thank you just the same.

Q: Then I suggest we continue on. You spoke of the gun the man— the killer—dropped. What can you perhaps tell us about it? If anything.

A: Well, it was like a revolver, I guess you'd call it. Anyway, he just let loose of it, dropped it right down on the floor next to the man that was shot. But I didn't get what you might call a real good look at it, I'm sorry to say.

Q: And were you able to observe what the man you saw drop the gun do next?

A: He just ran up some stairs right there to the street.

Q: And have you had occasion to see and recognize this man again? To your knowledge?

A: No, sir. I wouldn't want to.

Q: Members of the police department are in the process of rounding up men capable of this type crime, Mrs. Wilson. You may be asked to view some of these men in what we call a line-up in which you could see them but they could not see you. May we count on your cooperation?

A: Yes, sir. I certainly will. I think it's a shame what's happening in our city these days.

Q: Yes. That would seem to be all—at least for the time being. Thank you very much for your time and patience.

4

They were sitting in Roche's office, the four of them, waiting for him to show up for the conference he'd called for five that afternoon. Wendt was the only one not smoking; George Wellman had one of his nickel cigars going, while Casey and Brennan puffed on cigarettes.

Michael Casey, a tall broad-shouldered Irishman whose flaming red hair rode atop the face of a dissolute choirboy, said, "This fella—couldn't be more'n twenty years old, if that, friend of the wife's younger cousin—anyway this fella gets this job bill collecting for this furniture store out on Halsted. Across from the Twelfth Street Store there."

"Sibilano's," Sean Brennan said. "The very finest in home furnishings. Much of it is imported from Italy."

"That's the one," Casey said. "Anyhow, this young fella—name escapes me but he's no dago—he's been trying to collect this bill from a customer out around Townsend and Oak—middle'a Little Sicily, you know? Never can find the guy home. So six in the morning he goes out there, climbs up these outside stairs, pounds on what turns out to be the kitchen door.

"Way he tells it," Casey said, "this big spaghetti-head finally yanks the door open, wants to know what the hell he wants. Our boy tries telling him about not paying his bill. Only the guy don't listen, he just reaches over to the sink and grabs up this butcher knife had to be damn near two feet long.

"Well sir," Casey said, "the kid takes one jump for the stairs, hits the tenth, sixth and third step and takes off down Oak like a fucking bullet. Gets back to the store shaking like a leaf, tells . . . Sibilano? . . . about it and that he's quitting as of right now. Well, Sibilano about craps his pants laughing. But he manages to talk him into staying on—and here a couple days later in comes the guy, pays up, tells the kid he's sorry. And damned if he don't slip him a cee. How d'ya like *that* for a topper?"

"I can't say that I'm at all surprised," Brennan said. "From what I hear, Dominick Sibilano is an honest, forthright gentleman highly respected by his people."

George Wellman said, "You wanta talk about bill collectors, I got one for you." A squat, balding, bull-necked man in his late thirties, Wellman was a recent transfer from the city police force to the state's attorney's staff. "This guy I know does collecting for Mandel Brothers. Well, some'a these married dames up around Lincoln Park West and in through there, they get behind in their bills a lot. Not they can't come up with the dough; they just let things slide, you know? Well, he gets invited in once in a while for coffee or even a drink, and next thing you know they got their clothes off and pushing their cooz right in your face. It's not—"

The office door banged open and Roche strode in. He said, "Is it a pool hall you people think this is? Least you could open up a window, you gotta smoke."

Cigarettes were quickly extinguished; Wellman masked his cigar behind a meaty hand; Wendt, who was not smoking, eased over and opened the window while Roche was getting into the desk chair.

Roche said, "I just this minute left *Mis*ter Swanson." He took a slip of paper from his jacket pocket. "On my way out, *Mis*ter Swanson hands me this."

Reading aloud in a tightly controlled voice, Roche said, "'You, as chief investigator for the office of state's attorney, will immediately assign your most capable department members to the task of apprehending, arresting, and preparing for immediate trial the person or persons responsible for the heinous murder of Alfred J. Lingle. It is high time that the criminal elements in our city learn once and for all that lawless disregard for the lives and property of its citizens will no longer be tolerated.' "

Roche looked up. "Signed: John A. Swanson, state's attorney in and for Cook County, sovereign state of Illinois." He spread his fingers and the paper dropped to the desk top.

Casey was the first to find words. "I wouldn't know about this 'most capable' shit, Pat, but let me remind you it was you yourself right here in this office told me not to let nothing nor nobody pry me offa that Al Kearney rubout."

Roche said, "Right now the man upstairs don't give two hoots in a bathtub about Kearney getting knocked off or who did it. What we have here's a sterling member of the Fourth Estate getting shot in the head. That all by itself's got to get big headlines in half the country. On top of that the *Tribune* put up twenty-five thousand in reward money a couple hours ago for anyone nails the shooter for them."

He picked up the memorandum. "You have some idea the part in here about getting rid of the criminals in our fair city's just for my bonny blue eyes? It's in here because the man upstairs intends to make damn sure a copy'll be on every front page in the state this time tomorrow. Now we clean this one up for our Mister Swanson, he figures to get the press behind him and ride into the U.S. Senate or the governor's chair, may God in His infinite wisdom forbid.

"Where we start," Roche said, "is with the poor unfortunate victim himself. Mike, Sean: take a swing around the newsrooms. Talk to reporters. Like Jack McPhaul, Buddy McHugh, Walt Burns, Fred Pasley, Harry Reed, Clem Lane. Try and get some idea whose shit list Jake got himself on here lately. And another thing: every time I ran into Jake he had this roll big enough to choke an elephant on him. Papers just don't pay that kind of money—least not that I ever heard of. He must have kept some of it in a bank. Let's find out *what* bank."

Roche paused, fingered a lip reflectively. He looked at Wellman.

"George: Jake Lingle spent half his life in station houses. Check on them, get in a little chin music with desk sergeants, lieutenants, maybe a captain or two; the patrol-car lads. Like that. Start with the West Side precincts; I'll get a couple fellas to work Central and the North Side."

He moved a hand in dismissal, said, "Stick around, will you, Walt?" as the others filed out, and left his chair to close the window. Wendt straddled a straight-backed chair, waited till Roche was back behind the desk, then said, "Red Forsythe."

Roche lifted a questioning eyebrow. "What about him?"

"I got this call a minute or two before you showed up. Some guy—no name, naturally—says, 'Red Forsythe's the one put that bum Lingle to sleep and the witnesses will finger him for the job,' and hung up."

"Not from the descriptions I read, they won't," Roche said. "First place, Forsythe's got red hair, not blond. But what the hell; I'll ask Stege to have him pulled in for a line-up."

He leaned back, clasped his fingers behind his head and yawned. ". . . We got us a tough one here, laddybucks."

"Unless we end up lucky, I gotta agree with you," Wendt said. He looked past Roche's shoulder and out the window at the late afternoon sky. "I see where the funeral's set for Friday. You'll be going?"

"I don't think so, no," Roche said. "Tell you the truth, I wasn't all that crazy about Jake to begin with. In too thick with the mob guys for my taste. Anybody was to up and ask me, his comings and goings should've been looked into a long time ago. But what the hell, the man's dead, let him rest in peace."

He picked a pencil off the desk top, drummed the point lightly against the surface while sorting through what he had to say. "This fella Wellman there," he said abruptly. "Would you be after giving me your personal and private opinion on the man, Walter?"

"George? Pat, he's fitting in, okay? Still bothers you, don't it? Him coming in offa the P.D. and all. Be reasonable, Pat. That by itself don't make him bent. The man had four commendations, high marks on his sergeant's exam, two years pre-law. You want my opinion like you say, I gotta put him down as a standup guy. All right; so

4 5

Upstairs pushes him in on you. It doesn't *have* to make him Swanson's pigeon, if that's what's in the back of your mind."

The telephone rang. Roche picked up the receiver, said, "Roche speaking. . . . No, nothing in particular. . . . Yes. . . . None at all. . . . Ogden Grill, seven o'clock. Please thank the commissioner for me and tell him I'll be prompt. . . . Yes."

He put back the receiver, saw Wendt's expression and smiled wryly. "Seems the time has come to have a sit-down with the commissioner. To—how'd his deputy put it there?—'exchange information and coordinate our respective investigations.' Try playin' that one on the old piano.

"I won't be needing my gift for second sight," Roche said, "to fill in the blanks on this one, Walter, me boy. The good commissioner'll shake my hand, give me a fatherly pat on the back, pour me a couple snorts of pre-war Scotch, fill my belly with one'a Gibby's steaks . . . and lower the boom. Out will roll the words in that foine rich voice 'a his: 'I'm sure I don't have to be reminding you, Mister Roche, that it's both the obligation and the duty of the Chicago Police Department, of which I have the honor to be in charge, to investigate crime in this city, to locate and question witnesses, to gather all pertinent evidence, interrogate suspects, and arrest the perpetrator. *Then* the office of the state's attorney will of course be free to go after a conviction. I am speaking particularly of yesterday's dastardly murder of Alfred Lingle, Mister Roche. You'll be kept fully informed, I can promise you, of the progress in our customary thorough investigation of that case.' He has a way with the words, does the commissioner. Long as you don't get him flustered, that is. That's when he starts sounding like your everyday street cop.

"Like our Mister Swanson," Roche said, "the commissioner'd like nothing better than to get his manicured fingers deeper into the pork barrel. Maybe the mayor's office? A grand position indeed for lining the pockets. Judging by what's being bandied about down at City Hall, Big Bill the Builder has many a deposit box stuffed with the coin of the realm there.

"This isn't some alky-cooking-dago-dead-in-a-ditch knock over, my kraut friend. The body in question was once a reporter in the employ of the *Tribune,* owned lock, stock and printer's ink by the good Colonel Robert McCormick. Should the spirit of gratitude so move the colonel, he'll hand you any political plum your little heart desires—up to and including an upholstered chair in Congress.

"Nobody knows this better," Roche said, "than Commissioner Russell and our own Mister Swanson. They're gonna go at it hammer-and-tongs to get credit for putting Lingle's shooter in the little green room at Joliet there. Top of that, take this twenty-five thousand in reward money so far. That's gonna put us up to our tight little arses in reporters, stoolies, and private dicks—all out for that dough, along with the boost in reputation. . . . Let me have one'a your smokes."

They lit Sanos from Wendt's pack. "It wasn't a big lecture I was meaning to unload on you, Walter," Roche said. "It was more myself I was talkin' to—letting myself know what the score is, so to speak. Now I must be stepping over to Gibby's and butter up the good commissioner of police—an art I was never one to get the good marks for."

5

Ever'body kept saying now he was the man in the family, that 'cause Papa had "passed on" it would be up to him to take care of his mother and sister. Uncle Ted had told him so two times already, and once Aunt Grace had put her arms around him and cried and said the same thing.

Maybe that meant he'd have to stop school and get a job and earn some money to buy food and stuff. Once Papa told him about how a long time ago he started work on the paper as something called a copy boy. Maybe *he* could be a copy boy. He was six-going-on-seven years old and good in school. (Sister Agnes told Mama he was the best in his whole class in arithmetic and reading and he could say his holymarymotherofgods without forgetting one single word.)

Even though the whole church was almost full, people kept coming in and it was getting awful hot in there and he was beginning to sweat with a coat and a necktie on. In the *summer*time for gosh sake. People coughed and whispered and made quiet noises. And there were flowers all over, millions of 'em, and his head was starting to hurt they smelled so.

He wriggled uncomfortably and scratched where it itched. His mother put a hand on his arm and whispered, "Sit still, Buddy. It won't take long once they start."

Try as she might, Helen Lingle couldn't seem to shake off a deep-seated feeling of resentment. If Jake hadn't walked out on her six months ago, she kept telling herself, he wouldn't be dead now, leaving her with two small children to raise and no money coming in except what her father could spare. There might be an insurance policy; she didn't know one way or another, since Jake never was one to talk about such things. And a boy Buddy's age needed a father to bring him up right, something a grandfather couldn't really do. Maybe she might end up getting married again; she was still a good-looking woman, everybody said so. But how many men were around willing to take on bringing up some other man's kids?

With her resentment came a concomitant rush of guilt. The poor man not yet in his grave and here she was thinking about roping in a new one. Jake had had his faults, sure; show her a man who didn't. He had never struck her, he wasn't stingy about money, he paid his bills on time. Why, he was even buying a summer home on the lake shore in Long Beach, just over the Indiana line, where she and the children could spend the hot months. If only he didn't . . . *hadn't* had a job that forced him to associate with gangsters and bootleggers. . . .

The Requiem High Mass began. The celebrant, the Reverend Father Mulhearn, cut an imposing figure in maniple, stole, and chasuble emblazoned with large silver crosses front and back. The polished walnut coffin, closed, rested on a black-draped catafalque in the center aisle outside the sanctuary gate of the altar rail. Tall candles of unbleached beeswax flanked the casket, three to a side, with a seventh candle and a tall crucifix at its head. Sunlight through stained glass added an oddly cheerful counterpoint to the somber rites of the Mass of the Dead.

As the liturgy continued, Helen Lingle glanced at the other family members in the pew. Her daughter Delores, barely five, dozed beside her, a casualty of lifeless air and the weighted fragrance of flowers. Emily Durst, Jake's mother, sat with bowed head, a handkerchief pressed to her lips, Jake's stepfather next to her; they had arrived that same morning from Kansas City.

From the choir loft came the majestic, ominous chant of the *Dies*

Irae. Buddy yawned hugely, prodded his mother with an elbow, started to whisper something, subsided at her warning glance. And then finally the Last Gospel was said, the four supporting priests moved to positions at the side of the sanctuary, and Father Mulhearn slowly ascended the short flight of steps leading to the ornately carved pulpit at the left of the altar.

He stood facing the congregation, hands lightly clasped, and waited till the last throat was cleared and silence took over.

"Alfred Joseph Lingle," he began, "was a parishioner of Our Lady of Sorrows all of his years. As were his late father and his mother. He was baptized at its altar, as were his wife Helen and his two children, Alfred Junior and Dolores. He was a devoted son, a good and providing husband, and a caring father. His friends were legion, and largely because of his vocation, came from all walks of life. They grieve with us over the untimely passing of this good man."

The reverend father's voice deepened. "Alfred Lingle was a respected member of an honorable profession. As a skilled reporter for a great newspaper, a major part of his duties was to keep the public informed of and alerted to the machinations of the lawless and corrupt at all levels of society.

"To this duty, Alfred Lingle was wholeheartedly dedicated. His lofty ideals, his unwavering honesty, made of him a fearless and implacable foe of those who prey brutally on society and scoff at its laws.

"For this, Alfred Lingle was struck down, coldly murdered by those whose criminal activities he sought to expose, martyred at the hands of an underworld assassin. Let society mark well the manner of his passing and hereby resolve that Alfred Lingle did not die in vain."

Descending from the pulpit and returning to the sanctuary, Father Mulhearn began swiftly to bring the ceremonies to a close. Prayers of absolution were recited as he slowly circled the coffin, sprinkling each side with holy water. As he finished, the honorary pallbearers left their seats, moved to either side of the catafalque, and rolled it soundlessly up the center aisle and through wide double doors leading to the street.

Outside, both sidewalks overflowed with spectators drawn there an hour or so earlier by the procession that had escorted the coffin to the church of Our Lady of Sorrows. Column after column of uniformed police officers, city firemen, legionnaires and sailors from a lake shore naval station had marched to the measured beat of muffled drums block after block past thousands of the curious and morbid.

As the coffin was placed in the waiting hearse for its last journey, the open tonneaus of seven limousines were already being loaded with flowers removed from the church. Mourners emerged from the cathedral, forcing a pathway down the wide flight of crowded steps to enter the seemingly endless line of cars waiting to leave for Mount Carmel cemetery.

Jerome "Jerry the Bookie" Shapiro, a minor member of the Davey Miller mob, nudged his companion and muttered, "You'd think fa' chrissake they was buryin' Al Capone!"

It was to be Alfred J. Lingle's final eulogy.

6

In his spacious office on the twenty-fourth floor of the Tribune Tower, Colonel Robert Rutherford McCormick, in jodhpurs and a short-sleeved knit shirt, was playing polo. Controlling the mallet with effortless ease, he skillfully intercepted an errant pass, made a nearside backhand shot under the neck of his pony and drove the willow ball between the goal posts.

The telephone buzzer sounded briefly. The colonel glanced at the wall clock, then dismounted from his electrically powered "horse" and took the call. "Tell them to wait, Margaret." Characteristically, the colonel used the locution "tell" in place of "ask."

Securing the polo mallet next to its twin in a wall clip, he entered the office bathroom, washed up, and changed into a pale blue shirt, striped tie, and a three-piece suit of lightweight gray twill from one of London's Bond Street tailors. A band of black cloth pinned earlier to the jacket's left sleeve furnished a somber note.

After running a comb through his iron-gray hair and using the tip of an index finger to smooth the bristles of his gray, toothbrush-sized moustache, the colonel left the bathroom, crossed to his desk and pressed the intercom button twice.

He remained standing behind the desk as the door opened and four men, hats in hand, filed in. The colonel, not one for hearty hand-shakes and warm words of welcome, said, "Thank you for stopping by, gentlemen. Since it seems likely we shall be here a while, I suggest you pull up chairs and get comfortable."

It was the first time Roche had even so much as laid eyes on the man. One big son of a bitch, he thought: had to be a good four inches over six feet and likely no fat on him. There was a whiff of English accent in the deep voice, and those two years or so in the military showed plain enough in his squared shoulders and stiff back. You'd think he had a ramrod shoved up his aristocratic butt there.

Once his visitors were seated, the colonel deliberately turned his back to them, strode over to the wall of tall wide windows, and stood looking out at the leaden swells of Lake Michigan to the east.

Roche glanced idly at the others. Cook County's state's attorney John A. Swanson, known to his staff as "the man upstairs" or "that dumb fucking Swede," sat stiffly erect, his mouth hanging slightly open and his delft-blue eyes vaguely troubled. Stupid—no question; but at least he was honest. Something you couldn't on your kindest day say for Bob Crowe, the guy Swanson had replaced in the last election.

Seated to Swanson's left was Police Commissioner Bill Russell, wrapped in a tan suit that failed to camouflage his considerable paunch. His broad shoulders were aggressively hunched, his feet placed solidly on the short-piled broadloom, the deeply etched lines of his craggy face set in an expressionless mask.

Number three, Roche decided, was one of those birds you'd lose in a crowd of two. Little guy, skinny, small bones, slicked-back mousy hair, decked out in a classy tailor-made suit. Kind of pouty lips on him and a pair of pop eyes in back of rimless cheaters stuck on a button nose. Some kind of an accountant or maybe a lawyer. He sure's hell didn't look like no newspaper man.

And here we sit, Roche thought, asses planted, loafing around till the colonel makes up his mind on how to handle these guys. Maybe start off with a little pep talk, Knute Rockne style? Here's this fear-less reporter, goes out in the streets to expose crime and corruption for God, the people and the paper (well, maybe not in that order), and ends up getting hisself bumped off. Then follow that up with a load of malarkey about how the cops and the state's attorney's staff must "put aside their differences and work together in a relentless war against an enemy striking at the very roots of society's first bastion of freedom: the press."

In short, the kind of high-toned bullshit that showed up in a *Tribune* editorial any time the colonel felt like lecturing the public.

Okay, Colonel McCormick, sir. You told us to get over here and we came running. Now if it's all the same to you, would you lay off rehearsing your lines like some two-bit play-actor so we can get on with it instead of sitting here admiring your backside?

Seated next to Roche, Russell was beginning to fidget. He crossed his knees, found that his protruding belly made the position uncomfortable, uncrossed them, folded his arms instead. No matter how much clout that stiff-necked bastard packed, William F. Russell was the city's police commissioner, boss of some sixty-five hundred cops. Not by God somebody you could order around like some wet-nosed rookie. For a plugged nickel he'd stand up right now and walk the hell outta there.

The colonel turned from the windows and strode to the desk. With no explanation for the delay, he introduced the slender man with the rimless glasses as Charles Rathbun, a member of the law firm handling the legal affairs of the *Tribune*. Hands were shaken, polite acknowledgments made and seats resumed. McCormick took the desk chair, leaned forward and rested his elbows on the desk top.

"As I'm sure you've already surmised," he said, "I've summoned you here to discuss what steps are to be taken, first to find and then prosecute Alfred Lingle's assassin."

He impaled Russell on the blue lance of his eyes. "What progress have the police made thus far, Commissioner?"

Russell cleared his throat. "Little too early to say, Colonel. But I can assure—"

McCormick's gesture cut him short. "You've had four days," he snapped. "Am I to understand you've turned up nothing of consequence in that time?"

"I'd hardly say *nothing*, Colonel." Russell was choosing his words with care. "I've personally selected and assigned fifteen of the department's best investigators to work around the clock on the Lingle murder and to make daily reports directly to me. I fully expect to have something positive inside of a day or two."

The colonel leaned back in his chair and eyed Russell levelly for a long moment. Then: "I have this to say to you, Commissioner. In the past nine years alone, there've been six hundred and twelve gangland murders in Cook County—most of them within the Chicago city limits. And not one—I repeat, *not one*—has been solved. Believe me when I say *this* one *will* be solved and the killer convicted. Alfred Lingle's murder was a blatant attempt by the underworld to intimidate not only the *Tribune*, but every other newspaper in this country.

"I tell you here and now," the colonel said, "that I accept that challenge. Two hours after Lingle was shot, this paper announced that a reward of twenty-five thousand dollars will be paid for information leading to the killer's arrest and conviction. Other city newspapers have brought the total to over fifty thousand. While I doubt that the offer will get results, we can't neglect any possibility."

His eyes swung to Swanson. "John, what do you have for me at this point?"

Swanson stirred uneasily in his chair, appeared to weigh the question, said, "Well . . . uh—" then glanced helplessly at Roche. "Pat?"

"If it's a solid suspect you're wanting, Colonel," Roche said bluntly, "we don't have one. Eight witnesses—and not two descriptions of the shooter close enough to mean much. We got pickup orders out on eleven known possibles, but most of them—if not all—would be after taking it on the lam while Lingle was still on a table in the morgue there."

McCormick was staring at Roche with unabashed interest. "Are you a native American, Mr. Roche?" he asked.

Made abruptly aware of his accent, Roche felt his cheeks burn, reminded that it wasn't all that long ago since "No Irish Need Apply" signs were common outside employment offices. He bit back the first rush of anger, waited till he could trust his voice.

"If it's the story of my life you'll be needing, Colonel," he said coldly, "I was born in the County Galway, Ireland, and was barely yet seventeen when I came to this country. Six years I was on the cops in this town, moved over to working Prohibition cases for the U.S. government till Mister Swanson hired me, it'll be two years now."

While it seemed unlikely, Roche thought, the colonel's lips twitched in what could have been a smile. Probably allowed himself three a month. "Thank you," McCormick said mildly. "My own roots go back to Ulster. But that, of course, was generations ago."

He lifted an eyebrow questioningly at the others. "Is there something any one of you is prepared to add before I get into my purpose in calling this meeting? John?"

Swanson moved a hand vaguely. "Nothing comes to mind, Colonel. Not right off, anyhow."

"Commissioner?"

"Well, yes sir." Russell inched forward on his chair, his expression solemn. "I'm wondering if maybe we're not getting a little ahead of ourselves here by calling this a gang killing."

The publisher frowned skeptically. "Why do you say that?"

"In the first place," Russell said, "no gang leader in his right mind is gonna order a reporter knocked off. Gotta be bad for business—and believe me, with these birds business comes first. In fact, word I get is that the Capone and Aiello-Moran mobs are sore as hell about this. And when it comes to the small fry like Joe Saltis or the Touhys or them West Side sheenies . . . well, I can just about guarantee you *that* stupid they're not."

McCormick's face mirrored his revulsion. "The vermin Prohibition has saddled us with. Disgusting!"

"Yes sir," Russell said. "My point is, some . . . citizen could be behind shooting Lingle. A grudge or something. I don't have to tell you reporters step on a lotta toes."

It took a monumental effort on Roche's part to keep his expression blank. A rookie three days out of the academy would've known a statement like that was the bunk!

"It's possible, I suppose," the colonel said. "Mister Roche?"

Roche said, "This was an out-and-out gang knockoff, sir. Handled by a professional shooter. Probably on orders from Al Capone or any one of the three men running the North Side rackets. From the looks of the powder-burn pattern, I'd be after saying the gunman put the one shot in the head from no more'n three inches away. Amateurs just don't get that close; it's the body they mostly go for, and empty the gun. Plus the identification numbers being filed off and the gun dropped next to the body. A dead giveaway, that. What I'm saying, Colonel, is we got us a mob killing and no two ways about it."

The last few words seemed to hang in the still air. Russell sat stiff-lipped, furious at being openly contradicted but aware that this was not the time, place, or audience to say so.

McCormick said, "I'm told that unless a murder of this type is solved within the first few days, the odds are that it won't be solved at all. Has that been your experience, Mister Roche?"

"More often than not," Roche said.

"I don't propose to let that happen in the Lingle case," McCormick said. "To make sure it does *not* happen, this newspaper will assemble its own staff of qualified men to handle the investigation. With no help—or interference—from outside agencies."

He looked squarely at Russell. "And that, Commissioner, includes the Chicago Police Department."

He had left Fort Wayne shortly after eight that morning, keeping the needle at a sensible 35 till he reached Decatur. There he switched to a side road and crossed the Wabash river at Linngrove, some forty miles northeast of Muncie.

The '27 Reo Speedwagon lurched steadily ahead, its cargo of forty cases of Old Overholt bourbon covered with alfalfa bales under a black tarpaulin. Cottonwoods and elms met overhead to form a leafy tunnel. This was corn, wheat, and hog country, level as a billiard table, dotted with small white farmhouses, large red barns and an occasional silo. The sun shone, the air smelled of new-mown hay, birds sang and swooped and crapped on the windshield.

Leo Brothers, at the moment known as Lewis Blake, would have swapped all of Indiana and its bucolic charm for a sack of White Castle hamburgers and a couple of beers. Denied these, he settled for a Camel, got it burning and dropped the pack on the seat next to him. Moments later, shortly after crossing the Salamonie River, the truck rounded a sharp curve, sending the cigarettes skittering across the passenger seat and onto the floorboards.

Easing up on the accelerator, one hand controlling the wheel, Brothers bent to grope for the pack . . . and a hail of slugs from twin barrels of a shotgun ripped through the open window on his right, passed harmlessly over his head and shattered the windshield.

Brothers yelled "Shit!" jerked erect and slammed his foot against the gas pedal. The engine sputtered, came close to stalling, then steadied to a roar as the truck shot ahead. He glanced at the rearview mirror as a late-model Ford Sport Coupe, barely visible through a boiling cloud of dust, swung out from behind a clump of trees and took up the chase.

Crouching over the wheel, the accelerator jammed to the floor, Brothers watched the needle pass the sixty mark as the Speedwagon bounced wildly against the road's rutted surface. The thought of what might be happening to those forty cases of Old Overholt crossed his mind briefly. Fuck 'em! Right now his job was to get *himself* out of this. In *one* fucking *piece!*

The gap between the two vehicles had narrowed to less than a hundred feet and was closing rapidly. Brothers flicked a glance at the mirror. A man's head and arm were stretched outside the Ford's passenger window, a gloved hand aiming the truncated barrels of a shotgun at the truck's rear right tire. Brothers mentally crossed himself, dug his fingers deeper into the wheel and waited. . . .

When the explosion came, it seemed oddly muffled. Brothers, awash in cold sweat, waited for the Speedwagon to start spinning on its three remaining tires. . . . Nothing! The bastard'd *missed!* He caught the mirrored image of the Ford, its right front tire in shreds, careening wildly across the road before crashing head on into the trunk of a huge cottonwood.

Brothers pounded a fist on the wheel and broke into a fit of gasping, high-pitched giggles bordering on outright hysteria. A brand-fucking-new Ford and it up and blows a fucking tire on them! 'Less the car maybe hits a bump at the exact same second the guy's all set to pull the fucking trigger and ends up shooting out his *own* goddam tire!

It wasn't until he was a mile or so farther down the road that Brothers became aware of a wetness trickling down his left cheek. He ran fingers lightly across the skin, peered at them. Blood. Maybe not enough to get excited about, but blood just the same. *His* blood! He put his head out the window, brought it close to the mirror and made out at least a dozen tiny, superficial cuts put there by slivers of flying glass from the exploding windshield.

Alex Schoenburg's small run-down frame house fronted on a dirt road at the northern outskirts of Muncie. At the rear, between the house and a sagging barnlike structure, were three dark blue Autocar panel trucks, the stripped chassis of a Kenworth truck and a black Jordan sedan only days off the assembly line.

Alex was sixty-one, balding, a shade under five-four, and, given a pound or two either way, tipped the scales at two-ten. He wore bib overalls, no shirt, a field-hand's straw hat and was draining the crankcase of one of the panel trucks when the Speedwagon pulled into the yard and Brothers dismounted.

Schoenburg straightened, stared slack-jawed at the ruined windshield, then at Brothers's blood-streaked face. "The fuck happen to you?"

"I'll tell you what the fuck happened to me," Brothers said. "I run into a couple of hijackers's what the fuck happened to me. Okay?"

"The load?" Schoenburg said. "They didn't go get that load offa you?"

"They got shit is what they got," Brothers said. "Two feet behind me with a shotgun up my ass and they go and blow a tire. Headfirst into a fucking tree is where I left them cocksuckers.

"Now you ast me about the load," Brothers said. "Them bottles must've got bounced around some when I hit all the ruts in that fucking dirt road, running. But the boxes being made'a wood that way, and under all that alfalfa, probably nothing too much broke, okay?"

"A fucking hijack," Schoenburg said. "Can't hardly believe it. It's costing me a good seventeen hunnerd a month just to ice the law between here and Fort Wayne alone. So I gotta doubt any'a the off-duty bulls're gonna try it. I did hear some talk about how the Traum boys from around Terre Haute maybe might try moving this direction, but I figger it's just talk, you know."

Brothers said, "Anyway, I'm not ready to take on this kinda shit. The impression I got going to work for you was me making milk runs to the roadhouses and speaks on your list, plus two-three trips a month picking up a loada wet goods from your Fort Wayne supplier.

"So if it's all the same to you," Brothers said, "and no hard feelings, I'd like to be paid what I got coming to me and dust out. Even without what happened today, three weeks of going to bed with the chickens is about all I can take. Anyhow, that beef on me in Chicago's buried by now."

"Going to leave me kinda shorthanded," Alex Schoenburg said, "you pulling out on me and all. But what the hell, I don't like getting shot at any more'n you do."

"What I'd like to do," Brothers said, "is get down to the station and grab that four-ten to Chicago."

Schoenburg said, "Tell you what, Blake. Give me a hand unloading them boxes, then go on in the house and let the missus fix your face up for you. Looks to me like you still got some little pieces of glass stuck in you there. Then we settle up what I owe you, and I'll get you over to the station. You got plenty time till then."

At four-fifteen that afternoon, Leo Vincent Brothers, alias Lewis Blake, alias George Friedlander, alias Louis V. Bader, was comfortably seated in a day coach of a Chicago-bound C.C.C. & St. L. local. The man across from him, one Adolph Groat, a drummer for a

Cleveland cutlery firm, finished leafing through a copy of the previous day's Cleveland *Plain Dealer* and offered it to Brothers.

"They're burying that Chicago reporter today," he said. "He was shot down in cold blood by some gangster back there several days ago. A fascinating story, actually."

"New one on me," Leo Brothers said, and took the paper.

7

Barely able to get the words out, Police Commissioner Russell said, "With all due respect, Colonel, I can't believe I'm hearing you right. The *paper's* taking over the Lingle case? My department's entirely out of it? *That* what you're trying to tell me?"

"That is precisely what I *am* telling you, Commissioner," McCormick said.

"Other words," Russell said, "you're saying the police can't do its job, right? But that a bunch of reporters can? That, sir, is pure bullshit."

"Indeed?" McCormick said. "Six hundred and twelve gangland murders, Commissioner, and no convictions. Why is that? Let me hazard a guess. Perhaps it's because something like seventy percent of the Chicago police force, top to bottom, is in the pay of bootleggers, vice-mongers, racketeers and gamblers. And because that seventy percent has no intention of biting the hand that feeds it."

Russell said, "While we're handing out guesses, Colonel, let me give you another one on why there's been no convictions on gang murders in this town. Say you finally *do* manage to get a torpedo from one'a the local mobs into a courtroom. The prosecution witnesses get up there on the stand, and all of sudden something funny happens. Them witnesses? By this time they can't even identify one'a their own kids, let alone the guy they saw pull the trigger. The jury? Can't wait to get back to the judge and say, 'Not guilty, Your Honor,' loud and clear.

"It's not that they don't wanta do their civic duty, Colonel," Russell said. "Best intentions in the world . . . till the wife maybe gets a phone call middle'a the night. 'Hear you gotta couple'a nice little girls in the family, Missus Jones. Might remind your husband how terrible he'd feel, something happens to them.' A thing like that can sure play hell with your sense of civic duty, take it from me.

"Anyway, Colonel," Russell said, "what I guess I'm trying to get at is, it's going to take my department *and* John's, here, to locate Lingle's killer and get him in front of a jury. What happens after that, nobody can say. But there's no way on God's green footstool a bunch of reporters working on the case can run down the guy, let alone get enough on him to even hope to convict."

"Commissioner," McCormick said, "what you seem to overlook is that I'm a newspaperman myself, have been for nearly thirty years, and am perfectly aware of what takes place in our courts. But I see the brutal slaying of a *Tribune* employee as the impetus to launch a . . . crusade, if you will, with its goal the end of the reign of terror our citizens have been subjected to these past ten years.

"But it is the *Tribune*'s fight," McCormick said, "and the *Tribune* alone will wage that fight. It will be waged without the help of or interference from the police department. In any way, shape or manner. And that decision, sir, is not subject to further debate."

Police Commissioner Russell, his hands trembling, his face a flaming magenta, stood up slowly. It's a stroke the poor man'll be having, Roche thought, and looked away.

Russell said hoarsely, "No debate, like you say, Colonel. But if you think for one fucking minute you're running the police department, you're out-and-out crazy.

"Crazy is what I'm saying, Colonel," Russell said, "and crazy is what I meant. For your information, sir, I was appointed to my post by the Honorable William Hale Thompson, mayor of this city. Try telling him my department's off the case. Considering what he thinks of you *and* your paper, you got about as much chance of making it stick as a fart in a Texas cyclone."

During this McCormick's expression remained politely attentive. When it was evident that Russell had nothing further to add, the publisher, his voice icily calm, said, "I won't detain you further, Commissioner. Thank you for stopping by."

The commissioner took a slow, deep breath, hesitated, then turned on his heel, stalked over to the door, jerked it open and stormed out, not quite slamming it behind him.

The room had become preternaturally quiet. The colonel looked down at his hands resting on the desk. A little pink around the ears, Roche thought. Probably hasn't been talked to that way since he put on his first pair'a long pants, more's the pity.

McCormick glanced at the state's attorney. "John?"

Swanson swallowed convulsively, said, "If you don't mind, sir, perhaps you'd outline for me something of how you propose to conduct the investigation?"

What little respect Roche had for the man vanished at that moment. Stupid *and* a cream puff! Here's this guy, the county's chief prosecutor, elected to that post by a solid majority of the voters, and he's gonna set there on his skinny Swede ass and let this arrogant son of a bitch fold him up like a fucking cafeteria napkin!

McCormick said, "I'll get to that, John. . . . Mister Roche. This morning three members of the Chicago Crime Commission, at my request, sent me the names of departmental investigators they regard as competent and thoroughly honest. Both, it seems, are in woefully short supply. Of the few recommended, your name was first on all three lists.

"I've asked Mister Rathbun," McCormick said, "to work with you in putting together a staff of seasoned investigators—men whose honesty is beyond question. Their job—and yours—will be to find Alfred Lingle's assassin, gather whatever evidence it takes to insure a conviction and, if at all possible, to get the man executed.

"I have no idea," McCormick said, "what the state is paying you, sir. But as of this date, your salary will be doubled. Hire whomever you need, arrange for adequate office space at some central location.

All expenses incurred will be met by this newspaper . . . and they will continue to be met for as long as it may take to bring this matter to a successful conclusion."

Swanson said hesitantly, "If I may bring up a point, Colonel? Take away my chief investigator and key members of my staff, and my entire operation is crippled. I'm sure you're aware of what I'm up against, even without being shorthanded. Not to mention a budget already strained to the breaking point."

McCormick gestured impatiently. "I can't be concerned with that, John. Put whomever Mister Roche selects on unpaid leaves of absence and use those funds to hire temporary replacements.

"To operate lawfully," McCormick said, "Mister Roche and his staff must have unassailable legal status. I'm told you can arrange this by appointing Mr. Rathbun as an assistant state's attorney. Correct?"

"A matter of swearing him in," Swanson said.

"The *Tribune*," McCormick said, "will make the announcement in tomorrow's home edition. . . . Mister Roche. Commissioner Russell brought up the reluctance of juries to convict local gang members on murder charges. Am I to assume that doesn't apply when the gunman is from out of town?"

"Pretty much so," Roche said. "But it almost never happens. The local big shots like to keep their shooters in easy reach, case they show signs of going soft somewhere along the line."

"Yet it *does* happen?" the colonel persisted.

"Only twice that I'd be knowing of," Roche said. "That Mexican standoff Capone set up last year? Where they killed those seven Moran guys in that garage on Clark Street there. The two shooters in police uniforms they sent in ahead came outta this East St. Louis mob nobody in there would be apt to recognize."

"As long as the possibility is not overlooked," McCormick said. He stood up, said, "That will do for now, gentlemen."

As the others got to their feet, McCormick said, "Please keep me informed, Mister Roche, if anything pressing crops up during the investigation."

Swanson stopped off in the publisher's outer office to make a phone call while Charles Rathbun and Roche went on ahead. As they waited side by side for the elevator, Rathbun put a hand on Roche's shoulder in a gesture of camaraderie. "I can't tell you, Pat, how pleased I am to have a man with you experience working for me on this case."

Roche smiled, looked the attorney squarely in the eye and said, "As himself put it while we were in there, Mister Rathbun, it's working *with* you I'll be doing. Not *for* you."

Within minutes after Russell left the Tribune Tower, word of his meeting with the colonel had reached the street. An hour later, the commissioner walked into his office at City Hall and found five reporters lying in wait.

"Well, well," Russell said heartily. "Always a pleasure to meet with the gentlemen of the press. What can I do for you?"

A reporter with the City News Bureau said, "What was your meeting with the colonel about, Commissioner?"

"Nothing particularly newsworthy," Russell said. "Progress on the Lingle case, the steps being taken, what the police have come up with to date. Naturally Colonel McCormick is vitally interested in what's going on."

"You *are* gonna get the son of a bitch, right, Commish?" a second reporter said. "Or is this gonna be open season on all us news guys?"

Russell, his affable manner suddenly gone, waited until the wave of laughter subsided. "Put this in your papers, gentlemen," he said. "The murder of my friend Jake Lingle spells the end of gangsterism in Chicago. I have given orders to make this town so quiet you will be able to hear a consumptive canary cough."

The office door opened and his secretary put her head in. "Commissioner? Mister Ettelson's office calling. Says it's urgent."

Russell held up a hand to silence the reporters, picked up the receiver, said, "This is Commissioner Russell. . . . Afternoon, Sam," he said jovially. "What can I do for you? . . . . Don't see why not. Give me ten minutes to get there."

On the Tuesday following the Lingle funeral, Roche's office phone rang. He identified himself, listened to the voice at the other end without interrupting, then said, "Thanks, Lily," put back the receiver, and looked up at Wendt sprawled in a chair across the desk from him.

"Corporation Counsel Ettelson's office," Roche said, "has just announced that Russell is out on his well-upholstered arse. Replaced by Deputy Commissioner Alcock as of nine A.M. this lovely June morning, he was."

"I will be damned," Wendt said. "Goes to prove you don't fart around with a guy owns a big newspaper, huh?"

"Had to go shoot his mouth off," Roche said. "Sat there, he did, and said to the colonel, 'You're crazy. Out-and-out crazy,' he said to the man. His exact words.

"Kind of pitiful, it was, Walter," Roche said. "Seein' a grown man go to pieces like that. Here all along he's been thinking how he's gonna catch up with whoever it was put Lingle to sleep, get the big headlines and have the colonel—and maybe even the mayor, they manage to pry the bottle outta His Honor's fist long enough—shake his hand on the steps of the City Hall there, with maybe a brass band to play 'Hail to the Chief' for him. After that, who could guess? Run for mayor? Wouldn't be the first of this town's police chiefs to take a shot at a political plum that size. . . . Let me have one'a your smokes, huh?"

They lit Sanos from Wendt's pack. Wendt said, "Got down here kinda early, didn't you? Everything at home all right?"

"Depends on what you mean by 'all right,'" Roche said. "Least when I got home last night the furniture was still there. But I do have to say it's been better'n two months now since I walked in the house and found nothing but empty rooms. Funny how nobody's ever been able to figure out why Margaret keeps doin' that to me.

"Not that she's a bad woman," Roche said. "Not at all. But come next April it'll be twenty years we're married and right off the bat she had a troubled mind, so to speak. As I say, Walter, not a bad woman at all, though. Her folks back in New York there, they kept telling her that in taking me she'd be after marryin' beneath herself. And her with an old man'd drink a bathtub dry, it had enough booze in it."

Wendt said, "I haven't heard too much about that girl of yours here lately. How's she been doing?"

"The breath of me body, Mary Patricia is," Roche said. "The light in my eyes, that girl. Eighteen she is now, and you'll never come upon another as pretty or as smart. Nor as much a lady, for that matter. Goes to Mass with me now and then; fact the big reason I got down here early this morning is I accompanied Mary Patricia to the seven."

Wendt flicked cigarette ash into the desk tray and said, "Mike Collins called up. Said to tell you we got us sixteen hundred square feet at Seventy-seven West Washington, fifth floor. Carpenters're in there now; oughta be ready Friday, the latest. Gonna cost the colonel a piss-pot fulla dough, hurry-up job like that."

"And just the start," Roche said. "Time we get our dukes on that torpedo, himself maybe won't be so all-fired rich."

Wendt said, "I made up that list last night. Comes out to twelve men, including you'n me. Let me know when you wanta go over it."

"Something wrong with right now?" Roche said.

OPENING MOVES

You might as well put President *Hoover* on
the spot!

—Al Capone,
1930

8

Roche scanned the letter rapidly, grunted with satisfaction, and tossed the single sheet across his desk to where Rathbun was seated.

COLONEL CALVIN GODDARD

Northwestern University
Evanston, Ill.

June 19, 1930

Mr. Patrick Roche
Suite 503
77 West Washington Street
Chicago, Ill.

My Dear Mr. Roche:

The following is the information you requested pertaining to the weapon used in the murder of Alfred J. Lingle on June 9, of this year.

Weapon: Colt Detective Special revolver, .38 caliber, double action, 2-inch barrel, weight 17 ounces, blued finish, checkered walnut stock. Rifling, 6 lands and grooves, inc. left.

Ammunition: .38 caliber, Remington/UMC, lead, rounded nose.

Summation: Comparison tests establish that the bullet taken from the body of Alfred J. Lingle was fired from the above described weapon. Efforts to restore obliterated serial numbers have proved successful. They are as follows: t.k. 231701.

Respectfully submitted,

Calvin Goddard

Col. Calvin Goddard
Director, Crime Laboratory

Rathbun read the neatly typed lines twice before glancing up at Roche. "Then he *did* come up with the numbers. I thought that, once filed off, there was no way to restore them."

Roche said, "Now, there is. Under where the factory stamps the number is what Goddard calls a 'tattoo' of it. Here a month or so back, he comes up with some kinda etching solution that fetches out that tattoo—a little something the local hoods aren't wise to. Least, not yet."

An oscillating electric fan atop a bank of file cabinets battled the day's heat and humidity and stirred the papers on Roche's desk. From beyond the closed office door voices rumbled, typewriters clattered and phones rang. With the remodeling finished thirty hours ahead of schedule, the workmen had packed up their hammers, power saws, and paintbrushes and disappeared. Four private offices—two reserved for interrogations—now lined the suite's west wall. At the north end, behind double doors, floor-to-ceiling windows of a large conference room overlooked Washington Street five floors below. The suite's remaining space was crowded with a motley collection of battered desks, chairs and wooden filing cabinets, thereby creating the comfortably seedy ambiance of a detective bureau squad room.

Tucked into a far corner was a small telephone switchboard manned by Sophia Drombosky, a slender, soft-spoken blonde in her late twenties, whose husband, a police sergeant, had been shot dead by a crazed cocaine addict three months before.

Knuckles rapped briefly on the door's pebbled glass panel and Walter Wendt came in. Ignoring Rathbun, he put a manila folder on the desk blotter in front of Roche, said, "She's all there, Patrick. But take a good look at that last page. Casey turned over a couple new rocks this morning and hit himself another jackpot."

Roche grunted sourly. "As if we don't have enough already." He handed Wendt the Goddard letter. "Would you be after shooting a wire off to the Colt people in Hartford on this, Walter? Tell 'em we'd appreciate an answer at their convenience . . . as long as they hurry it up."

Wendt said, "Okay. And the boys'll be in the conference room in ten minutes."

Roche nodded, said, "Now if you could spare me a couple of your cigarettes. . . ."

Wendt got out his Sanos, placed two of them with exaggerated care in Roche's waiting palm. "Fifteen cents a pack they'd cost you, Mister Roche. I could loan you that much."

" 'Tis a bad habit, the smoking," Roche said. "Seven weeks now it's been since I gave it up."

"Congratulations," Wendt said.

He left, closing the door. Roche lit a cigarette and opened the manila folder. From it he extracted several typewritten pages, leaned back in his swivel desk chair and began reading.

Charles Rathbun's lips tightened into an angry line. An arrogant bunch, every mother's son of them. Joking among themselves, letting him know he really didn't belong in their tight little clique, determined to freeze him out. Nothing obvious, of course. All very polite. "Yes, Mister Rathbun." "Good idea, Mister Rathbun." "Let me take that up with Mister Roche, sir."

Didn't matter. Getting credit for putting the Lingle killer away could move his own career right up the ladder. A matter of outmaneuvering this cocky harp, Roche. Hadn't ought to be too difficult, once the chips were down.

All fourteen chairs around the conference table were occupied. On the scarred wood at each place were a dime-store ashtray, a legal-size tablet, and two freshly sharpened pencils. Layers of cigar and cigarette smoke moved sluggishly in the harsh light of overhead fixtures.

Roche was seated at the far end of the long table with several manila envelopes stacked in front of him. He said, "It's one job we have: to get the bozo that put the bullet in Jake Lingle. No question it was a shooter for one of the city's mobs. Seeing as how we don't know which mob, we'll be putting the squeeze on all of 'em till the pressure hurts bad enough for somebody to hand us our man.

"*Where* we put the squeeze is where it hurts them the worst: their fat wallets. We raid their breweries, we close their speaks and whorehouses, we cut off their trucks hauling wet goods in from around the country. Every handbook and gambling joint we can find gets shut down.

"It's the politicians and judges they got on their payrolls that's gonna be after our hides," Roche said. "But we got Mister Rathbun, here, to be doing his legal best to hold them off."

Roche picked the envelopes off the table, held them up. "Three warrants. Signed by a superior court judge with some reluctance. To close down one of Mister Alphonse Capone's breweries, to clean out a warehouse crammed with some of that cat-piss Giuseppe Aiello sells as booze, and to take apart that gambling joint on Kedzie and Roosevelt run by the Miller boys."

Shortly after the meeting had ended, Roche opened Rathbun's office door, said, "'Tis my belly reminding me a bite of lunch is called for. Would you be joining Wendt and me?"

"Like to," Rathbun said. "But I've got a few things to catch up on. And Colonel McCormick is expecting the two of us at three-fifteen. Sharp."

Roche dug an aging Ingersol from the watch pocket of his pants, glanced at the dial. "You'll be finding me in the good man's outer office at exactly three-ten."

At two-thirty on that same afternoon, the Big Fella lay face up on the living-room rug in his Lexington Hotel suite while grunting his way through a series of exercises involving a twenty-pound barbell. Perspiration darkened his gray sweatsuit, and his face had taken on an alarming shade of red.

Frankie Rio, Capone's chief bodyguard and constant companion, was a slender, taciturn Sicilian in his late twenties. He was seated on a couch covered in a soft-rose damask, his black bench-made oxfords propped against the edge of a walnut coffee table inlaid with Carrara marble. On one of the end tables flanking the couch, a white candlestick telephone was placed next to the base of a dark green cloisonné lamp, its off-white shade matching Venetian blinds, half-drawn, at the row of four tall narrow windows overlooking Lake Michigan four blocks to the east.

Rio said, "C'mon, Al. Will ya for chrissake cut it out already? You can kill yourself, them fucking exercises."

Capone released the barbell, but remained sitting on the huge Kirman rug. Finally, after a third effort, he managed to get to his feet and, panting, glared at Rio. "How many . . . times I gotta . . . tell you . . . keep your dirty shoes offa the furniture?"

Rio shrugged, lowered his feet to the rug. Capone dropped heavily into a lounge chair, head tilted back, while his breathing slowed and normal color seeped into his porcine features. He belched loudly, said, "Pour me some'a that red."

Rio left the couch, crossed to the bar alongside the room's closed door. Selecting a bottle of recently imported Chianti, he filled a water glass and brought it to the man in the lounge chair. Capone drank half in a single gulp and bent to place the glass on the coffee table. He raised an arm, turned his face, sniffed, jerked his head back, said, "Jesus! I *stink!*" He stood up and ripped open the sweatsuit, exposing a fish-white expanse of bulging belly dripping with sweat.

A knock at the door. Rio moved smoothly over to peer through a peephole set into one of the panels, then opened up and stepped aside as four men filed in.

Removing their hats, they greeted Capone effusively but, because of the man's tendency to sudden fits of rage, with an underlying uneasiness. Despite differences in build and facial features, all four seemed scissored from the same pattern. They wore faultlessly styled suits of pinstriped gray flannel, their neckwear was subdued in design and color, their linen immaculate. It was the granite faces, the coldly arrogant expressions, the opaque eyes that marked them for what they were: highly placed members of a powerful criminal organization.

At Capone's curt gesture, three of the visitors found seats. The fourth, Claude "Screwy" Maddox, went directly to the bar. He was uncapping a fifth of prewar cognac when Capone said harshly, "Hey you. Maddox. You can't live five minutes without the stuff?"

Abashed, Maddox mumbled an apology, replaced the bottle and sat down. Capone finished the wine in his glass, turned back the cover of a small lacquered box on the coffee table and took out an open pack of Melachrinos. By the time he'd placed one between his thick lips, his visitors were on their feet, lighters out and flaming.

The honor was bestowed on Danny Stanton. Capone exhaled a streamer of smoke and said, "Pour yourself a drink, boys." He turned away, strode briskly to the door and disappeared. Despite his bulk, the ganglord was light on his feet and never waddled.

There was a marked lessening of tension in the room. Maddox headed for the bar and the cognac bottle. Ted Newberry, a stocky, thick-necked Jew in his mid-thirties, said, "Hey, Frankie. Since when's he been on them coffin nails?"

Rio said, "The sawbones tells him lay offa cigars, is all. Won't last."

Stanton, slim, sandy-haired, with a normally sunny disposition, said darkly, "Ask me, I say somethin's eating on him. Hardly even said hello."

"It's this shit about Lingle," Rio said. "They don't nail that shooter quick, Al knows fucking well they'll try hanging it on him."

The fourth visitor, Francesco Maritote, alias Frank Diamond, a squat, swarthy Italian in his early thirties, said, "So what of it? Couple weeks—month—it'll be old news. Like when them seven Moran guys got it last year, you'da thought they was gonna bring in the fuckin' marines on us. Blew over. Al knows that."

At the bar, Maddox drained his glass and reached for the bottle. "Reminds me the time Hymie Weiss's boys go and shoot up a solid blocka Twenty-second Street, damn near. Back in 'twenty-six, that was. Here's Al tryin' to have hisself a nice quiet cuppa java when Hymie and his guys drive by, open up with the choppers and blows hell outta that cafe he was in. Al hisself told me he like to shit his pants! You was there, Frankie. Al always said, hadn't been for you they'd sure as hell got him."

Rio said, "Knocked him down and set on him. One of the papers comes out with this big headline: 'This Is War.' And they weren't all that wrong, either."

"And *that* blew over," Diamond said. "What I'm trying to tell you: so will this Lingle crap."

Newberry had walked over to the bar and put together a Scotch highball. "You're forgetting something, Frank," he said. He took a long swallow of his drink. "And I'm going to tell you what it is. Jake Lingle was a reporter, right? Only that's not the point. He had to go and be a reporter for the *Tribune.* Run by a fucking bulldog name of McCormick. Well, let me put you wise to something, Frank: a bulldog gets his teeth in your ass, they don't let go."

In the twenty-six hundred block of Monroe Street, three miles west of the Loop, stood a low, sprawling structure of red brick, the color long since buried under layers of soft-coal smoke. A row of narrow windows fanning out from either side of the entrance had been boarded up, giving the place a dreary, abandoned look.

Pasted to a wire-enforced panel of opaque glass in one of the double doors was a white cardboard placard:

These Premises
CLOSED FOR ONE YEAR
FOR VIOLATION
NATIONAL PROHIBITION ACT
By Injunction: U.S. District Court
Chicago, Ill.
Dated: November 9, 1929

A dusty Ford Tudor sedan carrying four men moved slowly past the building, made a U-turn at the next intersection and stopped at the curb directly across from the building entrance.

Fred Joyner was behind the wheel. His face was knife-blade thin, his eyes deep-set under craggy brows, his nose like an eagle's beak. He said, "Another couple minutes to make sure the back doors get covered, then we go in."

Michael Casey said, "I was still in high school, living over on Talman, when this was the Hoffman Brewery. Johnny Torrio took over right after Prohibition came in. Got closed down, in 'twenty-six I think it was; then Terry Druggan paid off City Hall and opened her up again. A patrolman out at Fillmore tells me whoever's running the plant nowadays's been sticking one'a those 'Closed by Uncle Sam' signs on the door every year."

Sean Brennan, sharing the back seat with David Levin, said, "From the appearance of those doors, they'll take some getting past."

Levin, a Talmudic scholar, said, "That's why Yahweh, in His infinite wisdom, invented the axe, bubalah."

At the Washtenaw intersection, a block to the west, a small Chevrolet delivery van swung into Monroe. It slowed, began angling toward the curb a few yards short of the brewery entrance. Lettered on its side were the words:

GOLDBERG'S DELICATESSEN
"Catering Our Speciality"

| Weddings | Bar Mitzvahs |
| 3715 W. Roosevelt Rd. | LAWndale 7896 |

Suddenly Joyner was out of the car and racing across the street. He reached the van as it coasted to a stop, yanked open the door and grabbed the startled driver by the front of his white jacket. Before the overweight young man could do more than sputter a protest, Joyner snapped, "Police! Not a sound outta you, hear?" and yanked him off the seat and into the street.

With the side of the van between them and the brewery. Joyner released the driver, flashed his badge, said, "You got a delivery for twenty-six twenty-one?"

"Yessir. Just some sand—"

"Where are they?"

"In front. The basket on the floor. Listen, I—"

"Give me your coat and cap."

"Wha' for? Jeez, I can't—"

"C'mon, dammit!"

The jacket came off; Joyner slipped it on after removing his suit coat. A tight fit, but it would have to do. He snatched the white cap from the dazed driver's head, clapped it on his own at a jaunty angle. Reaching into the van, he removed the ignition key, then pointed to a wicker basket on the floorboards. "That it?"

"Yessir."

Joyner hauled the basket out, shoved his Police Special under the white cloth covering its contents. "Plant your ass on that running-board and keep it planted till I tell you different. Clear?"

". . . Yessir!"

Joyner glanced over at the men watching from the Ford, got an understanding nod from Michael Casey. He slipped his left arm under the basket handle, circled the van, and went quickly up three wide cement steps to the building's twin doors.

A peephole had been installed in the one on the right. Joyner positioned himself so that only his left shoulder and the basket would be visible, then pounded a fist on the heavy planks.

Twenty seconds ticked off before a heavy voice from within snarled, "Yeah?"

"Goldberg's," Joyner said loudly. "Got your order out here."

Sounds: a bar being removed, the snick of a drawn deadbolt. One of the doors swung back and a bull-necked, olive-skinned young man in shirt-sleeves was standing there. He had small flickering eyes, a thin black mustache, a scowl and, under his left arm, a holstered gun.

Joyner said, "How's about a nice corned beef on rye?" reached into the basket, brought out the .38 and leaned its muzzle against one corner of the mustache.

Shock froze the man into slack-jawed silence. Behind him, far back in the cavernous, high-ceilinged room, five men in white coveralls and rubber hipboots were filling wooden barrels with freshly fermented and carbonated beer from two of the six huge glass-lined vats spaced evenly along the side walls.

Joyner's crew was already out of the Ford and running toward the brewery doors. Levin and Brennan carried axes, Casey a Baker/Batavia twin-barrelled shotgun. A late model Chrysler coupe, tires squealing, skidded to a stop; the klaxon on a passing flatbed truck blasted a warning. A horse-drawn ice wagon pulled up at the curb; the driver called out, "Go get 'em, boys!" and settled back to catch another segment of that ever-popular melodrama, the Prohibition Follies, now in its tenth year.

As the rest of the raiding party joined him, Joyner dropped the basket, yanked a small automatic pistol from the guard's holster and shouted, "Police! Nobody move!"

Heads jerked up and around, the nozzle of a beer transfer hose clattered against cement, a voice said, "Oh, *shit!*" in total disgust. Then hands lifted resignedly as the four officers moved quickly in on the group.

Joyner said, "Cuff 'em," and moved with swift silent strides to the far end of the room and on into a short hallway. He stopped at a closed office door, caught the sound of a muted voice from inside, then lifted a foot and kicked it open.

A well-dressed, middle-aged man with male-pattern baldness, horn-rimmed glasses, and an unruffled expression was seated behind a gray metal desk. His right hand, resting idly on an arm of the swivel chair, held the receiver of a candlestick telephone.

Joyner said, "Hang it up."

The man said, "The call's for you, Officer," and placed the receiver gently on the desk top.

Joyner gestured with his gun. "On your feet, hands against the wall."

The man shrugged, stood up without hurrying and assumed the position. Joyner patted him down briskly, came up with nothing more deadly than a Conklin fountain pen. He stepped away, leaned a hip against a corner of the desk, picked up the phone and said, "Joyner speaking."

A deep masculine voice said, "I get this call, there's a raid going on over there. Police raid. That right?"

Joyner said, "Close enough."

"I suppose you have a warrant."

"Wouldn't leave the office without one."

"Name Sam Grossman mean anything to you?"

"Uh-huh," Joyner said. "Alderman, Twenty-ninth Ward."

The voice said, "Now here's what I got in mind, Mister . . . Joyner, you said?"

"Uh-huh," Joyner said.

"You wanta pinch that crew out there," the voice said, "that's okay and no harm done. But it's the equipment won't be easy to replace. So, I'd appreciate you leaving it as is. Do that, then stop down at the Hall at your convenience and let me show you how *much* I appreciate it. Understood?"

Joyner said, "I hate to—" He stopped there as the sounds of ripping metal and shattering glass from the building's brewing area thundered through the small office.

The voice at the other end of the phone yelled, "What the hell was *that!*"

Joyner said, "Somebody must've dropped a beer bottle, Mister Grossman," and put back the receiver.

Roche, reading from his notes, said, "The *Tribune* was paying Lingle sixty-five a week. He had a three-hundred-dollar-a-month suite at the Stevens. He owned a Lincoln limousine, used a part-time chauffeur. His family lives—or did live till here lately—in a high-class West Side apartment building owned by Louis Mondi, brother of one of Al Capone's hoods. Lingle had just finished putting fifteen thousand down on a twenty-three-thousand-dollar summer home on the Indiana lake front. The man bet big at the track, as high as a thousand a race; and he died with fourteen one-hundred-dollar bills in his wallet."

Frowning, Colonel McCormick lifted a silencing hand. "Mister

Roche. You have substantiated this information? Beyond any possible doubt?"

"It's all been verified, Colonel."

"Then where the devil," McCormick said harshly, "did all this money *come* from?"

Roche, Rathbun, and Robert Lee, the paper's city editor, were seated across the desk from the colonel in the publisher's private office. Lee, a lanky, red-haired, soft-spoken man in his early forties, said, "I think I can furnish the answer to that question, sir. And put a stop to the kind of nasty innuendoes we've been listening to here."

McCormick's stony expression seemed to soften a shade. He said crisply, "Then by all means let's hear it."

Lee said, "The truth is, Jake was actually quite well-to-do. His father died eight-ten years ago and left him in the neighborhood of a hundred thousand dollars. Later on, an uncle of his willed him something like fifty thousand.

"And Jake did play the market," Lee said. "Some very close friends of his were stockbrokers: men like Arthur Cutten and, as I recall, Alvin Kramer at Federal Securities. By selling out shortly before last October's crash, Jake came out with a clear profit—by his own statement, Colonel—of close to a hundred fifty thousand."

By this time, McCormick was close to showing a smug smile. He said, "It would seem you've been looking through the wrong end of the telescope where Lingle is concerned, Mister Roche. Would you care to comment on what Bob has just told us?"

Alphonse Capone said, "I go to this new croaker the wife keeps telling me about. Some Hebe, he's supposed to know his onions. He goes over me like a guy looking to buy a used car or something, says, 'Mister Capone, just how old a man are you?' So I tell him: thirty-one. He says, 'Starting right now, no more pasta, no more wine, no more cigars, get some exercise or you don't make it to fifty.' So I say to him, 'I fired my last doctor for that kinda talk.' You wanta hear what the little bastard said to me? He tells me, 'Go back to your last doctor.'"

His audience accorded him the forced chuckle a loyal staff reserves for the company president. Freshly showered, shaved, and cologned, Capone had donned pale yellow silk pajamas, brown alligator house slippers lined with lamb's wool, and a thin robe of brocaded silk in subdued purple.

The gang leader settled his formidable bulk into a wingback chair, reached for a cigarette and accepted a light from Maddox. He motioned for Rio to refill the wineglass and looked at Newberry. "What'd you find out, Ted?"

Newberry leaned back in his chair, placed his palms together in an oddly prayerful position. He said, "Something might interest you, Al. 'Member that wheel joint the North Side boys operated over on Waveland? Got closed down year or so back? Well, here last month they go to Lingle for an okay to open up again.

"Anyway," Newberry said, "Jake says it'll cost 'em a grand. A fucking *week*, can you believe it! They say screw that; we open without you. Jake says, try it and you'll see more squad cars 'n you can count in a month. So, they don't open and Jake's got some people sore at him."

Capone said, "What people?"

"Well, there's this big fat fella," Newberry said. "Name of McLaughlin—John McLaughlin. Runs a wire room out around Belmont and Clark. And some guy they call Potatoes. They were both supposed to be in on opening the joint."

"McLaughlin's a bag'a wind," Capone said contemptuously. "And this Potatoes you mention? He's a two-bit, no-moxie punk name'a Kaufman I wouldn't wipe my ass on. What else you got?"

"Well, so far that's about it, Al," Newberry said lamely. "There's one or two other possibilities I'm still working on could pay off."

Capone, scowling thoughtfully, sampled his wine. He put the glass aside, leveled his gaze at Maddox. "All right. Now let's hear from you."

Maddox's eyes darted nervously at his companions, then came back to the man in the wing chair. He said, "I got to talking to Maxie Eisen here a night or two back. He's in tight with some'a the Morans; but then I guess you know that. Anyhow, Maxie tells me Lingle was into Joe Aiello for a C-note a week to keep the heat offa that bookie layoff joint over at Division and Halsted. Well, here last month damned if Jake don't up the ante on him an extra hundred. Way Maxie tells it, Joe kept saying it's about time somebody dug a nice deep hole for Lingle."

In a sudden burst of angry disgust, Capone slammed a hand down on the lamp table next to his chair. "Same fucking story all over again! First it's O'Banion, then it's Hymie Weiss; now it's Moran and Aiello. Six years I been trying to knock some sense into them peasants and all I get back is trouble. They—just—won't—*listen!*"

Newberry said philosophically, "Guess this's one time you can't hardly blame 'em, Al. The way Lingle was puttin' the boots to a lotta the racket guys around town, anybody'd get sore."

The observation earned Newberry a look of pitying contempt. "You wanta know something, Ted? You're stupid, you know that? You're like the resta the cement-heads in this business. Somebody looks at you cross-eyed, right away you're ready to grab a gun and start shooting."

Newberry, stung, said, "Aw, c'mon, Al. How many times you yourself set up some—"

"I'm not talking about some crummy hood steps outta line," Capone said impatiently. "Him you drop in the alley, it gets on page ten next to a brassiere ad and who gives a damn. But a reporter, for godsake? Even worse: a reporter works for McCormick? That's like you put President *Hoover* on the spot!"

In the charged silence that followed, the sudden ringing of the phone was like an explosion. Rio answered, listened briefly, said, "Lemme find out." He covered the mouthpiece, glanced at Capone. "Sam Grossman. Wants to talk to you."

Capone took the receiver, said affably, "Well, good afternoon, Alderman! This *is* an unexpected pleasure. Now, what can I do for you?"

Reading from his notes, Roche said, "Lingle's father, Alfred, was killed in an accident at Grays Lake in August 1920. Probate court records show he left his son five hundred dollars out of an estate valued at seven thousand two hundred. Jake's uncle Fredrick died of natural causes in April 1928, leaving his nephew one thousand dollars."

Lee said, "Colonel, I simply can't believe what I'm hearing! It's not possible to work with a man as closely as I did with Jake and not know what was going on."

"That," McCormick said levelly, "has already occurred to me, Robert."

Lee felt his throat tighten with something close to panic. He said, "Colonel McCormick, I can assure you all this is news to me. I simply can't believe . . ." He stopped there and looked blindly down at his hands.

Nothing changed in the publisher's expression. He shifted his gaze back to Roche. "Continue, sir."

Returning to his notes, Roche said, "Lingle had accounts with three LaSalle Street brokerage houses. One of those accounts was a partnership with former Police Commissioner Russell. It was closed out with a net loss for the two men of a hundred and seventy-three thousand dollars."

He paused, glanced up, and saw a face carved in granite. "The implication," McCormick said, "is not lost on me, sir. Please go on."

Roche turned a page of the notebook, said, "About the middle of May, this year, Lingle covered a market shortage with fifty thousand in cash. At the time he got himself killed he was pretty much out of the market, leaving a debt to one firm of a little over eleven hundred dollars."

McCormick said, "We've heard at length about the money Lingle was spending—money you say was not inherited. Now, can you state unequivocally where it *did* come from?"

"To be putting it flat out, Colonel," Roche said, " 'tis a crook the man was. Through and through. Connections with them highest up in the police department was what he had, not to mention a lot of pals in the station houses. A raid was set on a handbook, let's say; word was passed along to Lingle and he tipped off the operator—for a price. Same went for breweries, gambling clubs, whorehouses, speakeasies. He was go-between on payoffs by the mobs to judges, lawyers, and a good half of City Hall. And, if the truth be known, sir, to some on the state's attorney's own staff, more's the shame of it.

"The man was a close personal friend of Al Capone," Roche said. " 'Tis a fact that on the day Jake Lingle died he wore around his waist a belt with a gold buckle set with diamonds—given him by Capone. And to be topping it all off for you, Colonel, the man openly bragged it was him set the price of beer in Cook County."

Robert McCormick was no longer listening. While coldly furious at the extent of Lingle's treachery, the publisher was not one to let anger vitiate good sense. Airing the late reporter's criminal involvement with gangsters was bound to bring a cynical curl to a lot of lips from coast to coast. But what might be even more damaging was the risk of alienating many readers loyal to the *Tribune* and its policies. He was reminded of the mantle of martyrdom the city's press had bestowed on Lingle; of the seemingly endless columns of uniformed police, firemen, and naval cadets in that funeral procession, of Father Mulhearn's eulogy with such glowing phrases as "his lofty ideals, his unwavering honesty." There'd be a lot of red faces, McCormick told himself wryly, once the truth came out. Faces red with embarrassment and a concomitant anger directed, for lack of a more visible target, at him and his newspaper.

If the truth came out. Must it come out? He could quietly disband this newly formed crew of investigators and turn the case back to the police for burial once public interest flagged. One more coverup. Like the one after the murder, a few years back, of that young assistant state's attorney, Bill McSwiggin. Or the slaughter of those seven hoodlums in the so-called St. Valentine's Day massacre.

Coverups *pro bono politicus.*

Watching McCormick's expression, Rathbun thought: The man wants out of this. Except he's too stubborn, too damned egotistical to admit his taking over before the facts were in was a big mistake. Now he's looking for an excuse—any excuse!—to get the hell off the spot he's put himself on.

"Colonel," he said, "Lingle is dead. He can't defend himself. From what Pat's turned up, an investigation can only blacken his reputation, hurt his family, his friends. But more to the point, it can start a flock of wild rumors that could do a lot of harm to the *Tribune*. I suggest that has to be considered, sir."

He stopped there, thinking: Okay, Colonel. You want an excuse to drop your investigation without losing face, you now have it. It's called advice of counsel, Colonel—and nobody can fault you for taking it.

Roche held back a cynical smile. Now that it was starting to look like nabbing Jake Lingle's killer wasn't to be all that easy, seemed Charlie was getting a little nervous about maybe ending up on a losing team. Not a risk to be taken lightly, that, since 'twas a well-known fact the good colonel didn't cotton to losers.

McCormick's pale blue eyes seemed slowly to chill over. He said, "Mister Rathbun. Please understand that I'm quite capable of looking after this newspaper and its reputation. Our city's criminal element is responsible for the death of a *Tribune* employee. The murder of Alfred Lingle must mark the end of gang rule in Chicago. I tell you here and now there is to be no turning back. In short, gentlemen, either Justice will triumph or Justice will abdicate."

Roche sat, bemused. Would you be listening to the man! Even *talks* in editorials, the colonel.

She should have known, Angela Terrell told herself bitterly, that going to Jake's funeral would be a big mistake. Having to sit through all that Latin shit and the stink of incense and the silly circus the priests put on—that was bad enough. But what kept coming back to her was the memory of sitting forty feet from that polished walnut box, knowing it was Jake in there, knowing that once they finished talking God into giving him a harp and a halo, they'd haul him out and stick him in the ground. . . .

She angrily brushed away a tear, went to the bar, and refilled her glass with Gordon gin (or so the label claimed). After adding a miniscule amount of vermouth, she dropped in two ice cubes from the silver-trimmed bucket and crossed to one of the living room's wide windows. The newly installed Lindbergh beacon, revolving from high atop the Palmolive building a few blocks to the south, put a slashing path of light against the night's cloudless sky. Loop-bound traffic drifted soundlessly along Lake Shore Drive, past the Potter Palmer castle and the long stretch of beach at Oak Street and on into Michigan Avenue.

Sure beat the hell out of Brooklyn's Bensonhurst section.

It had been ten—no, come to think of it, it was closer to twelve years now, since her old man caught her and the O'Connor (O'Connell?) kid fooling around in the back seat of the family Packard. At the time, it seemed safe enough: two in the morning, the garage door closed, the light off. And they were holding down the noise—anyway they thought so till the car door was jerked open and Giuliano Torenello yanked Sean out of the car (and out of her!) and threw him clear across the three-car garage.

While he'd let Sean off with a whole skin and a warning to keep his Irish yap shut or end up in the East River, the old man turned on her, snarled, *"Puttana!"* and used his belt to whack her bare ass purple. And a week after that, despite a screaming fit by her mother (carried on like some *contadina* fresh out of Sicily, yelling how she'd throw herself in front of a streetcar!), she was out of St. Anne's and into a private school for girls at the ass end of Staten Island.

The place was run like some kind of reform school: no leaving the grounds even during the holidays, no visitors outside the immediate family, classes six days a week and homework half the night. And get caught even *bending* one of their stupid rules and you got buried up to your eyebrows in crap.

Once during the second year there, they did let her out. For a whole four hours! Pneumonia had killed her mother, and the old man sent one of his "business associates"—some "dese and does" asshole—to bring her to the funeral and back. Even then, the way her father acted you'd'a thought she had halitosis or something! Maybe because she was his only kid; if he'd had a couple sons he might not've stayed so mad for so long. Twelve years! And for what? Fooling around with some Irish kid at sixteen. It wasn't like she'd gone and got herself knocked up for godsake!

Her glass was empty. She returned to the bar, put a fresh drink together and switched on the radio. She lit her fifth Wings in the past hour and dropped into one of the matching chairs across from the couch.

Damn it to hell, she missed Jake! She wondered what his wife was doing tonight. Kids in bed, house quiet, reading a book, husband six feet under. And here sits Jake's best girl, all by her lonesome, swilling booze and eating coffin nails and listening to the music of Ben Bernie and all his lads comin' at you from the College Inn high atop the Hotel Sherman, yowsah, yowsah.

She rose impatiently and returned to the window, glass in one hand, cigarette in the other, watching the reflection of city lights prowl the restless reaches of the lake.

. . . She and this lawyer were in the headmistress's office, just the two of them sitting there, with an early spring rain pelting the windows.

He'd introduced himself as Anthony Balasari, attorney-at-law—a skinny little flat tire, patent-leather hair parted in the middle, dandruff thick on his coat collar, and a pair of beady black eyes that never seemed to blink.

"Miss Torenello," Balasari had said, "your father has instructed me to act as his representative in this matter. It will not be necessary—or even possible, I regret to say—for you to reach him."

He opened his briefcase, took out an envelope, and placed it on the desk pad in front of her. "A train ticket. One way, to Chicago. And a bank draft in the amount of five thousand dollars. You are to—"

"*Chicago?* What kind of sap you take me for? I wouldn't be caught dead in that lousy burg!"

Balasari lifted a hand, his expression pained. "You are now eighteen, Miss Torenello, and have the equivalent of a high school education. Your father feels it is time you set about living your own life in different surround—"

"Far from him as I can get, that it? Well, the old son of a bitch's fulla happy dust if he—"

"Please hear me out, Miss Torenello. A gentleman by the name of John Torrio—a trusted friend of your father's—will meet your train in Chicago, assist you in establishing a bank account, help you find suitable living quarters—"

"Oh sure. And go blabbing to my old man every move I make. Well, you can tell *Papa* for me he can go fuck himself he thinks for one goddamn—"

Balasari slammed a palm against the desk top. "Shut your filthy mouth, young woman!" He leaned across the desk and thrust a finger at her. "You have a choice. Go to Chicago, stay there, keep your nose clean . . . and you get three thousand a month. Refuse, and you can end up in the gutter and nobody'll give a damn. Least of all, Giuliano Torenello."

Three days later, during a mid-April snowstorm, Angela Terrell stepped off the Twentieth Century Limited at Chicago's LaSalle Street station.

A powerfully built young man approached her. He wore a faultlessly tailored suit, a vicuña overcoat, pearl-gray spats and fedora, and a winning smile. The three thin scars creasing his left cheek and jawline were barely noticeable.

"You Angelina Torenello?"

"The name," she said icily, "is Miss Angela Terrell."

The young man shrugged. "Close enough, I guess. I come to tell ya Mister Torrio's got some business he couldn't duck out on. So he wants I should take care'a you, okay? I'm Al Capone."

9

The boy from Western Union caught the quarter, said, "Gee, thanks!"—here lately even a dime was a good tip and not all that many of those—and left the office whistling a loose arrangement of the "Pagan Love Song."

Roche tore open the envelope, glanced at the contents. "From the Colt people," he said to Wendt sprawled in the chair across from him. "Says here, 'Your inquiry re thirty-eight. Police Special t.k. 231701 stop Item one of six shipped June twelve 1928 to Von Frantzius Sporting Goods, 608 Diversey Parkway your city stop Our invoice number 8247.'"

Wendt grunted sourly. "Shoulda guessed. How many times you heard me say close that guy's business and half the shooters in this burg'd end up using bows'n arrows."

Roche reached for the phone. "Sophie, see if you can get hold of Judge Lyle's bailiff for me."

He pronged the receiver, held up the telegram. "We got us our key, laddybuck. Now we start looking for the door it'll open."

He flipped the paper aside, tilted back the swivel chair, and propped a foot against the desk top. "Walter," he said, "could you be up to sparing one'a them foine cigarettes you keep hiding away in your pocket there?"

*　　*　　*

Harry Voiler said, "You sure you're clean, Louis? I don't want coppers come shoving into the club some night looking for you, see? Stirring up a fuss, annoying the customers. I got no patience for anything like that."

"Nothing like that's gonna happen, Mister Voiler," Brothers said. "I guarantee you. That little matter you maybe heard about—that's been taken care of while I was outta town."

They were seated in Voiler's cubbyhole office on the third floor of the Green Mill Gardens, a swank cabaret and gambling club in Chicago's Uptown area. An oversized desk and four battered green filing cabinets left barely enough space for the two chairs.

Voiler was in his early forties, a short, slight-bodied man, foppishly dressed, with a receding hairline and a thin black mustache, which he constantly fingered. He said, "I have to admit Gus's not cut out to handle the troublemakers. Matter of fact a couple times there I come close to letting him go altogether."

Brothers said, "I'd certainly appreciate you taking me back on, Mister Voiler. You know I can do the job for you."

"What was it I was paying you, Louis? Hundred a week?"

"Yes sir. That's right."

". . . Okay. Start tonight, eight till closing. How you fixed till payday?"

Brothers gestured apologetically. "Guess I'm a little short, at that, Mister Voiler."

Voiler took a folded sheaf of currency from his pants pocket, stripped off several bills, and handed them over. "That's fifty you owe me. Just make damn sure you don't give me any problems on the job."

When the door closed behind Brothers, Voiler picked up the phone, dialed a number. ". . . Morrie? Put Louis Bader back on the payroll as of today; same money. . . . I *know* that. But if you ask me he's a standup guy, and I'm here to tell you I've had all'a that schmuck Gus I can take."

The phone was answered on the second ring. "Yeah?"

A deep voice said, "Sal? Mario. This extra load just showed up here. Find room for it; the truck'll be there inside an hour."

Salvatore Moretti said, "How big a load?" But the caller had already hung up.

. . . Hoskins said, "Think he went for it?"

Leonard Nevins shrugged, pushed the phone aside. "Don't see why not. Mario Fanelli's the guy who'd make the call; he's got one'a these heavy kinda voices that all tend to sound a lot alike."

"It'd by God better work," Joyner said. "Otherwise we could get our asses shot off."

Clark Street intersected with Diversey Parkway three miles north of the city's Loop and a few blocks west of the lakefront. Because the area's two major hotels catered largely to underworld figures and the corner cigar store ran a huge bookmaking operation, local residents had dubbed the intersection Gangster Gulch.

The nearest open parking space was a few doors west of the new Elks National Memorial. They left Wendt's Ford Runabout there and ducked through heavy traffic to the north side of Diversey.

Roche said, "Seeing as how His Honor wasn't available to us this morning, Walter, let's go about pulling a little something slick on Mister Von Frantzius. As I'm asking the questions, maybe you could be floating around the shop, sticking your nose into this and that. I'm told a man's guard can let down once his attention is divided."

Number 608 was squeezed in between the Rienzi Hotel and a B/G Coffee Shop. Lettered across the single window were the words VON FRANTZIUS SPORTING GOODS, with an untidy display of golf clubs and bags behind the smeared glass. A buzzer sounded as they pushed open the door and went through.

It was a narrow room, deep and badly lighted, with a long blond wood counter. Metal racks supported rifles and shotguns. Shelves on the opposite wall held a miscellany of sports items. Some distance farther back stood a tall glassed-in display case stocked with bows, steel-tipped hunting arrows, and a thick bundle of paper targets.

Alerted by the buzzer, a slender, neatly dressed man in his midthirties appeared from behind a partition at the rear of the shop. His thin, high-pitched voice said, "Is there something I—" He stopped short and his expression went slowly blank.

Roche said, "Been a while, Peter. I think you know Mister Wendt here."

Behind thick, horn-rimmed glasses, Von Frantzius's close-set black eyes seemed to glaze over. He said tonelessly, "What is it you want, Roche?"

Peering closely at him, Roche said, "Well now. Would it be something new we're seeing here, Peter? A mustache. Must say it looks good on you, lad. What there is of it."

Von Frantzius said coldly, "Am I to assume you just dropped in for a . . . friendly visit?"

During this exchange, Wendt had turned away and drifted over to make a casual inspection of the boxed merchandise. Roche said, "I'm normally a man to be friendly, Peter. Keeping it friendly is up to the other guy. With that firmly in both our minds, I'd like a little information from you." His tone hardened imperceptibly. "About a gun."

He brought out the telegram from an inner pocket of his jacket, unfolded it and carefully smoothed out the creases in the yellow paper. Wendt had left the shelves of boxes and was eyeing the archery equipment with mild interest. Von Frantzius, distracted, flicked an uneasy glance at him.

"A Colt .38 Police Special," Roche said. "Shipped out a couple years ago this month. One from a batch of six alike they tell me. I'm here to find out the man's name who bought it."

"Two years," Von Frantzius said, frowning. "Naturally I want to be all the help to you I can. But that far back—"

Roche said, "Don't be dancing me around, Peter. You keep records on handgun sales back to the day you opened this shop. So you get a choice, bucko: either dig 'em out for me or I do the job for you. Right this minute."

Von Frantzius stiffened angrily. "I won't permit anything of the kind!" he snapped. "And certainly not without a warrant. I know my—"

By this time, Wendt had reached the gun rack. He held up a Winchester self-loading rifle and called out, "How much you get for this baby, Pete?"

Von Frantzius, rattled, glared at him. "I don't—I'm not sure. I'd have to—"

Roche said, "A warrant you say? 'Tis that very thing I have here in me pocket, friend Peter." He took a folded document with a blue cover from his jacket, held it an inch from Von Frantzius's chin. "And a lovely fresh one it is, signed by His Honor Judge John Lyle no more than a single hour ago."

The badgered man shoved the hand holding the warrant roughly aside, snarled, "My office," and stalked toward the rear of the store.

Number 620 proved to be a single floor of aging red brick extending a hundred feet along the north side of Hobbie Street. Faded white letters below the roofline spelled out WHOLESALE MEATS—HITCH-COCK AND NORRIS—WHOLESALE MEATS.

Joyner said, "Take a left, back her up the driveway to the doors and give 'em a toot on the horn."

Hoskins, at the wheel, cut the speed of the Diamond T flatbed to a crawl and made the turn. Crouched behind the rear flap of the truck's hooped dark-green tarpaulin were Casey and Brennan, each gripping a handgun.

Inside the warehouse, four olive-skinned young men were deep into draw poker. A fifth dozed in a backless kitchen chair near the double doors. Stacked cases of alleged bourbon and Scotch lined the walls. As was normal for this hour of the day, all trucks were out covering routes ranging from Gold Coast mansions to swank nightclubs and on down the scale to back-street speakeasies.

Outside, a motor growled in the driveway and a horn swore briefly. Salvatore Moretti said, "That's gotta be Mario." He dealt himself two cards, missed a spade flush, yelled, "Rocco! Get off your dead ass and let the guy in!"

In the truck, Joyner, eyes intent on the rearview mirror, said, "They're moving. Back her up . . . slow . . . slow. . . . Hit it!"

The heavy truck shot through the opening, narrowly missing one of the doors, and slammed to a stop as Rocco vanished. The tarpaulin's rear flap jerked aside, Sean Brennan yelled "Police!" and the card players were staring into the muzzles of two leveled guns.

For a frozen instant nobody moved. Then Moretti's shoulders twitched, a small black pistol sprouted in his hand, swung sharply toward Brennan. A gun roared. A black hole appeared below Moretti's left eye, blossomed into a red gout. His jaw sagged in disbelief, then he put his head gently down on the table and died.

The remaining three mobsters were standing, hands lifted, faces blank, as Joyner and Hoskins, their guns out, came into the scene. Brennan said, "The stupid son of a bitch *drew* on me! He's looking straight down the barrel of my fucking gun. And he *draws* on me!"

No one spoke. The three Italians, hands still raised, looked on stoically. Brennan took a few quick steps, bent down and pounded a fist against the table next to the dead man's head. His voice breaking, he yelled, "You guinea prick—why? For what? Aiello's stinking booze? Come on, you dumb shit! I wanta know *why!*"

Peter Von Frantzius swung back the safe's heavy door, brought out a stack of cloth-bound ledgers and slapped them down on the kneehole desk. He said, "Irregardless of who buys a weapon from me, you can rest assured they must have a legitimate license."

Roche said, "Sure. And for a sweet smile and fifty bucks, seven judges I can name off the top of my head will hand one over. Under any name that pleases and not so much as a question asked."

"Legal just the same. Two years, you say?"

"Shipped from the Colt factory June twelve, one-nine-two-eight," Roche said. "One of six .38 caliber Police Specials. Could take, say . . . four to seven days to get here."

Von Frantzius selected one of the ledgers, leafed quickly through the first half, then slowed as he examined the remaining pages. Finishing, he leaned back in his chair and spread his hands. "Gentlemen, I regret having to disappoint you. But I have no record of any such shipment."

Roche said, "Try your invoices."

Von Frantzius shook his head. "No reason to hold onto them.

Every shipment received is entered on a separate page. As each item is sold it is recorded on that same page."

Roche looked over at Wendt. "You hear the man, Walter? Made a mistake, the Colt people. Pity."

And then Roche was on his feet. Grabbing Von Frantzius's jacket lapels in both hands, he yanked the gun dealer out of his chair and half across the desk. "Friend Peter," he said, "they can't afford the mistakes, the Colt people. And more to the point, boyo, neither can the likes of you."

He shoved Von Frantzius back into the chair, leaned down, and speared him with a cold-eyed glare. "Now hear my words," Roche said softly. "Should I leave without what I came here for, every ledger, every sales slip, every shipment record in and out, leaves with me. And let me find among them one—*one*—gun sale to any man with a fake license and a crime sheet and I will close down this foine shop of yours, ceiling to basement."

Roche straightened, stepped back, took the telegram from his pocket and glanced at it. "The number taken from that .38 is t.k. 231701. Feel up to giving it another go around, friend Peter?"

By the time they left the gun shop and were back in Wendt's car, the temperature had climbed into the nineties, with the humidity close on its heels. Coats came off and ties were loosened, then Wendt made a U-turn and headed for the Loop.

Traffic fumes drifted through the open windows and settled in around them. A streetcar gonged aside a horse-drawn wagon and tempers flared. Jackhammers were tearing apart a stretch of pavement south of Fullerton Avenue.

Roche said, "Citro ... Frank Citro. 'Tis a name that chimes a faint bell with me, Walter."

"Name like that," Wendt said, "must be some spaghetti head, I'd say. Sure don't figure to be the Lingle shooter, him blond and white-skinned the way those witnesses keep on telling it."

Roche said, "Not all wops have black hair and dark skins. Go up

Italy a ways—'round Florence and Pisa there—you'd think you're in, say, Sweden almost."

Wendt said, "You're not gonna find many like that in this town's mobs, Patrick. Not from what I run across. What we get is all these greaseballs from around Naples. Palermo. The Mafia guys. And not a blond or anything near it in the bunch."

A mile or so later, Roche sat up sharply, said, "Some years back it was, Walter. Whilst I was yet on the P.D. Election day, and some ballot-box stuffing was going on out in one'a the Nineteenth Ward precincts as I recall.

"Anyhow," Roche said, "we made the run and picked up a couple tough eggs, booked 'em. After that, I don't know. But, Walter, sure as hell's hot one'a them called himself Frank Citro. Blond or dark I couldn't say offhand, but Frank Citro was the name. And the minute we get back, I want somebody put on it."

On the way up in the elevator Wendt began to chuckle. "Let me ask you something, Pat. Let's say Von Frantzius *had* wanted a look at that phoney warrant of yours. What then?"

Roche grinned, said, " 'Tis the pure of heart has the good Lord in his corner, my kraut friend. Never once doubt it."

Rathbun said, "So far, the raids are bearing fruit, Your Honor. As of now we've closed down seven of the town's largest breweries, as well as a good number of gambling dens, houses of prostitution, speakeasies and outlying roadhouses. Truck convoys hauling wet goods into the city have been intercepted and their cargoes confiscated. The loss of revenue to Capone and the Moran-Aiello mob is considerable. But for our primary purpose, Your Honor, it's not enough."

He was seated opposite Municipal Court Judge John Lyle in the latter's chambers. The court was in noon recess and Lyle, forty-eight, a tall, rangy native of Tennessee, was having coffee and a tuna sandwich at his desk.

"Your primary purpose," Lyle drawled, "being to smoke out the Lingle killer."

"Exactly," Rathbun said. "In time, I suppose, those tactics would force whoever gave the order to hand over the man who pulled the trigger. But the colonel is impatient, Judge. He wants the process speeded up."

Lyle chewed ruminatively on a mouthful of sandwich, washed it down with a draught of coffee. He said, "Why've you come to me on this, Charlie?"

"You're familiar with section two-six-seven-nine of the city ordinances?"

Lyle gave an amused grunt. "Well, sure's hell not right offhand, no."

Rathbun produced a sheet of paper from a jacket pocket, unfolded it. "I've taken the liberty of editing two-six-seven-nine down to fit my purpose. Mind listening?"

"Shoot."

"It's headed *Vagabonds, Vagrants.*'" Then, reading aloud: "'All persons who are idle and dissolute . . . and who neglect all lawful business, and who habitually misspend their time by frequenting houses of ill-fame or gaming houses . . . and having no lawful means of support, shall be deemed to be and are hereby declared to be vagabonds, and shall be fined two hundred dollars for each offense.'"

He stopped there, refolded the paper and waited for a response from the man across from him.

Lyle leaned back, fished a handkerchief from a pocket of his robe. Removing his rimless eyeglasses, he breathed gustily on the lenses, polished them vigorously, replaced them. He said, "Make your point, Charlie."

Rathbun said, "Give me arrest warrants charging vagrancy against the town's top gang figures, Judge. Capone, Aiello, Moran, Zuta, Jack McGurn, Humphrey, et al. We'll put them in front of the bench; they refuse to answer, you find them guilty. If they plead inability to pay, as accused vagrants they'll be required to work off the fine; if they pay it they must disclose their source of income. Let them try lying about *that*, and we prove it, they get nailed for perjury."

Nothing showed in Lyle's expression. He said, "Sounds to me like you been doing your homework, Charlie."

Rathbun said, "Let me give you what I think's the real clincher. Here lately Uncle Sam's been doing some digging into these big shots' tax returns. Jack Guzik, Frank Nitti, Ralph Capone. And the biggest shot of them all: Al Capone. A slip of the tongue while on the stand in your courtroom could end up helping the government's tax fraud investigation against any one—or all—of them."

Lyle took the last bite of his sandwich, pushed the plate aside, brushed crumbs from his fingers, and picked up his cup. He said, "Let me remind you, my friend, that mine is an elective office. And I don't mind telling you I like being a judge, like being called 'Your Honor.' Now just what do you think my chances would be for re-election if I was to go along with what you're asking me to do?"

Rathbun said, "The people are sick of gang rule, Judge. They want those sonsabitches behind bars."

Lyle snorted. "The people? Come on, Charlie; you know better than that. It's the politicians that have the say on who gets elected. Would you care to hazard a guess on who fills *their* pockets?"

Rathbun left his chair, walked over to a window and stood there looking down into the sun-tortured street three floors below. From atop a bookcase behind him an oscillating fan fought a battle already lost against the chamber's pervasive humidity and heat.

Rathbun said, "There are higher offices to aspire to than a judgeship, John."

When there was no immediate response, the lawyer turned. Lyle sat unmoving, his eyes revealing nothing of the thoughts behind them.

"Let's take an obtainable example," Rathbun said. "The mayor's chair. Bill Thompson is through. Naturally he'll be seeking another term, but he won't make it past the primaries. . . . I'm saying you could have that nomination, Your Honor."

Lyle said, "It's a nice thought you have there, Charlie. One I'll admit that's popped up in the back of my mind from time to time. And I have to agree that Thompson has worn out his welcome. Too bad it didn't happen years ago.

"But the consensus around City Hall," Lyle said, "is that the Democrats will sweep the ticket next year, that Tony Cermak is to be the new mayor. Considering his record, I shudder at the thought, but all the signs are there."

Rathbun said, "Not necessarily, John. With the backing of the right people and, let's say, a highly influential newspaper, Mister Cermak could have his pushcart upset."

A small smile tugged at the corners of Lyle's lips. "An influential newspaper. Such as the *Chicago Tribune!*"

"Colonel McCormick," the lawyer said, "wants Jake Lingle's killer brought to justice. Executed by the state, if at all possible; a life sentence at the very least. Those who get solidly behind that effort will find the colonel . . . grateful."

Knuckles tapped against the closed door. From outside it, the bailiff's voice said, "Five minutes, Your Honor."

Lyle said, "We're alone here, counselor. Are you saying flat out that McCormick will back me in the mayoral race? If I do my part in harassing the mobs into turning over Lingle's killer?"

Rathbun nodded. "That's what I'm saying."

"I'll need your personal word on this."

"You have it, John."

The jurist stood up. "I've got to get back." He stuck out a hand and Rathbun shook it. "Get your list together, Charlie," Lyle said. "The warrants will be issued."

Roche was on the phone when Herbert Seyferlich put his head in and was waved to a chair. He waited till Roche was finished with the call, then leaned over, dropped a white six-by-eight-inch card in front of him and said, "Frank Citro."

Roche snatched it up, read the neatly typed words. "Well, well," he said softly. "Frankie Foster." He settled back in his chair and glanced up at Seyferlich. "Would you be knowing of the man, Herb?"

"Can't say's I do, Mister Roche."

"Four aliases," Roche said, "but Foster would seem to be his rightful name. Started out with Capone a few years back, he did. Rode shotgun on booze trucks down from Canada there. Then seems he had this falling-out with Frank Nitti—two winters it's been now—and switches to the Moran-Aiello crowd. A shooter for them, 'tis said. Could be true."

He ran fingertips lightly across the smooth surface of the card, let it drop to the desk top and picked up the phone. "Sophie, see if you can find Walter for me, that's a good lass."

Patient file #37B, June 29, 1930. Physician: Dr. David V. Omens, 1225 Independence Blvd., Chicago, Ill.

Name of patient: Albert Brown, address 7244 South Prairie Ave, Chicago, Ill., Tel. Triangle 5871. Occupation: salesman.

Upon examination, I informed the patient that the lesion on his penis was a fully developed chancre, the primary stage of syphilis.

The patient became agitated and verbally abusive, called me a "cheap croaker," and stated that I did not know what I was talking about. Upon my suggestion that he get a second opinion, the patient calmed down and asked for a prognosis. I informed him of the second and third stages of the disease, during which he would be highly infectious, and cautioned against further sexual activity during those periods.

The patient then asked for details on treatment of the disease. When informed that a series of injections of arsphenamine over a period of weeks was indicated, he paled visibly and stated that nobody had ever stuck a needle in him in his life and never would. When I attempted to explain the probable consequences of refusing or delaying treatment, the patient refused to hear me out, mumbled something about thinking it over and abruptly left my office.

David V. Omens, M.D.

(Addendum: Although the patient gave his name as "Albert Brown," his resemblance to newspaper photographs, including distinctive facial scars, leads me to believe he actually is the notorious gangster Alphonse Capone.)

From the Chicago *Post*, dateline July 3, 1930.

Police yesterday recovered the body of a young woman identified as Ruby Wynoski, 24, from Lake Michigan near the Indiana line.

According to the coroner's office, Miss Wynoski had been badly beaten, then strangled. Burnham authorities state that she was an employee of the Arrowhead Inn, a roadhouse said to be run by the Capone syndicate, and had a lengthy record of arrests on prostitution charges.

CRESCENDO

If I'd thought there was gonna be this much
of a stink . . .

—Jack Zuta,
1930

10

Jerry blew two shrill blasts on his doorman's whistle. A Checker cab untangled itself from the line of traffic and angled toward the curb.

He said, "Another hot one, hey, Miz Terrell?"

"I'm afraid it is, Jerry," Angela said. "Do you *have* to wear that uniform jacket when it's like this?"

"Boss's orders," he said. "But you get used to it."

He opened the taxi door, thanked her for the dollar she slipped into his waiting hand, and watched the cab move off along Lake Shore Drive.

A real lady, that one. Class. Best damn tipper in the building. *And* one helluva shape on her!

A Yellow cab pulled up and he helped the elderly couple from 7E get out. They brushed past him and disappeared into the lobby. No tip there—and with the old fart owning this big factory or something on the West Side.

He moved farther back under the canopy, away from the sun, and thought about Angela Terrell. Here lately looked like she'd lost some'a the old bounce. Kinda—well, *sad*, you could say. Ever since, come to think of it, that reporter boyfrienda hers got hisself bumped off last month. She even might have some idea why. Him sleeping with her and all, he could easy as not opened up to her, told her who was out to get him. Say some copper comes along, asks her a couple questions, she slips him the info—and he gets that big reward the *Trib*'s putting up. Except the cops don't know about her and the *Trib* guy. But if somebody was to tip 'em off and it worked out, somebody could get their mitts on a hunka that reward money, right?

He was known as Jack McGurn, a slim, wiry Italian gunman attached to the Capone gang. In addition to the twelve murders on his personal scoreboard, he had been the brain behind the mass killing of seven members of the North Side Moran mob in a Clark Street garage a year earlier.

At the moment he was on top of, and into, a twenty-year-old blonde in a room at a downtown hotel.

McGurn climaxed, grunting heavily, then rolled off the blonde. She moved closer, ran a hand across the damp hair on his chest and cooed, "Good, honey?"

He brushed the hand aside. "Go find me a towel, for chrissake. I'm sweatin' like a fuckin' pig here."

"Sure, honey." The blonde sat up. "Now you just stay right where you are, dearie, and I'll—"

The corridor door crashed open and Hoskins and Levin, guns drawn, were in the room. The blonde screamed, McGurn's hand dived under a pillow, froze there when Hoskins yelled *"No!"* and slowly reappeared, empty. Hoskins took one swift smooth stride, swept the pillow aside and snatched away a snub-nosed .38.

McGurn said, "I got a license for that," and stood up with slow care. Levin came out of the bathroom, holstered his gun, scowled at the blonde, said, "Go get some clothes on, sister."

The blonde gave him a murderous glare, scooped a dress and teddies from the back of a chair, and marched into the bathroom.

Hoskins had taken a folded document from his jacket. He held it out to McGurn and said formally, "James DeMora, alias Jack McGurn, I have a warrant for your arrest."

McGurn said, "Stick it up your ass, copper."

Hoskins said, "Sure," and buried a fist in McGurn's belly, knocking him into the wall. The swarthy-skinned hoodlum sank to his knees and doubled over, gasping for breath. Hoskins grabbed a handful of brilliantined hair, yanked McGurn to his feet, said, "You're charged with being a common vagrant. Now, would you like to put on your pants or do we take you in buck naked?"

Roche said, "If there's one fault a man can find with this town 'tis the heat of its summers." He opened a desk drawer, took out a fresh handkerchief, pushed back his wilted collar and mopped his neck. "It is the look of a cat full of the cream you're wearing there, Walter."

Wendt took the chair across from him and lit a cigarette. He blew out the match, tossed it into the ashtray. "Has to do with Frankie Foster, Pat. The Seneca was one of his hangouts. I got to talking to one of the bellhops. Foster had something going with a woman name of Kellogg living there. Evelyn Kellogg. Divorced, maybe forty, no record on her. A real lady, Pat; this is no bimbo we're talking about here.

"Anyhow," Wendt said, "she tells me her understanding was that Foster owned some kind of trucking outfit. She ran into him one day in the hotel lobby, they get to talking, he was pleasant and attentive, and they start seeing each other. Then here around the middle of June sometime, he tells her he's got to be outta town, just how long he can't say offhand, he'll call her when he gets back."

Roche nodded thoughtfully. "Middle of June, huh?"

"Not that it has to mean all that much by itself," Wendt said. "You know damn well half the top shooters in Chicago lit out for the sticks right after Lingle got it."

"Fact remains," Roche said, "Foster disappeared around the same time a bullet was put into the late Mister Lingle. A bullet out of a gun bought by the aforementioned Mister Foster."

Wendt said, "Anyhow, what I was getting at. Four-five days ago, damned if Evelyn Kellogg don't get this letter from Foster saying he's sorry about being too busy to write before and it could be a while till he gets back."

Roche sat up abruptly. "Return address?"

"Maybe yes," Wendt said. "He used hotel stationery but didn't say anything about staying there."

"Where?"

"The Hollywood Hotel," Wendt said. "Out in Hollywood, California." He grinned. "Maybe the man's looking to get in one of those gangster movies."

"You call the hotel? See if he's registered?"

"I thought it better not to, Patrick," Wendt said. "In case a bellhop or a clerk should whisper in his ear as to how somebody in Chicago was asking about the state of his health."

Roche leaned back, gazed thoughtfully at a corner of the ceiling. He absently patted his shirt pocket, Wendt pushed his cigarette pack across the desk, Roche shook one out and got it burning. From atop the filing cabinet the fan droned futilely, traffic sounds from Washington Street, five floors below, crawled limply in at the open window and died on the floor. Beyond the closed office door, phones rang and typewriters ground out a steady stream of reports.

Presently Roche extinguished the cigarette, said, "Time we got us a little legal advice, Walter." He stepped across to the closed connecting door of the adjoining room, knocked, said, "You in there, Charlie?" and went through.

Rathbun was at his desk. He put aside a typed report, said, "Morning, Pat. Walter," without warmth, and gestured for them to sit down.

In contrast to the second-hand austerity of Roche's office, the attorney's had been outfitted by an interior decorator from Marshall Field's. Royal blue broadloom extending to the baseboards gave regal emphasis to a large solid walnut desk, a well-stocked bookcase in the same wood, a high-backed swivel chair in black leather, a burnished-copper desk lamp, a state-of-the-art telephone, and tastefully framed hunting prints spaced along the walls. On the desk, next to a Waterman pen desk set, stood a photograph of a handsome dark-haired woman and two teenaged girls.

Rathbun leaned back, put one leg across a corner of the desk, and said, "Something I should know about, gentlemen?"

Roche said, "We're told Frankie Foster's on the West Coast. Maybe in Hollywood. While he's being rounded up would you be after preparing the necessary papers to pry the man loose and back into our eager hands?"

It was known as Gil's Place, an eight-table poolhall on West Sixty-sixth, two blocks off Halsted and three steps down from street level. Two shirt-sleeved men were deep into a snooker match while a few hangers-on watched from a respectful distance. Layers of smoke from cigarettes and cheap cigars drifted under the overhead lights.

Up front, Gil Mahoney was gluing a fresh tip to a cue stick when the door opened and Joyner and Brennan came in. They went past him without a glance and on down the room. New faces to Mahoney, but he had rubbed elbows and tempers with the law and the lawless enough years to recognize either element on sight. He stayed where he was, called on his patron saint to intercede in protecting the joint, and began smoothing the cue tip with sandpaper.

It was said of Danny Stanton that, for a man well up in the Capone organization's hierarchy and close to the Big Fella himself, he also associated with some pretty crummy types. In the early years of the beer wars he had been connected with Polack Joe Saltis's "back-o'-the-yards" gang and was reliably reported to have at least seven gangland scalps to his credit.

At the moment, he was stretched half across Mahoney's snooker table, one foot on the floor, while preparing to sink one of the red balls.

From behind him, Joyner said, "You're under arrest, Danny."

Stanton's hand twitched, the cue ball spun off at an angle and plopped into a side pocket. In the sudden silence nobody moved and the kibitzers' expressions went slowly and carefully blank.

Stanton slammed the butt of his cue against the floor and spun around. "Who the hell you think—?"

He stopped short, stared hard at Joyner. ". . . Hey. Don't I know you from somewheres?"

Joyner said, "Fred Joyner, state's attorney's office. We went round and round out at the Brighton Park precinct some years back. When I was still on the force."

Stanton's expression cleared, took on its normal good humor. "Yeah—sure. That jewelry store knockover, right? I spread a little dough around and got it cut to illegal entry."

A burly truck-driver type with a wide loose-lipped mouth and salami-on-rye breath pushed between them. "What the fuck *is* this— old home week?" He shoved a prognathous jaw at Joyner. "We got two cees ridin' here, buddy, so back the hell off till we're done."

Joyner said, "You're already done, fella," and turned away. The player grabbed his arm, yanked him back. In one blurred movement, Joyner snatched a red ball from the table and shoved it completely into the man's mouth.

There was a collective gasp from the onlookers as the man stumbled back, gagging, and clawed wildly at his face. Joyner swept a sharp glance at the others, then lifted an eyebrow at Stanton. "How's about it, Danny?"

Stanton grinned. "If it's all the same to you," he said, "I druther have me a pork chop."

Gil Mahoney, brow furrowed, was sanding a fresh cue tip at the front desk. He didn't look up as Joyner and Brennan escorted Stanton out the door.

For the past five days a brutal heat wave had clamped clammy talons on the city's throat. Nightfall brought no relief. Entire families sought respite in parks and the lakeshore beaches, hoping for a full night's sleep under the stars. Others crowded the Byzantine and French Renaissance interiors of movie palaces where huge noiseless fans blew air currents across cakes of ice, raising the number of common colds in audiences to epidemic levels.

Senseless violence flared in the streets. Two South Side gangs, the Batwings and the Kenwoods, tangled in a bloody border dispute that put seven of them in the County Hospital's prison ward. When asked if it was hot enough for him, a recently divorced bank guard shot dead the conductor of a Milwaukee Avenue streetcar.

Gaetano Morici, maitre d' of the Alcazar Ristorante, entered one of its small private dining rooms and set a laden tray on a serving stand. With smooth grace he filled three wineglasses from a large cut-glass carafe, placed them on the table where Giuseppe Aiello, George "Bugs" Moran and Jack Zuta were seated.

A scowl creased Moran's lumpy face. He said, "I don't want this dago milk. Get me a bourbon, water on the side."

"At once, Signor Moran," Gaetano Morici said, icily polite. To the well-born, racial slurs from *contadini* were as an idle breeze. He placed the carafe and a platter of sausage, olives, celery stalks and hulled walnuts on the table.

"Our thanks, Gaetano," Aiello said.

Morici said, "It is my honor to serve you, Don Giuseppe," and left the room, closing the door softly.

Zuta stirred impatiently in his chair. He said, "All right. You boys called this sit-down. Something special bothering you?"

Aiello carefully selected a walnut meat, bit into it. Despite the night's smothering heat he wore a three-piece suit of lustrous brown Italian silk. He had a narrow, olive-skinned face, overly large ears, and deep-set soft brown eyes that, in anger, took on the impenetrable sheen of wet paving stones. A graduate of Palermo University, he had come to America while still a young man and prospered as a wholesale produce merchant. Now, at thirty-nine, he was a high-ranking member of the city's Mafia and, together with Moran and Zuta, leader of the North Side mob.

He sipped briefly from his wineglass, set it aside, said, "Nineteen of our best spots've been closed down, what with four warehouses knocked off we're running low on booze, some of our best horse joints are gone, our delivery trucks get grabbed left and right, two of my brothers are up on vag charges, and our total take is running at damned near two million below what it should be. So yes, Jack, something's bothering George and me."

He reached for an olive, said, "And why is it these things are happening to us? Because some *assassino* puts a hole in Jake Lingle's head. Whose idea, Jack? Yours?"

Zuta said evenly, "You're asking me how I run my business?"

Aiello spread his hands. "*Your* business, Jack? We're partners, no? We run this thing of ours together."

"Sure," Zuta said. "But don't expect me tell you every time I take a piss."

Moran, in his late thirties, pot-bellied, with a thick neck and a receding hairline, glared at Zuta. "Whatta you crackin' wise for? It's a legit question. Was it you had Lingle bumped off or not?"

A discreet knock at the door. Gaetano Morici came in, set two glasses in front of Moran, disappeared. Zuta settled back in his chair, took up his wineglass, and stared at it moodily.

"The son of a bitch comes to me," he said. "In May, this was. Open a dog track, he says, and you make more money than the fucking mint. I said to him, 'Don't you read the papers, Jake? They got a law in this state against dog tracks.'

"Then he tells me," Zuta said, "Judge Fisher's thinking of retiring but wants to build up a bank account first. Slip his honor fifty grand through me, Lingle says, then open the track. They try closing me down, I get a restraining order from Fisher. It's a tough legal question: if horse tracks can run, why not dog tracks? While Fisher's taking a couple months making up his mind, I'll be raking in the dough."

Aiello kept his contempt from showing. "So?"

Zuta shrugged, sampled his wine. "All bullshit," he muttered. "Jake made the whole thing up, then told me to go to hell when I wanted my fifty thousand back."

"And you have him killed."

"You damn right," Zuta said. "Let a thing like that go by and everybody marks you for a patsy."

Aiello sighed, shook his head. "You should've come to us, Jack. We could've worked something out."

Zuta set his wineglass aside, fumbled out a half-empty pack of Omars, lit one. "Maybe so," he said. "If I'd'a thought there was going to be this much of a stink . . ."

His voice trailed off. Moran was glowering at him. Aiello helped himself to a walnut, used wine to wash it down. A polite knock and Morici looked in, said, "Would the gentlemen wish to order dinners?"

Aiello looked at the others, saw a complete lack of interest. "It would seem not, Gaetano. Perhaps later."

"As you wish, Don Giuseppe." The maitre d' withdrew. In the weighted silence that followed, Moran, scowling, gulped down most of his whiskey, belched hugely, and sat staring at the glass.

Aiello said, "Who did the job on him, Jack?"

Zuta's expression went blank. "What's that got to do with it?"

"He's got to go."

". . . You telling me you want him dead?"

"Has to be, Jack," Aiello said. "Look at it this way. Put your boy on a slab, tip the cops he's the one shot Lingle, the witnesses'll make him for sure. Why wouldn't they? He's the one that did it. The *Tribune* is satisfied, Roche is out of a job and they stop hitting us with these raids."

Moran stared at Aiello in unabashed admiration. "Hey!" he said. "I like it!"

Zuta's jaw hardened. "You know what's the matter with you guys? You got a yellow streak. This thing's gonna blow over; they always blow over. Come on! All we hafta do is sit tight for a while."

"Jack," Aiello said. "Wake up and smell the coffee for chrissake. We got this mule-head McCormick to contend with here. These crackdowns won't stop till he's satisfied."

Zuta said, "And you want *me* to set him up, right?"

Aiello shrugged a shoulder. "He's your guy."

Zuta took a deep breath, let it out slowly, said, "Not a chance. Forget it."

Moran's face turned an angry red. "What's the matter, Jack? This bum a relative'a yours or somethin'?"

"Him I don't give a shit for," Zuta said. "It's me I'm talking about. I hire a guy to do a job, then knock him off for doing it, how long you think I stay in business? *Alive* even—everybody's got friends, you know."

He stood up without haste, drew up the knot of his tie, set his Panama firmly in place. He said, "You're so anxious to hit somebody, go hit Pat Roche. Just lay the hell offa my people, that's all."

Zuta turned, stalked to the door, jerked it open. From behind him, Moran said, "Wanta know somethin', Jack?"

The stocky panderer, fuming, half-turned, glanced back impatiently, said, "Yeah?"

Moran said, "From what I been hearin', Al Capone's got some idea maybe one'a us had Lingle pushed. This heat don't let up pretty soon, he's just screwy enough to take a crack at all three of us. So think it over, okay?"

Zuta said, "Fuck Al Capone," went on out, slamming the door and leaving Aiello and Moran staring thoughtfully at each other across the table.

Moran's laugh was brief and without humor. He said, "Fuck Al Capone, huh? Can't count how many times I said exactly the same thing. Up till a year ago last February, that is."

Aiello rose, took the wine carafe from the serving tray, refilled his glass and sat down. He said, "Let me ask you something, George. How bad would you say we actually *need* Zuta?"

Moran gave him a lopsided grin. "Well, they tell me he runs a mean whorehouse. But I'd put the figure he brings in at around four-'n-half million. Maybe five. What with them new slots and the unions."

Aiello absently pawed through the walnut meats, selected one. He said, "I'm going to say this, George—and you're not talking me out of it. We take over . . . and we lose Jack Zuta. We can't afford him no more."

Moran, aware pulling something like that could snap back on you, finally shrugged in assent. He said, "But you gotta remember somethin', Joe. You heard him: 'Ever'body's got friends.' It comes out *we* put Jack on the spot, we could end up taking it in the ass ourself."

He leaned back, got out his watch, snapped open the cover, frowned at the hour. He said, "I gotta get some shut-eye, Joe. Three truckloads of Log Cabin bourbon supposed to get in here six A.M." He grunted sourly. " 'Less a'course Pat Roche's boys bust it up for us."

The two men got to their feet, shook hands. Aiello said, "On your way out, George, tell Morici I want him?"

"Sure."

Alone, Giuseppe drained the wineglass, refilled it for the third time. His decision to remove Jacob Zuta permanently had been made two days before, along with a possible way to bring it off. And now he had Moran's approval, no matter how reluctantly it had come.

The door opened and Gaetano Morici slipped in. "You wish to speak with me, Don Giuseppe?"

"Do sit down, Gaetano," Aiello said. He gestured at the carafe. "Will you join me, my friend?"

"*Grazie, patrono,*" Morici said. He accepted a filled glass and sank onto the edge of a chair. Aiello sat facing him, lifted his own glass, said, "*Salude.*"

They drank, put the glasses aside. Aiello took a small black cigar from a vest pocket, dipped one end into Moran's untouched wine and bent to the match-flame Morici proffered.

In a Sicilian dialect common to both men, Aiello said, "What I say to you now, Gaetano, is in confidence. You understand this?"

"Certainly, Don Giuseppe."

Aiello said, "I seem to recall hearing that you have a family member in the pay of the Signor Caponi."

Morici shrugged as only a Sicilian can shrug. He said, "The son of my elder brother," then added with faint distaste: "From Taylor Street."

"You regard him as a friend?"

"We have never quarreled."

Aiello said, "It is necessary that I call on you, as a friend of the friends, for a personal and confidential favor."

"How may I be of service to you, *patrono?*"

Aiello leaned closer. He said, "Arrange to notify the son of your brother that on this night I met here with the Signori Zuta and Moran; that you heard Signor Zuta openly boast of arranging the assassination of the reporter Lingle; that both Signor Moran and I were deeply distressed and angered by his stupid act. Beyond that you heard nothing. Is this understood?"

"It is understood," Gaetano Morici said.

11

The apartment building at 8126 Vernon Avenue was four floors of red brick with a yellow facade. It had three entrances off a foliage-choked central court.

In the third-floor apartment of Howard and Abigail Wilson, Leonard Nevins said, "In your statement given to officer John Stege on June tenth, Mrs. Wilson, you described the man who shot Alfred Lingle as being around five-feet-six or -seven, a hundred and fifty pounds or thereabouts. Is that correct?"

Mrs. Wilson, a slightly plump woman with light brown hair and soft features, said, "Near's I can remember, Mister. . . ?"

"Nevins."

". . . that's about what I said, yes, sir."

"You also said, I understand, that you would recognize this man if you saw him again. Is *that* correct?"

Abigail Wilson said, "Well now, I think I could, Mister . . . Nevins. I'd have to see, you see. They had me down with some other people to look at what I was told was a . . . 'line-up'? and he certainly wasn't any of *those* men."

Nevins opened his briefcase, took out four eight-by-ten glossy prints, spread them across the dining room table in front of the woman. He said, "Would you take a close look at these four photographs, Mrs. Wilson, and tell me if any one of them is, or could be, the man you saw shoot Alfred Lingle? And please take all the time you need to be sure one way or the other."

One by one, Abigail Wilson scanned the pictures closely, frowning in concentration. Finishing, she hesitated, went back to one, peered at it intently, then handed it to Nevins. "If it wasn't for his hair, Mister Nevins, I'd say I'm almost sure he's the man I saw shoot that gun."

Nevins glanced at the face, said, "His *hair*, ma'am?"

"This man I saw took his hat off in that tunnel and he had kind of blond hair, you see." She pointed at the photo Nevins was holding. "*His* is black, it looks like to me. Even if it's the right face."

Nevins produced a fountain pen, handed it to her. "Just to make sure I don't get it mixed up with the other three, Mrs. Wilson, would you write your name on the back of it?"

". . . I guess that would be all right," Abigail Wilson said.

It was a photograph of Frankie Foster.

The New York, Chicago & St. Louis Railroad terminal was located at the southern fringes of the Loop. The entrance to the cathedral-like edifice, hemmed in by office buildings, fronted on Van Buren Street, a busy artery made hideous by heavy traffic and the clanking thunder of passing El trains.

Warren Williams studied the four eight-by-ten glossy prints spread across the small table.

"Take your time," Sean Brennan said. "We both wanta be sure on this."

They were seated in the caboose of a freight train standing on a siding in the NY, C & SL marshaling yards. Despite the two open windows and door, the car's air was stifling.

Williams, wearing a brakeman's uniform and cap, was in his early thirties, well-built, with a shock of cinnamon-hued hair, pale blue eyes, and a bad overbite. Finally he thumped a grimy-nailed finger against one of the photos.

"That's the guy," he said, "and no two ways about it." He leaned back in the flimsy chair. "Hair had me fooled there for a minute—

too dark—but I got a good memory for faces and that one I'd know anywhere. Just who the hell is he anyway?"

"They don't tell me these things," Brennan lied. "They just hand them over and send me out."

He reached for the picture, eyed it briefly, said, "No question, huh?"

"Absolutely not," Williams said.

Brennan got out his pen. He said, "Mind signing your name on the back? I want to be sure I don't get it confused with the rest."

"Glad to help," Williams said, and took the pen.

The man in the photograph was Frankie Foster.

Here lately she'd been smoking too much. A fresh pack of Wings, opened right after breakfast, now down to three, not even noon yet and lighting another one. But she *had* cut down on lapping up the booze—before dinner anyway.

And the place was a mess. That nigger cleaning woman had gone out on her ass for swiping a pair of emerald earrings. At least they'd turned up missing, and she on her worst day wasn't one to lose things. Till she could get off her dead butt long enough to hire a new girl, the bed stayed unmade and nothing much was put away. At least the living room was presentable (maybe a loaded ashtray or two but no dirty glasses on the tables or bar).

Not that anybody was invited in; since Jake got himself killed there'd been nobody here except that salesman she'd picked up, screwed and thrown the hell out. First and last time she'd been to bed with a man since Jake died. Not that she didn't get the old itch (sometimes it like to drove her crazy!), but she hadn't run across a man she could stand, let alone end up in bed with.

And this business of laying around all day with nothing on except step-ins and that slinky negligee Jake got her on her last birthday. Laying around like some twenty-bucks-a-night whore waiting for her john to show up.

The buzzer sounded. Probably the doorman with that dress she'd ordered at Carson's. She extinguished the cigarette, walked over and opened the door.

Roche thought: Holy Mother, what she's wearin' wouldn't make Sunday dinner for a moth!

Keeping his eyes resolutely above the negligee's neckline, Roche removed his hat, said, "Good afternoon to you, Miss Terrell."

Angela eyed him blankly. "Who're you?"

"The name's Roche. Patrick Roche, it is. I tried calling you but the girl on your switchboard there tells me you weren't taking any phone calls."

"What is it you want?"

Roche took out his wallet, flashed the silver-plated badge pinned to a flap. He said, " 'Tis but a few minutes of your time I'll be needing, ma'am. If I could come in. . . ?"

Angela thought: They found out about Jake and me.

She stepped aside. Roche moved past her, swept the room with one all-encompassing glance. Angela said, "You might as well sit down, Mister Roche." She took his hat, dropped it on the narrow table near the door. "Even if it *is* only for a few minutes."

He walked over to one of the two lounge chairs in yellow damask facing a low-backed chesterfield in the same material, and sank cautiously into it. A heavy coffee table, lacquered in off-white with a thin gold stripe, held a matching pair of ashtrays, along with the latest issues of *Smart Set, Liberty* and *Harper's Bazaar*.

Angela sat on the couch across from him and crossed her legs, exposing a generous section of shapely silken thigh. She said, "It's about Jake, isn't it?"

Roche nodded. "That's right, Miss Terrell. It's hoping, I am, that maybe you—"

"Who told you? Jerry what's-his-name, the doorman downstairs?"

She had it right. "Matter of fact," Roche lied, " 'twas a woman called in."

Angela stiffened. The robe gaped wider. "My God, not his *wife!*"

"Not the wife," Roche said. "That we do know."

Roche thought: Lady, for the love of God will you pull that thing together on you! Before it's a hard-on right here in your grand living room I'll be ending up with.

Angela sank back, only partially relieved. The cops didn't have a damn thing on her. She'd been seeing a married man. Okay, these days so were a couple million other women.

Roche said, "Reason I stopped by, Miss Terrell, I have these one or two questions you could maybe go about clearing up for us, you see."

What really scared her was the thought of this getting in the papers with front-page headlines a foot high. Minute her old man found out it was goodbye three grand a month!

Angela thought: Whatever this cop's after, I've got to stall him off long enough to . . . to what?

"Like you," Roche said, "we want who killed Jake caught. And punished, as they say. Now if—"

Angela stood up, said, "I need a drink. Even if it *is* too early in the day," and went over to the bar.

Roche thought: The arse on the lady! 'Twould tempt His Holiness himself!

Angela said, "While I'm at it, Mister Roche, could I offer you one?"

Roche, aware of a growing erection, crossed his legs, took a deep breath, said, "'Tis kind of you to be asking, Miss Terrell. Would you'd be having handy a wee drop of the Irish there?"

Angela thought: You know something? He looks a lot like Jake. Well, maybe not in the face so much. More the eyes and around the mouth, sort of.

Angela found a bottle, held it up. "How about this? Old Bushmill? Jake used to— Guaranteed to be the real thing, not that bootleg slop."

Roche said, "No man could ask nor hope for better. And without the ice in it would be foine."

She filled a glass for him, a large Scotch for herself, came back, the negligee rustling, and bent to hand him his drink. He uncrossed his legs while taking the glass; the robe's neckline gaped and the cool tips of her fingers brushed his hand. . . .

Before Roche could recross his legs she caught a brief glimpse of the bulging cloth at the crotch line. Her breath snagged and she stepped back, acutely aware of his embarrassment. "There," she said, forcing a smile, "that ought to hold you," and went back to the couch.

Angela thought: Poor guy. Minute he came in I shoulda got dressed, not go parading around like some Haymarket burlesque queen.

Roche said, "Guess there's no point in going back over how Jake was tied in with the mobs. It's been there in the papers." He took a long swallow of the whisky. "You being so . . . close to the man and all, only natural he would've confided in you. Like who he was on the outs with, anybody that mighta made threats to . . ."

Angela thought: He's bigger in the shoulders than Jake was. And better looking I gotta admit. Maybe hung better, too. Even if Jake did have a cock on him like a bull.

". . . get him and so on. What I'm saying to you, Miss Terrell, 'tis your help we're after here. Who wanted Jake dead—and why. That's it in a nutshell, as the saying goes."

A dampness there: a moisture born of desire, touching her pubic hair, reaching the inner surfaces of her thighs. . . . Calmly, she leaned forward, set her glass on the coffee table, rose to her feet. She said, "Would you excuse me a minute?" and left the room.

Roche slowly uncrossed his legs. . . . He got up, went over to the bar to freshen his drink. When he turned, she was standing there, smiling.

And she was naked.

Peggy Norris said, "I realize I should have gone to the police immediately, Mister Wendt. I kept telling myself not to get involved, that what I had to say wouldn't make all that much difference. But to be honest about it, I suspect I was . . . well . . . afraid."

They were seated in Roche's office, the door closed in an attempt to filter out the sounds of squad room activity. The hot spell, now in its fifth day, had dotted the young woman's face with tiny beads of perspiration and put dark underarm blotches on her severely tailored shirtwaist.

"One keeps hearing," Peggy Norris said, "that once you are identified in the newspapers as a witness to a gangland murder—particularly in Chicago—those men will do anything to intimidate you. Even if it means harming your family."

Wendt said, "I won't try to tell you different on that, Miss Norris. That's why we do our level best to keep those names out of the papers—least till the trial starts. But after you get up there on the witness stand and point out who it was did the job, the hoods are smart enough to leave you alone. Way they'll look at it, what's done is done; getting even won't change a thing; it's the jury they'll have to start worrying about. Understand what I'm saying?"

"Of course."

"Now from what you tell me," Wendt said, "you were able to get a close look at this fella did the shooting. So if you saw him again—even let's say a picture of the guy—you could identify him. That so?"

"Yes."

Wendt said, "That's fine, Miss Norris. And let me say how much I admire and respect you for coming in today with this information. Believe me, I'm well aware how hard it was for you to do. . . . Now if you'll pardon me a minute."

The door closed behind him. Peggy got out a handkerchief and mopped her face and wrists. Earlier doubts began seeping back. Despite this man's assurances, she knew it wasn't going to be all that easy—or even safe!—to get up in a courtroom and point to somebody and say *He's the man I saw kill that reporter.*

Wendt came in, his step jaunty, carrying a large manila envelope. Turning back the flap he removed four eight-by-ten glossies and fanned them out on the desk in front of the young woman. He said, "I'd appreciate your taking a good close look at these, Miss Norris. And let me know if you recognize any of the faces."

She scanned the first two quickly, discarded them. The third she stared at it for a full thirty seconds, then looked up, tight-lipped, and thrust the photograph into Wendt's hand.

"This," Peggy Norris said firmly, "is the man I saw."

Keeping his expression carefully noncommital, Wendt eyed the print. "You're all that positive, Miss Norris?"

"Yes. His hair wasn't as dark as it appears in this photograph. But that *is* the face of the man I saw."

Wendt said, "What if I had to tell you this fella's been behind bars in Joliet for the last seven months?"

"I wouldn't believe you."

Wendt grinned. "Good for you, kiddo!"

The man in the picture was Frankie Foster.

After showering, he dressed quickly and entered the living room. Angela, wearing a jaconet robe in pale blue, was in one of the lounge chairs, smoking a cigarette and idly leafing through the copy of *Smart Set*. She dropped the magazine on the coffee table, gave him a gamine grin, said, "You're one hell of a man in bed, Irish. The way you went at me in there, anybody'd think you hadn't been laid in years."

Roche said, "And it's right they'd be." The words were out before he realized it and he felt his face flame with embarrassment.

Angela said hastily, "Look, I'm sorry, okay? I didn't mean to . . ."

Roche turned away, strode to the bar, snatched up a glass. He forced a smile. "With your permission, Miss Terrell, I'll be having another drop or two of your foine whiskey. And you?"

". . . Yes. A little Scotch. With ice."

How long now since last he'd bedded Margaret? (Margaret—never Maggie!) Four years . . . five? How does a man go into a woman that lies frozen on her back there, eyes tight shut, mouth pressed into a bitter line. A length of stovewood with a knothole 'twould serve as well! Or lock himself in his bathroom and commit a sin of the flesh. Father Mahaffey'd be shitting in his cassock, he would, to hear that in the confessional from a grown man!

He returned with the two drinks, handed the Scotch to Angela and took the other chair. His grin a bit lopsided, he lifted his glass in salute, said, "'Tis a darling lass you are, aroon," and drank deeply.

Angela sampled her drink, lit two cigarettes with a gold Moncrief lighter, handed him one. Abruptly, she said, "About Jake. He took chances and sometimes he'd get people sore at him. Once in a while, when he was really bothered, he'd let me in on it. But if I open up to the fuzz, and it gets out . . . mister, I'm dead.

"And that's only the half of it," Angela said. "Not that I'm going to hand you the story of my life or anything, but it just so happens I'm from Brooklyn, and the way I was brought up you don't rat on *any*body."

Roche said, "Is it, then, that you can see Jake's killer get away with the deed? 'Tis a man once dear to you we're talking about here."

Angela winced and the fingers holding her glass tightened. But the stubborn glint in her eyes failed to soften. "You're looking for a stool pigeon, copper, go look somewhere else."

A sudden rush of rage flared in Roche. He said, "Straight from Giuliano Torenello, is it? *Omerta*. 'Keepa yuh mout' shut, don' tella nobody nuttin.'"

Angela Terrell sprang from the chair, yelled, "You *bastard!*" Roche ducked barely in time to avoid the thrown glass. "Dug up the dirt on me, did you? Okay, you got your free drink and your free fuck, now you can get your ass outta here! And don't come back!"

It wasn't at all easy, but Roche managed to hold onto his temper. "'Twas a pleasure making your acquaintance, miss," he said thickly, and headed for the door.

"Pat."

He turned. She was watching him from across the room, her face a rigid mask. She said, "There's this guy. Pimp named . . . Zuta?"

Roche nodded. "Jack Zuta."

Angela said, "Back in May, I think it was, Jake pulled some kind of a fast one on him. Don't ask me what; that he didn't go into. But I'm here to tell you Jake was plenty worried."

"It's grateful I am for your help, Miss Terrell," Roche said.

"Be damned sure you forget where you got it." Unexpectedly she flashed her gamine grin at him, said, "Just keepa yuh mout' shut," then left him standing there and vanished into the bedroom.

Roche let himself out and walked on down the hall to the elevators.

*　　*　　*

"Going by what I been told," Walter Wendt said, "the first floor is mostly this big room where the whores sit around waiting for the marks to take their pick. Any space that's left is where the supplies—towels, sheets, stuff like that—are. And maybe some other rooms; that I'm not sure of. The second floor is maybe fifteen-twenty rooms. Bed, a sink, a chair, and a closet. Ten bucks, ten minutes with the lady of your choice—and you're out in the hall butt'ning your pants."

Wendt and Roche were in the Ford Runabout, parked near the mouth of an alley behind the three floors of crumbling red brick that made up the former Monroe Hotel. A black Hudson sedan stood a few feet in front of the Runabout, with the motors and headlights of both cars switched off and the doors closed. Traffic was light; the only places still open were an army-navy surplus store and the Raklios restaurant at the intersection of Paulina and Monroe a half-block to the west. Night moths formed swirling veils around the corner streetlights.

Wendt said, "It's the top floor where his nibs has his office. The far end of the hall, last door on the right. And no way to get up the stairs without some kind of alarm tipping him off."

"It's not the stairs we'll be taking," Roche said.

A wino urinating into the darkened doorway of a dime store was the only pedestrian in sight. He finished, used a thumb and fore-finger to blow his nose and wandered off. In the Hudson's front seat the tip of a cigarette glowed briefly.

Wendt peered at the radium numbers on his wristwatch, said, "It's nine-thirty-six, Patrick."

Roche nodded. "Let's be paying the man a visit."

They took out workmen's cotton gloves, pulled them on and left the car, moving quickly toward the black mouth of the alley. As they disappeared into it, five men slipped out of the Hudson and headed for the hotel's side entrance. Two carried hand axes, one a crowbar.

In the alley, Roche and Wendt stopped underneath a badly rusted fire escape. Wendt, using his gloved hands to form a cup, boosted Roche to the secured swing-down section, and in turn was hauled up to join him.

The two third-floor windows within reach were locked. Using a glass cutter, Roche etched a semicircle in one of the upper panes at the juncture of the sashes, applied a strip of tire tape to the loose segment, removed it and reached in to turn the catch.

The warped wooden sash gave grudgingly. The two men climbed through and into a narrow dimly lit corridor lined with doors painted a dark scabrous brown. The lifeless air stank of mildew and rotting wood, and the only sound was the fading scream of a far-off siren. . . .

Holding the phone close to his lips, Jack Zuta said, "I don't give a shit *what* he says. There's plenty room, saw it myself, to stick three slots on that back wall next to the men's room. Now I want them, he wants to stay in business, I want them machines installed there and no two fucking ways about it, you hear me, Sam?"

The receiver made squawking noises. Zuta said, "Damn it to hell, Sam, will you do what—"

The desk lamp's bulb winked rapidly three times. Zuta slammed down the receiver, scooped several ledgers off the desk, crammed them into a recess behind a wall panel and replaced the cover. He was back in his chair and calmly lighting an Omar when the door crashed open.

Zuta, unruffled, dropped his cigarette into the ashtray, lifted his hands. Roche took three swift strides, yanked the chair from behind the desk and, with Zuta still seated, spun it across the room. Wendt jerked the unresisting pander to his feet, shoved him against the wall and made certain he was unarmed.

Zuta said, "You fellas are making a mistake. I'm in real estate these days. Strictly legitimate."

He was ignored. Wendt stepped over to a wall rack, picked off the gangster's jacket and began turning out the pockets. Roche, at the desk, had finished pawing through the drawers and was digging into loose papers.

The phone rang. Roche lifted the receiver, said, "Yeah? . . . Who wants him?"

For all his bulk, Zuta was quick on his feet. He lunged to the desk, tore the phone from Roche's hand, yelled, "Shut up!" and slammed down the receiver.

"Jack," Roche said chidingly. "Maybe it's a house the man was after buying. What with you so big in the real estate and all."

Zuta was sweating profusely. He fumbled out a handkerchief, mopped his face and hands. He said, "You've got no call to come at me like this, Mister Roche. If it's something to do with that reporter . . ."

He had said too much, knew it even before he saw the sudden coldness in Roche's unblinking stare. He spread his hands, forced a sagging smile and was silent.

Roche came around the desk, put a hand against the man's chest, pushed him not ungently into a chair, said, "Now that you bring it up, Jack, let's you and me talk about you and Mister Lingle. Was a close friend of yours I keep hearing."

His confidence back, Zuta said, "I can't help what people go around saying. Believe me, I hardly knew the fella to speak to."

Roche said, "That cathouse you got going downstairs there, Jack. How much's it bringing you in these days?"

". . . Nothing to do with me," Zuta said. "Talk to the people own the building. Maybe they can furnish you that information."

"Downtown says you own it, Jack."

"Guess they're behind in their records down there," Zuta said. "Up to last March, I did, yes. But then this opportunity came along, you might say, and I sold out."

"Who to?"

Zuta said, "Offhand, I don't think I have to tell you that, Mister Roche. Seeing how it was one-hundred-percent legal and all."

The room's humid air reeked of dust and sweat. Roche sighed, said, "'Tis a slippery one you are, me lad." He glanced at Wendt. "Would you be after handing the good man his coat, Walter? Time's come for us to be taking a nice ride downtown."

Wendt plucked Zuta's coat from a chair, tossed it to him. Zuta said, "This a pinch?"

Wendt said, "That it is, my whoremongering friend."

"You got nothing on me," Zuta protested. "I tell you I'm clean."

"Come on, Jack," Roche said wearily. "It's not a clean day you've had since you got in the pussy-peddling business."

It stung, but he'd heard it all before. Cops had this habit of looking down their nose at anybody in his line. You expected it, lived with it, knowing all along you could buy just about any'a these pricks for the price of a secondhand tin lizzie. Even less, they were hungry enough. He said, "I got a right to know what the charge is."

Roche nodded. "That you do." He took a blue-bound paper from his pocket, unfolded it, held it in front of Zuta's eyes. "Paragraph two, line two. Comes out about like so: 'The aforesaid Jacob Zuta, here charged as a common and notorious vagrant, is—'"

A sudden surge of rage jerked the pander out of the chair. "Vagrant!? I look like some kinda lousy bum? Listen, you cheap elbow. I got more dough than you're gonna see the resta your fucking life!"

Roche, grinning, said, "All that does, Jack, is make you a lousy bum with money."

George Wellman said, "Gah*damn*est thing I ever seen. These desks, like in grade school, you know? Even got inkwells in them, for chrissake, and this blackboard where some joker wrote down a lotta geography and arithmetic shit on it like in a regular school, you know?

"Anyway," Wellman said, "there's these desks like I said, and up in front is this regular desk with this prune-faced old maid; like she was the teacher, you know? Couple'a books on the desk, even got this *apple* up there, can you believe it? Like I was back in the sixth grade with old lady Burton all set to give somebody hell.

"And here's the kicker," George Wellman said. "Ever' one of them desks got'a kid in it. Girls. With these cute little dresses not even down to their knees and these big ribbons in their hair. Only they ain't kids at all. They gotta be a good twenty, the youngest, all the way up to I'd have to say maybe thirty. And no lipstick; nothing like

130

that. And a'course something tied around the tits to flatten 'em down. And they sit there, that's all, just waiting till some guy always wanted to stick his dick in a kid, picks one of 'em out. You know?

"Then we come busting in," Wellman said, "and you shoulda heard 'em. Screeching and carrying on, you'd'a thought a weasel got in the henhouse, for chrissake. On topa that this hood they had in there, supposed to protect the joint, he tries pulling a gun and ends up a few teeth less'n he started with. How it come out was, Warren Avenue sends a couple paddy wagons over, hauls in the whole kit'n caboodle and books 'em. Johns and all."

12

At 10:17 on the following morning the advance line of a cold front, sweeping out of Wisconsin, struck at the city. Within the hour the temperature had plunged nearly thirty degrees, reaching the low sixties. Gusting winds keened through the stone-and-steel canyons of the Loop, rearranged the omnipresent litter in the streets, whipped hats and billowing skirts from the grasp of frantic fingers, stung eyes with prairie dust, snatched papers from corner newsstands and, as serendipity, wiped out the pervasive stench radiating from South Side stockyards and abattoirs.

Jacob Guzik, reading aloud from a loose-leaf ledger, said, "In the past thirty days, the number of our liquor and beer outlets shut down comes to one hundred fourteen. Estimated uninsured loss through structural damage: eight hundred twenty thousand dollars."

Guzik was a short, paunchy man with a sagging face, dewlaps, skin the color of library paste, and the mournful eyes of a dyspeptic bloodhound. A former operator of a string of brothels, he was now, at forty-four, the financial brains of the Capone outfit.

Capone, in pajamas and bathrobe, stood at a window of his sixth-floor office at the Lexington Hotel, his back to the room. Danny Stanton and Claude Maddox, holding drinks, were perched on stools at the bar. Ted Newberry and Frank Diamond sat side by side on the office's leather couch. Frankie Rio, tilted back in a chair near the door, was idly flipping through an issue of *Black Mask*.

Guzik turned a ledger page, said, "Estimated uninsured loss on confiscated fixtures, gambling devices, motor vehicles, et cetera: nine hundred seventy thousand dollars. Bail bonds outstanding: three hundred fifty thou—"

Without turning, Capone said, "Shut up a minute, Jake. All I wanta hear right now is how much we're behind on the take for, let's say, middle'a May to the middle'a June."

Guzik said, "I'll need a minute or two, Al."

"Just do it."

Guzik drew a pencil from a vest pocket, began leafing through pages and putting down neat rows of figures. In the silence, Capone turned, eased his bulk into the swivel chair, leaned back, waited without taking his eyes off the man across the desk from him.

Maddox poured himself a refill. Newberry lit a cigarette, the match making a small sharp sound as it ignited. Windows shook under the impact of the gusting winds. Stanton picked his nose, inspected the prize, and flicked it away.

Guzik put back the pencil, looked up, met Capone's eyes and said, "It's down, Al. Little over six million."

Shock dropped the gang leader's jaw. "Six *million?* Jesus! In one *month?*"

Guzik gestured resignedly. "Afraid so, Al. And even that figure doesn't take in—"

"Get outta my sight!"

"Al. We had to expect—"

"Jake." That single word was little more than a harsh whisper but it lifted Guzik out of his chair. Clutching the ledger, he backed away, fumbled open the door and disappeared into the hall.

Capone sat like a man turned to stone, staring fixedly at nothing. The others in the room eyed him warily, braced for one of the man's epic fits of rage.

Forcing out the words, Capone said, "Six million bucks. Right—down—the sewer. The United fucking States mint'd be outta business losin' that kinda dough!"

He slammed both hands against the desk top, took a deep breath, released it audibly . . . then he turned back the cover of the leather-covered humidor, removed a cigar, lighted it and settled back in his chair. The inchoate explosion had at least been postponed.

Capone blew out a streamer of oily smoke, said, "Okay. You heard Jake. Pat Roche and his boys are kicking the living shit out of us. How we gonna get him to lay off?"

Bodies shifted uneasily, brows furrowed, throats were cleared. No one spoke up. Capone threw his hands wide in disgust. He said, "I'm trying to run a business here. I got payrolls to meet. On topa that I got City Hall to grease. I got all these judges, their fucking hands out. I got tank-town politicians in half the fucking *county* on the take! I got friends in Springfield to look after. I try telling alla these people the money's dried up, how long you think we stay in business? Or maybe we just give up, huh? Get outta the rackets altogether? Open some hot-dog stands? Set pins in a fucking bowling alley?"

Capone said, "Somebody around here's gotta come up with a few bright ideas on how to put a stop to these raids. I can't get to Murray Humphries—the Feds've got a paper out on him. Same thing with Nitti on this income-tax shit they're on his ass over. So? Whatta we do?"

Frank Diamond said, "Buy him off, Al."

Capone frowned, said, "Roche? C'mon."

Diamond said, "Why not? He's a cop, ain't he?"

Capone said, "I know the man better'n eight years. He'd spit in my eye, I even suggested it."

"I'm not talking peanuts here, Al," Diamond said. "He's costing us—what'd Guzik say—six million a month? You was to say a hundred grand a month for, say, a year? He could stick it away in a cigar box under the bed for that year, then go live in, in Florida or something."

Danny Stanton said, "That don't work, I gotta thought. There's this old limestone quarry out westa Elgin. Half fulla water. Roche could lay out there a hundred years and nobody'd know it."

Capone gave him a contemptuous glare. "You just won't learn, will ya, Danny. Like the man said, you can't make a silk purse out of a horse's ass."

Ted Newberry finished his drink, set the glass aside. He said, "Give Roche a patsy, Al. That'd do it."

Capone looked at him, weighing the idea. "A patsy. How?"

Newberry said, "You get copies of what the people saw Lingle killed said the guy looked like. Find some hood fits the description, knock him off, tell Roche that's the man he's after. The witnesses'll be glad to make him. And why not? That way they don't have to worry about maybe going into court and fingering some shooter's got friends that could give 'em a hárd time, you know?"

Capone said, "Let me get this straight. I walk in on Roche lugging this stiff. I say, 'Here you are, Pat: the guy that knocked off good old Jake. I took care of him for you.'" He looked at the others, grinning, said, "Wanta know something, Ted? You're starting to sound like Danny, here."

The others laughed, more relieved than amused. Newberry said, "I'm not kidding around, Al. The guy gets dumped inna ditch. Roche gets this phone call how it might be smart to have these people saw Lingle shot, take a gander at the stiff. I'm telling you, Al, it could work out."

Arturo Molina sat in a rear booth at the Beacon Grill, a small lunchroom located at the corner of Ninth and Beacon Streets in the Westlake Park section of Los Angeles. A small brown man, with guileless brown eyes and a self-effacing manner, he managed to eke out a modest living by peddling exotic drugs to a small but select list of clients and as a poorly paid informer for a police lieutenant out of Central Headquarters. At the moment Arturo was waiting for his wholesaler to show up with a week's supply of snow.

At 11:14 A.M., a late-model Buick coupe turned north into Beacon from Olympic Boulevard and parked at the curb in front of an aging three-story structure a few doors from the lunchroom. Frankie Foster got out, went past a sign reading FURNISHED APTS, INQUIRE 1A, entered the building, climbed two flights of steps and knocked on the door to 3B.

The sound of light, hurried steps. A man's voice said, "Who's that?"

"Eddie Ryan," Foster said. "It's okay."

A key turned, the door opened far enough to reveal a sliver of face. Foster said, "Hi, Arnie," went through and into the living room of the small, cheaply furnished apartment.

Jimmy DiFrancona, sprawled in a sagging lounge chair, said, "Looking good there, Eddie," and got to his feet. A battered table-model radio was tuned low, bringing in a recording of Fanny Brice deep into the lyrics of "Walkin' My Baby Back Home."

Foster said, "How'd we make out?"

Arnie said, "Like a fucking thief is how we made out. Whaddya expect?"

Arnold DiFrancona was short, stocky, with bad skin and a face life hadn't been gentle with. His brother was a few inches taller, with almost effeminate features and the smooth effortless movements of a ballet dancer. They took seats across from Foster at the breakfast-nook table. Arnie turned back the flap on a large envelope, removed a thick wad of currency, dropped it in front of Foster, said, "The stuff fenced for twenty-two grand, Eddie. Comes out seventy-three hundred apiece, give or take a few bucks. Go ahead; count it."

Foster grinned, said, "Why would I wanta do that? Joe Ross tells me you guys are honest crooks." He folded the bills, shoved them casually into a pants pocket, leaned back. He said, "Easy dough. Where do we hit next?"

The brothers exchanged deadpan glances. The radio station identified itself, spoke glowingly about Camay soap, and Miss Brice came back to sing "You're the Cream in My Coffee."

Arnold DiFrancona said, "Ain't gonna be a next time, Eddie. And lemme tell you why. Up till when Ted Yerxa got nabbed on a bank heist, the three of us had a nice little operation going: Jimmy, here, outside behind the wheel and a hand on the horn just in case; me and Teddy on the inside filling up the pillow cases. If somebody starts acting up we flash the iron—that's all it takes, no rough stuff, no trouble, nobody gets hurt but the insurance people and who gives a fuck about them?

"Going in, we told you this, Eddie," Arnie said. "So the old guy wakes up on us—and you had to go lay his head open, put him in the fucking hospital. The guy's family gets upset, they put the pressure on the cops, and we got to go around looking over our shoulder. Which is something we don't like and can't afford having happen, ya see."

Foster said, "Shit, Arnie. The old fart started to yell. I hadda shut him up."

"So, he yells," Jimmy said. "Next house's half a block away. So who's gonna hear him?"

"Maybe that's how you do it in good old Chi," Arnie said. "But out here we handle these things different. So we'll say goodbye to you, Eddie, and no hard feelings. Okay?"

In the Beacon Grill, Arturo Molina and his supplier, a middle-aged gringo with a mane of white hair, concluded their business meeting. They shook hands cordially and the white-haired man left. Arturo sat down and picked up his coffee cup.

At 11:38, Frankie Foster entered the lunchroom and took a counter stool near the rear. Four diners were at one table, three booths were occupied, as were several of the stools.

The lunchroom owner left the register, filled a coffee cup, set it on the counter in front of Foster and said, "Get you something else, Eddie?"

Foster said, "Guess not. I had some breakfast no more'n an hour ago."

The man said, "Little dessert oughta go good about now."

"Well," Foster said, dragging the word out. "Pie maybe?"

"Peach? Apple?"

"Let's try the peach," Foster said.

Arturo Molina sat very still, staring obliquely at Foster's profile. He watched him wolf down the slice of pie, finish a refill on the coffee, smoke most of a cigarette. He watched him rise, saunter to the register, pay the tab, pocket the change, go to the door.

"Drop in again, Eddie," the owner said.

Foster said, "I just might do that, Andy," and walked on out.

Arturo left the booth, stopped at the register, said, "I had three cups'a java."

The owner said, "Comes to fifteen cents."

While accepting change from a dollar, Arturo said, "I never seen Eddie White around here before. How's he doing these days?"

The owner eyed Arturo blankly. "Who's Eddie White?"

Arturo said, "Guy you was just now talking to. C'mon, Andy, you even *called* him Eddie, for chrissake."

The owner said, "That's Eddie *Ryan* I was talking to. Been coming in here last couple-three weeks now."

Showing a puzzled frown, Arturo said, "That's sure's hell funny. Dead ringer for Eddie White. *And* the same name. First one, anyhow."

"Way it goes sometimes, Artie," the owner said.

In the living room of their small suite at Los Angeles's Ambassador Hotel, Fred Joyner was on the phone while Johnny Greer took up a corner of the couch. Using the ingredients provided by a sympathetic bellhop, Greer was putting together a pair of bourbon and ginger ale highballs.

The voice at the other end of the phone said, "For a stoolie, Artie's pretty dependable. Insists the guy he saw matches that photo I gave him right down to the eyebrows on him. Even went so far's to get the name the fella's using."

Joyner said, "What name's that?"

The voice said, "According to what the lunchroom owner told Artie, it's Edward Ryan."

Joyner jerked erect. "Eddie *Ryan!* Hey, that's one of Foster's aliases! You'd think these stupid hoods would know better."

The voice chuckled. "Lucky for us they *are* stupid, Mister Joyner. Otherwise, how we ever gonna nab 'em?"

Joyner said, "Can't argue with you there, Lieutenant. Where's this café your boy saw him at?"

"Ninth and Beacon. And from what the owner out there says, the guy comes in his place a lot. Which sounds to me like he's holed up somewhere in that neighborhood."

Joyner put back the receiver. Greer was watching him expectantly. "Bingo?"

"Bingo," Joyner said. "Least it sure's hell looks like it."

Greer handed him one of the drinks, said, "Tell you the truth, I was kind of hoping this could drag out a while longer. Get a chance to see a couple movie stars? Clara Bow, maybe?"

Joyner lifted his glass in salute. "Clara Bow," he said.

Around two that afternoon, clouds had begun to form a dark gray wall to the northwest—a wall that continued to grow and darken. Far-off thunder snarled under its breath; lightning flickered near the western horizon. At a few minutes before three, the rain began, hesitantly at first, like a skirmish line testing enemy defenses: a scattering of drops the size and color of silver dollars.

Walter Wendt sat down across the desk from Roche, said, "Just finished talking to Joyner. Called up here like he was walking on air—and Fred's not a boy to excite easy."

"Is it you're saying they've picked up Foster?" Roche said.

Wendt said, "No, not so far anyway. But it sure sounds like they're breathing down his neck."

Roche said, "I'll be borrowing one of your cigarettes, you don't mind, Walter, while you tell me about how close the man's neck is to their breath."

A huge bolt of lightning ripped apart the sky directly overhead, a rolling hammer-blow of thunder shook the windows—and the city staggered under cascading torrents of water.

Roche turned on the desk lamp, accepted a Sano and a light, leaned back, listened to Wendt's summary of Joyner's report, spent a few moments weighing it. He said, "Jack Zuta. Did I hear it said he's out on bail on that vagrancy rap we had the pleasure of soaking him with?"

"The poor man had to sit out the weekend in a cell," Wendt said. "Monday, Lyle sets his bail at fifty grand, Judge Fisher cuts that to twenty-five hundred, Jack's on the street inside an hour."

Roche left his chair, went to the window, used a hand to wipe a clear spot on the fogged glass, peered out at a miniature Niagara. He said, "Time to bring the man in again, Walter. Before he gets too comfortable behind the desk in that swell office'a his."

Pasta drowned in clam sauce had long been a favorite dish of the Big Fella's. After finishing off two loaded plates, half a loaf of garlic bread, close to a quart of Chianti, and a cigar, he entered his hotel bedroom, shed robe and slippers and stretched out on the bed's silken coverlet.

Sleep refused to come. Too much on his mind. Like this thing of him catching the syph. No signs of it here lately; he'd known all along that sawbones was a fucking quack. But right in the middle of something else going on, he'd get this thought: what if the kike was right? Had to admit it bothered him.

And this crap about not paying his taxes. Not that Uncle Sam had a thing to go on; he'd been too smart to put anything down on paper. Too bad he couldn't say the same for his brother. Of course Ralph had never been what you'd call real bright to begin with.

But what was giving him all these gas pains was them raids of Roche's. He couldn't let it go on—not if he wanted to stay in business. If burying Roche was the answer, then Roche would already be six feet under. Turning a chopper on that fathead McCormick'd make more sense, seeing as how it was him back of it all.

The door opened and Frankie Rio stepped in. "You sleepin', Al?"

"Whatta you want?"

Rio said, "There's this fella on the phone. Says he's a wheelman on our booze runs outta Canada. Name's Vito Morici."

"So?"

"Wants to talk to you." Rio said. "All's I can get outta him is he's got something on who had Lingle knocked over."

It was close to nine that evening when they brought Jack Zuta in. Although a light rain was still falling, the fury of the storm had finally abated after flooding underpasses, cutting deeply into theater and restaurant business, forcing postponement of a doubleheader between the Cubs and the St. Louis Cardinals and canceling the weekly mah-jongg session of the Hibernian Ladies Social Club (president and cofounder, Mrs. Patrick Roche).

Wendt and Roche were in the latter's office when Sean Brennan and Michael Casey appeared in the doorway. Jack Zuta, his hands cuffed, stood between them.

Roche said, "How you feeling, Jack?"

Zuta said, "I don't understand the roust, Mister Roche. I figured you and me, we'd settled our business."

"You know how it is, Jack," Roche said. "New things keep popping up."

Away from his home base, much of Zuta's normal arrogance seemed to have deserted him. He held out his manacled wrists, said, "Would you mind getting these things offa me, Mister Roche?"

Roche said to Brennan, "Be taking the bracelets off for the man, Sean. Then the two'a you might as well go on home."

The cuffs were removed, Zuta's escorts disappeared. Roche said, "Go ahead, Jack; sit yourself down. Way it looks, we're liable to be here awhile."

The pander took a straight-backed chair across from Roche, rubbed the circulation back into his wrists. He said, "I'd like to call my lawyer? If it's okay with you?"

"Lines are all busy," Roche said. Then, with no change in inflection, he added: "What d'ya hear from Foster these days?"

Zuta's defenses slipped momentarily, revealing shock and a flash of outright fear. Then, the mask back in place, he said, "Foster?"

"Jack," Roche said. "Is it you're after thinking I'm fresh off the boat? We both damn well know who we're talking about here."

Zuta said, "If it's not too much trouble, you wouldn't happen to have a cuppa coffee around, would you?"

Roche leaned back, looked over at Wendt. "D'ya think we could accommodate our friend here, Walter? Might give him time to get his memory back into shape."

Wendt said, "Lemme see," and left the office. Roche swiveled his chair to face the window, sat silently staring through the rain-streaked glass. Zuta fidgeted a pack of Omars from his shirt pocket, lighted one, drew smoke deep into his lungs.

Presently Wendt was back, three cups of steaming liquid balanced on a clipboard. He handed them around, keeping one for himself, and settled into a chair near the window.

Zuta ground out his cigarette, sampled the coffee. He said, "If this fella Foster is the fella I guess you got in mind, I guess I *have* seen him around. Once or twice."

Roche said, "When was the last time?"

"Quite a while back," Zuta said. "Anyway, six-seven months."

Roche said softly, " 'Tis a cockeyed liar you are, my fat friend. Foster's been on your personal payroll better'n a year now. Bagman and all-around muscle. Here lately he's been pushing your slots into North Side joints."

Zuta said, "Mister Roche, I gotta tell you I honestly don't know what you're talking about here. People tell lies on me, I can't help that. Like I already said to you, I'm in the real estate business. Since at least last summer. I won't say I've always been on the up-and-up, but that was before."

Roche had stopped listening. He opened a desk drawer, brought out a folder, removed several pages of a typewritten report. Reading from it, he said, "March twelve, this year, you and one Willie Bioff opened three houses of prostitution between Throop and South Halsted. Jake Lingle was paid to block any police interference. On June twenty-eight, all three houses were raided and closed." He looked up, said, "Wanta tell me I'm wrong, Jack?"

Zuta said, "Somebody's sure been bullshitting you there, Mister Roche. Don't know a thing about any'a that."

Roche turned a page. "Early in May, this year, you paid Jake Lingle a lotta money to take care of a matter for you. Jake didn't deliver, you didn't get your dough back, and Jake ran headfirst into a bullet."

He looked up, saw only a bewildered expression on the face across from him. "The gun that fired that bullet? Sold by Peter Von Frantzius. Who'd he sell it to? Sold it to your boy Frankie Foster."

Zuta said, "Not that I'm sticking up for the fella, Mister Roche— and believe me he's not my boy as you're suggesting—but buying a gun don't mean too much. You can lose a gun or have it end up in a hock shop. Something on that order."

"Good thinking there, Jack," Roche said. "Except we got witnesses saw Lingle shot. People standing ten feet away. People that've already made Foster from mug shots. Once we stick him in a line-up he's halfway to the hot seat." He smiled. "And you next in line."

Squirming on the chair, Zuta said, "Pardon me, but I have to go to the men's room. Unfortunately, I got this bladder condition I take pills for."

Ethel Merman finished belting out "Can't Help Lovin' Dat Man" and left the stage. Ben Pollack's orchestra struck up a dance number and couples began filing onto the floor.

Standing near the rear of the cabaret, Leo Brothers was keeping an eye on a half-tanked young man in a faultlessly cut tuxedo. The girl with him was blonde, no more than nineteen, wearing a light-blue crepe de chine dress and a white cloche hat sporting a small perky blue feather. They were at a table well away from the bandstand, and an ongoing argument between them was rapidly coming to a boil.

A short sharp exchange, then the young man came off his chair and slapped the girl viciously across the face. She cried out, cowered away—and Brothers was at the table. He snared the young man's right arm, clamped it in a hammerlock, said, "Sorry about that, folks," to the couple at the next table. Before the young man could offer more than token resistance, Brothers had shoved him through a side door, along a deserted hallway, and out into Lawrence Avenue.

". . . Take yuh fuckin' hands offa me."

Brothers said, "Sure," released his hold, caught the young man on the way down and whistled at a Checker cab parked at the corner. The driver backed the taxi near them, got out.

Brothers said, "Take him somewhere."

The driver said, "Whaddayuh mean—'somewhere'?"

"One way to find out," Brothers said. A brief search turned up a wallet with a loaded currency compartment and an identification panel. Brothers slipped out two of the twenties, pocketed them, said,

"1102 Rockland, Wilmette," and put back the wallet. He opened the passenger door, said, "Hey, buddy. That girl you was with?"

"Fuck her," the young man said and fell into the cab.

The girl was still at the table, eyes half closed, shoulders swaying to the music. She was quite sober. She glanced up as Brothers sat down across from her.

She said, "Well, hello there."

Brothers said, "Thought maybe you'd wanta know I took care'a your friend."

"Thank you. Did he have anything to say?"

"He told me to fuck you," Brothers said.

She said, "I'm not at all surprised. Since he's not capable of it himself."

She opened a glittering evening bag, handed him a twenty, said, "Now run along and peddle your papers."

"Been nice talking to you," Brothers said.

Roche said, "We'll be bringing Foster back from the West Coast any day now. With that gun tied to the man and seven-eight witnesses ready to finger him, 'tis a cinch we'll be getting an indictment.

"Now we both know," Roche said, "that Frankie Foster is one tough monkey. But I guarantee you, minute he sees what he's up against on this, it's a deal him and his lawyer'll wanta make. And you wanta know something else, Jack? We just might go along with 'em." He stopped there, spread his hands, said, "Unless a'course you feel like beating Frankie to the punch."

Zuta sighed, shook his head. "You got it all wrong, Mister Roche. If this man Foster was the one shot Lingle, he sure didn't do it on account of me. Why would he? Anybody says I gave that reporter ten cents in my life, they're a liar. I keep telling you: I got out of the rackets least a year ago."

Roche returned the typed pages to the folder, thrust it into the drawer. He said, "You had your chance, Jack. And you muffed it. Go on; beat it."

Zuta glanced uncertainly from him to Walter Wendt, got hesitantly to his feet, took his hat from a corner of the desk. At the door, he turned, seemed on the point of saying something, saw only stony eyes and cold faces, and went out, closing the door quietly behind him.

Roche glanced at his watch, raised an eyebrow at the time. He said, "Been a long day, Walter. Let's knock it off."

"Fine with me."

Roche stood up, took a short-barreled Colt .38 and a belt holster from a drawer, clipped it in place, switched off the desk lamp, and put on his coat. Wendt said, "Give you a ride home?"

"Night like this—the rain and all—I'd appreciate that, Walter."

Leaving the overhead light on, they left Roche's office. At a corner desk, Julius Siegan was using two fingers to type out a report while a middle-aged cleaning woman emptied wastebaskets into a large cardboard box.

They were at the corridor door when it swung open and Jack Zuta was standing there, his expression drawn. He said, "I sure hate to have to ask this, but maybe I could get a lift from one'a you fellas?"

"You got a hell of a nerve, pimp," Wendt said. "Go grab yourself a cab."

"Have a heart for chrissake, will you?" Zuta pleaded. "You're the ones had me hauled down here; least you can do is get me somewhere it's safe."

Roche said, "And who might it be, Jack, would want to harm an upstanding businessman like yourself?"

Zuta said, "I got enemies, that's all. I go running around the Loop this time a'night, I can get my ass shot off. So give me a break, okay? I got a right to protection much as the next guy."

"For a fella in the real estate," Roche said, "'tis a lot of worrying you do. But all right; we'll be doing you this one favor."

The three men rode the elevator to the first floor, crossed the deserted lobby, and stepped out into the night. The earlier rain had slackened to hardly more than a light drizzle. At this hour, the storefronts along Washington Street were dark, the sidewalks empty and traffic at a minimum.

Wendt's Runabout stood at the curb. As the three men approached it, a small black sedan parked a few yards to the west swung out on squealing tires and roared toward them.

Roche was the first to see the barrel of a machine gun leveled through a side window. He yelled, "Down!" and threw himself against the others, sending them sprawling as a stream of .45-caliber slugs sprayed the area. Cement dust swirled up from the gouged sidewalk, shop windows disintegrated. Metal screamed in protest as bullets tore into the Runabout, riddling its body and turning windows and windshield into coruscating shrapnel.

By the time Roche and Wendt managed to scramble to their feet and draw their guns, the sedan was turning south into Dearborn Street. Summoned by the echoing sound of gunfire, a crowd began to form and there was a swelling wail of distant sirens.

Wendt said, "Lucky they didn't hold off till we got in the car." He touched a wet spot on his cheek: blood from a nick left by flying glass.

Roche, eyeing the circle of faces around them, said, "It's not that I want to sadden you, Walter, but 'twould seem Mister Zuta has taken it on the lam."

An older building, it stood at the southwest corner of Seventy-first and Drexel Avenue on the city's South Side: three large airy apartments, one to a floor, in weathered red brick with a facade of rough gray limestone. Behind an ornamental iron railing, steps led down to a paved areaway and an English basement.

Shortly after eleven that same night, Patrick Roche climbed a flight of worn stairs, let himself into the foyer of his second-floor apartment and quietly entered the living room.

It was a large room, fussily neat, furnished in L. Fish Traditional. In one corner a votive candle flickered at the foot of a figure of the Virgin Mary. Religious prints took up much of the wall space, copies of *The Youth's Companion* and *The Literary Digest* were neatly stacked on the coffee table near a half-completed jigsaw puzzle.

Roche passed the closed double doors to the dining room and was opening the hall closet when his wife's voice reached him from the darkened bedroom. "Pat? That you?"

It was a querulous, high-pitched voice, as abrasive as emery. Roche said flatly, "Yeah. It's me all right."

An end-table lamp went on, throwing a sliver of amber light across the hall carpeting. "After eleven o'clock, it is," the voice whined. "You mean to tell me you're just now getting home?"

"Out drinking the champagne," Roche said, hanging his coat and hat in the closet. "*And* dancing the Black Bottom. Now that you've heard my confession, would you be going back to sleep?"

He tugged out his shirt tails, began freeing the buttons. Margaret Roche said, "Why I put up with it. Coming in all hours and me spending half my days sitting around here. Like a bump on a log, I am, nothing to do and not a soul—"

"Any milk?" Roche said.

"What?"

"I said any milk?"

"Look in the icebox," Margaret Roche said. "And do it quiet for heaven's sake or you'll wake Mary Patricia *too*."

"Ha," Roche said, "you couldn't be waking Mae up with a twenty-one gun salute."

The light went out. Roche continued on down the long hallway, passed the bathroom and paused outside the closed door to the back bedroom. His daughter's bedside radio was playing, so faintly that he could barely make out the voice of Eddie Cantor singing "Louisville Lou."

Roche rapped lightly on the panel, called out softly, "Mae, is it asleep you are in there?"

The music ended abruptly, the door opened, and a girl of eighteen, a coral-hued robe over her nightgown, said, "Hi, Pops. And no, I was *not* sleeping. Come on in and shut the door. Before *she* wakes up and starts yelling her head off."

Roche obeyed, kissed her lightly on the cheek. "'Tis rings under the eyes," he said, "you'll be ending up with, awake at this hour."

"Poo," Mary Patricia Roche said. She was tall, leggy and slim, with shingled auburn hair and a face that missed being beautiful by a narrow margin. She said, "Want a cigarette?"

He stiffened, scowled, said, "Now just a damned min—"

She said, "Pops; you know perfectly well I don't smoke. But Timmy O'Rourke does, and when we had sodas after the movie I swiped a couple offa him for you." She ran a hand under the edge of the mattress, brought out two Camels.

He slipped one into a pocket, lighted the other, drew up a chair and straddled it, elbows resting on the back. He said, "Your mother smells smoke in here, it's a lotta trouble we're both in."

"She's not gonna smell anything. The window's wide open."

Roche said, "This O'Rourke fella. You like him?"

"He's a wet smack, Pops. Keeps trying to get his hands under my dress, you know?" She saw his expression, added hastily, "What he ends up with is a slap in the face."

Roche deposited cigarette ash in his pants cuff, said, "With some a slap's not enough. Maybe it's a talk I'll be having with the lad."

"You will *not*," Mary Patricia said. "I'd never live it down, you go and do anything like that."

In the kitchen, Roche field-stripped the cigarette, dropped the pieces in the garbage pail. He opened the General Electric refrigerator with its tiara of freezer coils, took out a fresh bottle of milk, poured the cream into a small chinaware pitcher, filled a tall glass, and sat down at the porcelain-topped table.

. . . That shoot-up. It wasn't him or Walter they'd been after. No sir; Jack Zuta it was—and tough-titty for anybody happened to be around at the time. Thing to do was bring the man in, stick him away somewhere for his health. Least till Foster was back in town and ready to name Jack as the one hired him to bump Lingle off.

He thought about helping himself to some of that cold chicken in the fridge, decided against it, lit the second Camel instead, and got up to open the window over the sink (that Margaret: nose like a creature of the wild!). He returned to his chair, slipped his shoes off, leaned back and rested his heels on the table's edge.

The phone rang.

Roche came out of the chair, snatched up the receiver on the kitchen extension before it could ring a second time.

A crisp voice said, "Am I speaking to Mister Roche?"

Roche said, "Who's this?"

"My name," the voice said, "is Joseph Stenson. If I recall correctly, we met some years ago?"

"That we did," Roche said. "Back, it was, when Uncle Sam tried drying up those breweries you and Johnny Torrio had your hand in."

"All ancient history," the voice said. "I do regret calling you at this late hour, Mister Roche. However I've just finished speaking with . . . well, the Big Fellow, and he was quite insistent that I telephone you at once."

Roche said, "Speaking of Mister Capone, here about two hours ago I came this close to getting my head shot off by a couple'a bozos with a tommy gun. Nothing personal; way I look at it they were shooting at a man Mister Capone's not too crazy about. But you might mention to him that if it happens again, I'll be having the pleasure of booting his Italian ass from one enda Michigan Avenue to the other."

Stenson said, "He's requesting a meeting with you, Mister Roche. Tomorrow, if at all possible."

"The hell you say," Patrick Roche said.

13

The architecture was early Norman: three floors and seventeen rooms in the center of ten flawlessly landscaped acres. The leaded glass of casement windows sparkled in sunlight reflected from the restless swells of Lake Michigan a few hundred yards beyond a tertiary road to the east.

Walter Wendt piloted the Chevrolet coupe, drawn from the department pool to replace the bullet-ridden Runabout, along a semicircular driveway and stopped under the porte-cochere. No other cars were visible. Roche, seated next to him, said, "If it's gunshots you hear, Walter, me boy, don't bother coming in to collect my mortal remains."

"This is Lake Forest," Wendt said. "Not Cicero. Long as you keep your hands off the silver and don't spit on the floor, nobody'll lay a glove on you."

Roche got out, went over to double doors of ornately carved teak, used a black enameled door knocker in the shape of a mailed fist. After a few seconds one of the doors swung back and a tall, spare man in butler's livery was standing there. "Mister Roche?"

"That it is," Roche said.

The butler took his hat with unobtrusive grace, said, "If you'll be good enough to step this way, sir."

They walked down the center of a huge circular hall under a stained-glass skylight, past three suits of armor complete with armet helmets and halberds, into an enormous living room furnished in French Provincial, Flemish arras on the walls, across that and along a wide hallway.

The butler stopped at a door near the far end of the hall, opened it, said, "Mister Roche is here, sir," and stepped aside.

"Come on in, Pat," Alphonse Capone said.

Fred Joyner said, "Take a gander over there, Johnny, and tell me if my eyes are lying."

Greer looked to where Joyner was pointing. "The guy getting out of that Buick?"

"Uh-huh."

They were in the front seat of a rented sedan, parked across the street from the Beacon Grill. It was shortly before noon and the lunch crowd had begun straggling in.

Greer said, "Well . . . I'm not sure. He's got the right build but it's hard making out the face with his hat on."

"One way to find out," Joyner said.

They left the car, strolled casually to the opposite side of the street and came up behind Frankie Foster near the café entrance.

"How's it going, Eddie?" Joyner said.

Foster stiffened, turned, gave both men a startled glance . . . and his expression settled into a blank mask. He said, "I s'posed to know you guys?"

"You believe this, Johnny?" Joyner said. "Eddie doesn't recognize us."

They edged closer. Greer said, "Eddie's kidding around, right, Eddie?" He gave the gangster a friendly pat under the left arm, smoothed his coat at the belt line.

Joyner said, "Want to step over to the car a minute, Eddie? No sense drawing a crowd."

Foster said, "The hell *are* you guys? Cops? You're makin' a mistake here."

Joyner said, "You're Eddie Ryan, right?"

"Yeah," Foster said. "Yeah. Eddie Ryan."

Joyner's tone hardened. "The lieutenant says bring you in. So get your ass over to that car."

Foster stood his ground. He said, "Not'll I see somethin' *says* you're the law, I don't."

Joyner and Green exchanged glances, then Joyner said, "Have it your way." He took out his wallet, found a card and handed it over.

Foster read it twice. His expression showed a sharp rush of relief, then the mask was back in place. He said, "With *Swanson?* You guys're jackin' me off here. This ain't Chicago. Ya got no jura—jury—"

"Jurisdiction?" Joyner said. "That we've plenty of." He grinned. "Had you going there for a minute, didn't we, Frankie? I'll bet you thought your pal Zuta'd sent out a couple of shooters to shut you up on that Lingle job."

He wrapped fingers around Foster's forearm. "Time to take a ride, Frankie. But not the kind you were expecting."

The three men rode in silence for a few blocks. Then Foster said, "Pull over a minute, will ya?"

"For what?" Joyner said.

"Just pull over, for chrissake," Foster said. "You in some kinda fuckin' hurry or somethin'? I wanta talk to you, is all."

The car angled to the curb, stopped. Foster said, "Listen, there's gotta be some way we can work this out, huh?"

Greer said, "What is it you have in mind, Frankie? Pay us off for a pass?"

"That what it'd take?" Foster said.

"No dice, Frankie," Joyner said. "Besides, you don't have that kind of dough."

Foster gave him a darting sidelong glance. "How much we talkin' about here?"

Joyner moved a hand airily. "Oh . . . a million ought to do it. Apiece, that is."

"Don't fuck around," Foster said, scowling. "Look, first place, about this reporter gettin' knocked off. Maybe Jack Zuta *did* have somethin' to do with it—I wouldn't put it past that lousy pimp—but

152

I been readin' the hometown papers, see—it's all in there about Lingle—and I know goddamn well there ain't *no* way the cops nor nobody else's gonna tie me in on that job.

"So you lock me up," Foster said. "I get myself a smart lawyer; he goes to the judge, tells him there's nothin' to prove my client's done a thing wrong in Chicago and you can't send him back just on the say-so of a couple outta-state cops."

Joyner said, "Cutting all that down, it means you're going to fight extradition."

"Yeah," Foster said. "That's it. Extradition. I'm gonna fight extradition."

Greer said, "Why would you want to do that, Frankie? If we got nothing on you."

"Reason I blew town," Foster said, "is I got in wrong with a couple guys. This Lingle shit's got nothin' to do with it, you understand. I'm waitin' till things cool off, is all."

Joyner said, "Nice of you to give us a couple extra weeks at the beach, Frankie. While we wait for the okay to take you back. But you *are* going back. The district attorney out here's a fella name of Buron Fitts. He's in tight with a man by the name of Chandler, owns a local newspaper. And Chandler's in tight with our own Colonel McCormick. *If* you get my drift."

Foster said, "You guys really want me dead. Minute it gets in the papers I been pinched and on the way back, I'm fulla lead somewheres between gettin' off the train and landin' in the jug. Another thing: you cops're liable to get yourself killed just bein' *with* me, you know that?"

Greer said, "It takes a real big shot to order up that kind of artillery, Frankie. Who would it be?"

"Fuck that noise," Foster said. "It's gonna happen is all."

Joyner rubbed his chin. He said, "Tell you what, Frankie. You waive extradition, we slip you back to Chicago, lock you up under an alias and out of sight. Not only it doesn't get in the papers, nobody even knows you're in town. Whatta you say to that?"

"Lemme think on it," Frankie Foster said.

Alphonse Capone said, "Classy joint, huh? Belongs to this fella I know from back East. Right now he's over running around the old country somewheres."

"George Remus," Roche said. "Took a good forty million outta distilleries from Ohio to Missouri. Paid off halfa Washington, D.C., he did, to get away with it. Now can we be knocking off the bullshit, get to what it is I'm doing here?"

Capone, freshly barbered, resplendent in tailored gray twill, white silk shirt, conservative striped tie and imported spectator shoes, sat behind a walnut Queen Anne desk with Roche in the depths of a leather wing chair across from him. Books lined two walls, a drop-leaf table held a pair of gilt Falconet bronzes, a wooden relief by Grinling Gibbons took up much of a third wall. French windows led to a covered patio and kidney-shaped pool.

Capone sipped Les Noirot from a crystal goblet, allowed the wine to caress his palate briefly, then swallowed. He said, "Pat, I'm not here to shit you. You and me've got to work out some way to keep from wrecking my business."

Roche said, " 'Tis the law business *I'm* in. And your business happens to be against the law."

"Some law!" Capone said hotly. "Nobody in this town wanted Prohibition. You know that. Six to one they voted against it. Man wants a drink, Pat, he'll find some place to get it. And that's what keeps me in business."

"And shoot the ass offa anybody gets in the way," Roche said.

"Oh, for chrissake, Pat! You think I *want* it like that? For years I tried to get across to O'Banion, Weiss, Moran, and now this prick Joe Aiello, how there's enough dough to go around without all this killing each other. 'Play it smart,' I kept on saying. 'Pay off the politicians and the cops, keep the hell off the front page, and we end up big as U.S. Steel.'

"Makes sense, right?" Capone said. "But not to these *imbecili*. Okay; they don't listen; you can't take them to court; so they end up in a fancy box. Has to be that way, Pat; this business it's either them or you." He lifted the wineglass, stared at it somberly. "Now you see why I hafta ride around in three tons of steel a fucking *cannon* couldn't put a dent in."

He drained the glass, refilled it from a cut-glass carafe and, with an abrupt change of mood, took on the role of cordial host. "Sure you won't have that drink, Pat? Or, say, how's about a cigar? You can't *believe* the kinda cigars this friend of mine smokes."

" 'Tis not all day I have here," Roche said.

Capone voiced an exasperated sigh, said, "It's not enough there's this Depression going on and the Feds out to hang a tax rap on me. No, I gotta have you on my ass, too." He put aside the glass, leaned forward in his chair. "I can't go on taking these raids, Pat. So I'm asking you—one businessman to another—what d'ya want?"

"The lad that put Lingle away," Roche said. "And with the goods on him that'll make a jury plant his arse in the cooker."

Capone said, "Pat, you're having yourself a pipe dream. Say they *do* bring in the right guy. If he's tight with one of the local outfits, can you see anyone in their right mind get up in court, say 'That's him, Your Honor'? Even if that was to happen, you still got the jury. You think for one fucking minute they're gonna send a connected guy up? Let alone fry him? Not in good old Chi, Pat; the mobs own this town. If you don't know that by now . . ."

Roche said, "A lovely afternoon it's been, Mister Capone. And I do thank you for adding to my education. If there's nothing else you have to say, I'll be running along."

Capone said, "Whatta you so sore about? Okay. Let me put it to you straight out, Pat. If it takes money to stop the raids, how much'll it cost me?"

Nothing showed in Roche's expression. He said, "Mister Capone. Is it you're thinking these raids come out of some kinda faucet? That one man turns off the tap, they stop?"

"Nobody's saying they have to stop," Capone said. "You still got Joe Aiello's North Side joints to work on. Along with the Touhy mob and them West Side bums'a Davey Miller's. And to make it look good, once in a while I'll slip you one'a my own spots to bust up."

He reached for the wineglass. "Stay offa my neck, Pat, and you get a hundred *Gs* a month. Every month for a solid year, even if this Lingle thing is over and done with. Fair enough?"

Sounds of a hedge being clipped somewhere on the grounds seemed unnaturally loud. Under the porte-cochere Walter Wendt lit a fourth Sano and looked at his watch.

Roche put his hands on the wing chair arms, rose to his feet. He said, " 'Twould seem it's nothing more we have to talk about, Mister Capone. I'll be finding my own way out," and moved toward the door.

Capone said, "Listen to me! You know damn well I didn't have Lingle pushed. Why so hot to make *me* the goat?"

Roche turned. "Nothing personal about it, Mister Capone. It's just that you're included in with the resta the hoods giving this town a bad name. And till I get what I'm after, ever' mother's son of you's a goat."

Capone gestured in surrender. "Let me see what I can do. I got a business to protect—and with me that comes first."

Roche went to the door, was opening it when Capone said quietly, "Let me ask you something, Pat."

"Sure."

"Whoever it was killed Lingle. Will you take him dead?"

Roche turned, his face suddenly white with rage. "And have halfa Chicago screamin' 'fix'? Now you hear me, you fuckin' greaseball! You pull a stunt like that and so help me God I'll see you counting towels in a Chinese whorehouse!"

The door banged shut behind him. Capone ran a hand slowly over his smooth cheeks, took a cigar from the desk humidor, lit it with a heavy silver table lighter, leaned back in the chair and lifted his feet to the desk.

Then he reached for the phone.

CHARADES

The mobs own this town.

—*Al Capone,*
1930

14

Angela Terrell said, "I just wish to hell I could think of something to *do.* Besides lay around watching the years float by. I took these classes at the Art Institute for a while, but I couldn't even draw a decent *ass,* can you believe it?"

Roche sat up, propped his back against the bed's headboard, picked his drink off the nightstand. He said, "I know this fella: some kinda buyer or something at the Boston Store. It's a job you could be using, I'll call him up."

"And be a saleswoman?" Angela said. "Fifteen dollars a week, stand on my feet eight hours a day, take a lot of crap from customers? No, thank you very much."

Roche said, "A job like that, there's plenty'a people would jump at it nowadays. I know this one man. The vice president of a bank, he was. Right now he's standing on a street corner peddling apples, five cents apiece and damn few takers."

"Jake kept talking about maybe finding me something to do at the *Trib,*" Angela said. "'Soon as I can find the right spot,' he'd tell me." Her voice faltered a little. "You know something, Irish? Maybe he *was* a bullshitter and a crook. But there were a lot of good things about Jake. He was fun to be with, he really cared about me—even though there were times he'd do things I could have killed the bastard for—and damn it to hell I m-miss him!"

She averted her head sharply, buried her face in the pillow. Roche emptied his glass, returned it to the night table, put a hand softly on her bare shoulder.

He said, " 'Tis no soapbox I mean to be getting up on here, girl. But a bad law got put on the books—Prohibition. And the burglars, the stick-up men, the safe-crackers?—they weren't cheap crooks any more. Oh no, they were businessmen. They sold people what they wanted—what the big shots in Washington said they couldn't have.

"With all that easy money around for payoffs," Roche said, "why go after businessmen for breaking a law nobody wanted to begin with? So it's get on the bandwagon, boys! The cops, the politicians from the governor's mansion to a ward heeler's desk in the back of a poolhall. With all that goin' on, can you wonder that Jake went after his share?"

Angela rolled over to face him. She said, "Then why, may I ask, didn't you?"

He grinned, said, "A dumb Mick like me? It'd never work."

She drew his face down, kissed him, said, "It was a very nice speech."

" 'Tis a silver tongue the Irish have," he said. "And now I'll hafta be getting outta this grand bed and going about my business, dull though it may be."

She moved closer, pressed against him, ran a hand along his belly and tight into his crotch. She said, "Maybe you could pretend I was a gun moll and arrest me for a little while?"

Ignoring a faint stab of guilt, Roche said, "No man lives that could say you nay, aroon."

"Whatever *that* means," Angela Terrell said.

Some amateur sharpshooter had recently used it as a target but the words on the staked sign alongside the Sante Fe tracks were still legible:

At 10:27 A.M., the east-bound Chief ground to a stop near the town's tiny station. Rising steam wreathed the engine and formed vaporous ribbons along the length of the train.

Three men, one of them wearing handcuffs, descended the steps of a Pullman car, hurriedly crossed the station's deserted platform to a nondescript black sedan, its motor running, and slipped into the rear seat.

From his place next to the driver, Wendt looked over his shoulder, said, "Welcome home, pal."

"Go fuck yourself," Frankie Foster said.

Ecola Cremaldi's '29 LaSalle coupe had two features that made it perfect for his purpose: classy enough not to seem out of place in exclusive neighborhoods and a trunk large enough to hold sixty neatly packaged quart bottles of liquor. As an employee of the Aiello-Moran mob, Ecola personally delivered the finest in imported wines and whiskies to an elite clientele on the near North Side.

Ecola was running a bit late; it was close to four that afternoon when he pulled the LaSalle into the curb in front of an apartment house on North Lake Shore Drive. He was out of the car and unlocking the trunk lid when a stockily built man in a ready-made blue suit came out of the building, exchanged a few words with the doorman and strode briskly toward Michigan Avenue.

He'd seen that guy's mug someplace, Ecola decided. Not one'a his customers; they didn't run around in off-the-rack suits from Goldblatt's. His picture'd been in the papers maybe? When you're in the rackets you gotta watch your ass, check up anytime you run into something even *looks* funny.

The trunk yielded a gift-wrapped package, camouflaged with Marshall Field stickers. Ecola tucked it under an arm, walked over to where the doorman was standing, and said, "How'sa boy, Jerry?"

"Can't complain, Mister Crimaldi," Jerry said. He cocked an eyebrow at the package, said, "Somebody's gettin' a nice necktie, I bet," and winked broadly.

"Close enough," Ecola said. "Say, I meant to ask you, Jerry. That fella just come out? You know him?"

The doorman said, "Mister Crimaldi. I ain't s'posed to talk about any'a the tenants live here. It could bounce back on me."

Ecola got out a sheaf of bills, removed the gold clip, stripped a bill loose, said, "For starters," tucked it into the breast pocket of Jerry's uniform. "You know him or don'cha?"

The doorman said, "Name's Roche. This cop they got huntin' for the guy shot that *Trib* reporter, you know?"

"Uh-huh," Ecola said. "Now tell me what he's doing around here?"

The doorman eyed the bills Ecola was holding. He said, "There's this broad in 6C. Used to be that reporter's girlfriend, see? This guy Roche's been up there two-three times I know about."

Another bill went into Jerry's pocket. "Don't stop now," Ecola Crimaldi said.

It had taken sixteen stitches and well over a month for the marks left by the beating they'd given Mildred Koslak to fade. On top of that she still owed Zuta over three hundred on her "shortage." But at least she still had her job; the "schoolroom," now under the protection of Lieutenant Phelan at the Warren Avenue station, had reopened four days ago.

Mildred was in the laundry storeroom folding bed linens when the phone rang in the adjoining office. Solly Vision, Zuta's second in command, answered, his words reaching her through the partially open door.

"Yeah? . . . Jack? Hey, how the hell are ya? . . . No, nothing much outta the ordinary. Business a little slow right now, but it'll pick up. Where are ya anyhow? . . . Wait a minute, you'll hafta spell that one out for me, Jack; lemme get hold of a pencil here . . . Shoot . . . Yeah . . . Yeah, I got that. Hey, ya gettin' any nookie up there? . . . Two grand? Sure, get it right'n the mail for ya . . . All over the papers down here for a while that it was Capone's boys behind it. Nothing much here lately though. Too bad they didn't get that fuckin' Roche while they was at it . . . Jack, c'mon. How's anybody gonna find out? From your mouth to my ears and that's where she stops, okay? Anyway, it'll all blow over pretty soon; you know how these things go . . . Yeah, sure. Okay, Jack. Lemme hear from you. So long."

The receiver went down, papers rustled, again the phone rang. "Yeah? . . . He *what?* . . . Well, like hell he will! I'll be right down there." A chair was thrust violently back, there was a rapid clatter of footsteps, a door banged shut.

Mildred Koslak stood frozen, a pillowcase forgotten in her hand. Then she had dropped it, was across the room, into the office, and staring at words pencilled on a memo pad on the desk:

J. H. GOODMAN
LAKELAND LODGE
UPPER NEMAHBIN LAKE
DELAFIELD, WISC.

Twenty minutes later, Mildred Koslak stepped into a United cigar store phone booth. Her hands trembling, she leafed hastily through the directory pages, found what she needed, dropped a nickel in the slot, dialed CAL 1840.

(I'll show *you*, ya lousy kike.)

A click, then a deep voice said, "Lexington Hotel."

John Hagan said, "Let me say right off how much I appreciate you gentlemen seeing me at all, let alone this time of night. You understand, it's just that I can't have it get out I'm talking to the cops."

At two in the morning, the Washington Street squad room was dark and deserted, the fifth floor cleaning crew gone. Hagan, Charles Rathbun, and Roche were seated in Roche's office, while Wendt rested a hip against a windowsill, smoked a Sano and listened in.

Hagan, a rawboned, soft-spoken man, was in his late thirties, with weathered skin, deep-set brown eyes and an earnest manner. He said,

"I realize you don't know much, if anything, about me, so I might as well level with you right off the bat."

Roche said, "Till around five years ago, you had this one-man detective agency at Jackson and Wabash. You tried blackmailing a client, had your license yanked and came damn near getting sent up altogether. You moved to Kansas City, picked up thirty-two arrests on charges from armed robbery to disturbing the peace; no convictions. Hauled booze in from Canada and Mexico, ran a hot-car farm, served a year in Leavenworth for car theft."

Hagan gestured resignedly, said, "You've got it all, Mister Roche. I might've known. Anyway, that's all behind me. I did my time, got out of the rackets, now I want to get back on the right side of the law."

Rathbun said, "I don't understand what all this has to do with the Lingle case, Mister Hagan. On the phone you said you had information for us."

"What I do have doesn't amount to a whole lot so far," Hagan said. "But here three days ago I run into this fella outta Chicago. In solid with the North Side boys, I was told. Anyway, this fella, he claims the rumble is that it was some outta-town shooter they brought in to do that job on Lingle.

"Who the guy was," Hagan said, "and where from, that wasn't mentioned—and you can be damned sure I didn't come right out and ask. But I've every reason to believe it's a kosher lead, and I'd like a crack at running it down for you."

Roche said, "What's in it for you?"

Hagan said, "Like I told you: a chance to square myself with the law in this town. If I can be of any real help to you, you might be willing to help me get back that agency license."

"Along," Roche said, "with a cut of that reward money?"

Hagan shrugged. "That would come in handy; sure. I'm not exactly rolling in dough right now."

"Then of course it's an expense account you'll be wanting to draw on?" Roche said.

Hagan held up both palms. "No sir, Mister Roche. I'm not out to chisel on anybody—just to help. But I'll be honest with you, the guy I really want to help the most is me."

Roche stared levelly at him for a long moment. Then he said, "Sorry, Mister Hagan. We're not interested."

Rathbun said, "Hold up a minute, will you, Pat? Let's not be too hasty here. Mister Hagan has something we don't have: ready access to criminal circles. I think you and I should discuss this further."

Turning to Hagan, Rathbun said, "Where can we reach you, sir?"

Hagan smiled, said, "Under the circumstances, I'd better be the one to do the reaching, Mister Rathbun."

"I understand," Rathbun said. "Call me here in a day or two." He looked over at Wendt. "Walter, would you mind helping Mister Hagan find his way out?"

The two men left the office. Roche stood up, opened a drawer, took out his gun, snapped it and the belt holster into place.

Rathbun said, "I *would* like to know your objection to using this Hagan fellow, Pat. Please keep in mind that you and I share the responsibility of bringing this case to a successful conclusion."

Roche removed his coat from the back of a chair, said, "Let me be laying this out for you, Charlie. Chapter and verse, as the saying goes. At this minute the man that shot Lingle is tucked away in a cell on the top floor of the Criminal Courts building.

"And there he stays," Roche said, "away from the newspapers and everybody else. Least till the witnesses pick him out of a line-up as Lingle's killer and give us sworn statements so they won't be tempted to change their minds when they wind up in court."

"And if they don't?" Rathbun said. "Pick him? Or have second thoughts later?"

"Charlie," Roche said patiently. "'Tis three positive makes we have on the man from photographs alone. Not to mention the four probables. The gun's been tied to him. He skipped out inside a day or two after the shooting. He's as good as cooked, my friend."

"No," Rathbun said. "There are simply too many loopholes. For a murder of this magnitude, the assassin had to be someone who could not be tied to any of the Chicago mobs. The fact Foster purchased the gun is not prima facie evidence it was in his possession when the trigger was pulled. Moreover, without exception, every witness insists the killer was blond; Foster's hair is almost coal black.

"What I'm saying to you, Pat," Rathbun said, "is that at this stage of our investigation, we dare not summarily dismiss a source of possible information."

"Meaning this John Hagan?" Roche said.

"And why not?"

"Because," Roche said, "I don't trust the mealy-mouthed son of a bitch."

Rathbun's expression mirrored his exasperation. "Pat. What's *wrong* with you? There's certainly nothing new about setting a crook to catch a crook. You've told me yourself you use informants."

Roche said, "A crook turns stoolie to settle a grudge or keep himself out of prison—fine. Him I use."

"Hagan wants to go straight," Rathbun said. "A second chance. Why shouldn't—"

Roche said, "With *his* record? Bunk! It's no trust I have in the man and want no part of him. That's final."

Unnoticed, Wendt appeared in the doorway. Rathbun said angrily, "Well, by God, it's not final with me. I intend to use him."

Roche shrugged. "Okay, Charlie. But if you don't mind a suggestion, make damned sure it's him you'll be using, not the other way around."

Rathbun, fuming, turned sharply, brushed past Wendt, and was gone, his heels beating a rapid tattoo on the squad room floor, followed by the slam of the outer office door.

"What," Wendt said, "was all that?"

Roche sighed, gestured resignedly. He said, "A worried man, our Charlie. 'Tis this nightmare he has in which the jury, afraid to send up *any* local mobster, finds Foster not guilty of killing Lingle. Should that be true, Charlie sees the colonel's disappointment as fatal to his own ambitions."

He slipped into his jacket, looked at his watch, said, "Past three, it is! This keeps up, Walter, your lovely wife'll be filing for divorce any day now."

"Not with this Depression going on, she won't," Wendt said. "I read where the divorce courts are damn near out of customers these days. Come on, I'll get you home. This time'a night it's a long wait between streetcars."

Roche said, "You might give thought to moving next door to me, Walter. Think of all the gasoline you'd be saving."

"An idea that's already crossed my mind," Wendt said.

They stood in front of a horizontally lined background: six men dressed in varying styles and of much the same height. Three were black-haired, two blond, one a washed-out shade of brown. Under a battery of strong overhead floodlights, they followed Fred Joyner's instructions, turning left, right, and back to full face.

In the room's unlighted area, seven witnesses to the murder of Alfred J. Lingle sat staring through the glass between them and the men on the platform. At the rear of the room, a young woman was seated at a stenotype.

Speaking slowly, weighing his words, Roche said, "Early on, you were shown photographs of possible suspects in the Lingle murder—some from out of town. Now that you've had a long hard look at those six up there, please tell us if you recognize any one of them as the man you saw fire that gun. They can't see you or hear what you say, so please don't hesitate to speak up. . . . Mister Applegate?"

A trainer and owner of race horses, Clark Applegate was a tall, heavily built man with a shock of unruly red hair. He said, "Well, sir, I'd have to say it's number three up there. The hair might not be exactly as I remember it, but that face I'd know in a dark alley."

"Mister Campbell?"

Patrick Campbell, a plumber in his late thirties, said, "Number three. Same guy's picture I picked outta the ones this cop came out to the house showed me a while back."

"Miss Norris?"

Peggy Norris said, "Number three, Mister Roche."

"Mister Dimvale?"

Sidney Dimvale, a foppishly dressed clerk employed by a LaSalle Street brokerage firm, said, "I, sir, am firmly convinced the person I saw that officer chasing is not among those men. Number three does somewhat resemble him, but the color of his hair is simply not right."

"Mister Stein?"

Albert Stein, an employee of the Cook County Recorder's office, said, "Maybe he had his hair dyed that day, or something, but number three's got the right face."

"Mister Beckwith?"

Dwight Beckwith, factory foreman, a middle-aged railroad switchman, said, "I hafta admit, Mister Roche, I actually can't put a finger on any one of them people. That blond guy on the far end of the line's hair's the right color and cut the same way and all, but his face don't look right to me."

"Mister Williams?"

Warren Williams said, "Number three's the same fella in the picture the cop came out to the yards to show me."

Roche glanced at the stenotype operator, got back a brief nod, then signaled Joyner to clear the platform.

In dismissing the witnesses, Roche said, "Copies of your statements will be ready tomorrow. You won't be asked to come all the way out here; somebody'll show up at your home or your job—whichever you say—to get them signed. Till then, should reporters question any of you on this, tell them they must come to me for their answers. And let me add this: 'tis my deep and sincere thanks you have for what you've done here this day."

Police officer Anthony Ruthy, seated near the stenotype operator, was the first to leave.

Later, over coffee at the building cafeteria, Roche said, "Four out of seven, Walter. And that traffic cop Ruthy. Not all I was hoping for, yet good enough I do believe."

Wendt said, "One thing I did spot."

Roche glanced at him sharply. "And what would that be?"

"Up to right near the end," Wendt said, "I didn't once hear that rich Irish brogue of yours."

"Now and then I do try," Patrick Roche said.

* * *

Danny Stanton said, "Comes out around a hundred miles, kid. Hundred ten maybe; some of it's back roads up there."

"Can't take me more'n three hours, Mister Stanton," Giangoro said. "Tank's full up startin' out, so we don't need to make no stops."

Barely out of his teens and already a high-ranked member of a street gang known as the 42s, Momo Giangoro was regarded as the premier wheelman on the entire West Side.

They were in a freshly stolen dark blue Buick sedan standing at the curb in a residential section of Cicero, a few blocks from the Western Hotel, a Capone gang hangout. With them were Claude Maddox and Willie Heeney, an emaciated gunman with sunken cheeks and acne-scarred skin. A sleek-lined Chrysler Imperial coupe, also stolen, was parked a few feet behind the sedan, Frank Diamond at the wheel, Ted Newberry seated next to him.

In the Buick, Stanton looked at his watch, nodded. He said, "Three hours, huh? That oughta get us there about ten at night. Just what the doctor ordered. So okay, kid, let's roll."

Roche said, "Recognize it, Frankie?"

"What am I?" Foster said. "Fuckin' blind or somethin'? It's a fuckin' gun. So what?"

"A bit more'n just a gun, Frankie," Roche said. " 'Tis a .38 Colt Special I have in me hand here. The same identical gun put that hole in Jake Lingle's head. *Your* gun, Frankie."

"Says who?"

"Says Mister Peter Von Frantzius, the well-known dealer in such items. And with his records to back him up."

"I dunno know what the fuck you're talkin' about," Foster said.

They were in an interrogation room on the top floor of the Criminal Courts building. With them were Wendt and Charles Rathbun. It was a small room: unadorned walls, a table, four straight-backed wooden chairs and a screened window open to the humid night air.

Roche got to his feet, came around the table, held the weapon inches from Foster's face. "Go on, Frankie, take a good close look. Little nick in the stock there? That help? C'mon, the thing belongs to you. As we both damn well know."

Muscles twitched along Foster's jawline. He said, "I ain't had a gun I mighta bought off that guy for a long time now."

"And this one? Fell through a hole in your pocket?"

Foster's lips curled in a small sneer. "Who the fuck knows? Maybe I swapped it for a mah-jongg set."

Instantly, with no change of expression, Roche slapped him hard across the mouth. Foster came up like a scalded cat, threw a fist. Roche let it slip past his ear and slammed a right hand deep into Foster's belly, sending both him and the chair crashing to the floor.

The mobster lay there, fighting for breath. Rathbun, appalled, lunged to his feet, said, "My God, Pat, this is no way to question a suspect. I refuse to stand by and allow this man to be physically assaulted!"

Roche turned his head slowly, stared expressionlessly at the lawyer, said nothing. Their eyes met, held . . . and Rathbun turned, stalked over to the corridor door and out.

Roche was still holding the gun. He let it drop to the table, righted the chair, then bent, grabbed Foster's coat lapels, hauled him to his feet and dropped him back onto the chair. "Seems to've slipped my mind what you were after saying there, Frankie. Be doing me the favor of repeating it, that's a good lad."

They found the clearing at the end of a sharp curve in the narrow road. A long, low, determinedly rustic building stood at the rear of a parking lot with a dozen or so cars strewn about its unpaved surface. Three floodlamps high atop metal poles illuminated the area.

Danny Stanton said, "Close enough. Pull off the road aways and stop. Under that tree's fine."

The heavy sedan rolled over grass, skirted a clump of lilac bushes and drew up beneath the branches of a huge cottonwood. The Chrysler swung in behind the first car; motors and headlights died.

Two minutes passed. Sounds: the rhythmic tick of cooling engines, the skirl of cicadas, and, faintly from the lodge, the strains of heavily syncopated dance music.

Stanton opened the door next to him. "Keep your eyes peeled," he told Momo Giangoro. "Any trouble, lean on the horn."

The lobby of the Lakeland Lodge was small and badly lit. Except for the desk clerk dozing under a cone of light at a small switchboard, the room was deserted.

The screen door opened and Maddox and Newberry sauntered in. The clerk left his chair, moved behind the counter, said, "Evenin', gentlemen," and was reaching under the ledge for the guest register when the four-inch barrel of a S & W .38 revolver prodded his chest. "You," Maddox said, "got a guy by the name'a Goodman staying here."

It was not a question. The elderly clerk, wide-eyed and trembling, said, "Y-yes sir. Mister John R. Goodman. F-from Aurora."

"Where's he at?"

"I-I-I—"

"Come *on!*"

A spate of words poured out. "I think Mister Goodman's possibly in the—probably in the p-pavilion, sir. Outside, around the corner to your left. You see, we have dan—"

"Shut your yap and sit down!"

Ted Newberry went to the lobby door and out. Maddox moved behind the counter, past the clerk to the switchboard, yanked it loose, kicked aside a tangle of wires and slammed it to the floor.

A player piano at the rear of the Lakeland pavilion finished grinding out "Tiptoe Through the Tulips" for the eight couples on the dance floor. A pause while a fresh nickel was fed into the slot and the strains of "Good for You; Bad for Me" took over.

At the piano, Jack Zuta, smiling, turned as four men holding handguns, wide-brimmed fedoras pulled low, came through the screen door. A heartbeat of stunned silence, then a woman screamed, another slumped to floor in a dead faint. The dancers shrank toward the side walls, clearing a path for the gunmen as they moved in on the terror-stricken man at the piano.

A dark stain began spreading across the front of Zuta's white flannel trousers. His voice barely more than a whimper, he said, "You got the wro—" then a bullet from Stanton's gun shattered his teeth, blew away the back of his head, and showered the piano with blood and brains.

The music played on.

Zuta was still falling when Newberry and Heeney shot him through the chest. Frank Diamond stepped up, planted a foot on either side of the body, bent over and fired a final round into the mangled skull. A middle-aged man dropped to his knees and vomited on a woman's shoes.

The music played on.

When three deputies from the Waukesha County sheriff's office arrived forty minutes later, the parking lot was empty and the lodge patrons long gone.

Malcolm DeVries, the desk clerk, admitted to hearing gunfire but reported he had seen nothing. He was unable to furnish names of possible witnesses.

Frankie Foster said, "Somebody stold it offa me, okay? Swiped it right outta my fuckin' room, ya know? I—"

"Take 'fuck' away from you bums," Roche growled, "you'd hafta talk on your hands. How long's this gun'a yours been missing?"

Foster said, "Who the fuck knows? Six months, maybe. Maybe more. I—"

The door opened and Rathbun entered with a loaded cafeteria tray. He put a coffee cup in front of Roche, another at his own place at the table, handed Wendt a third, and sat down. Foster scowled at being slighted but said nothing.

Roche leaned back, said, "Thanks, Charlie." He took a swallow of the steaming liquid, lit one of Wendt's cigarettes, said, "When was it you took off for the Coast, Frankie? Right after this Lingle thing, wasn't it?"

"I dunno for sure," Foster said. "Maybe around then somewheres."

"Maybe even the same day?"

"Coulda been, I guess. I didn't look at no fuckin' cal—"

"Why?"

". . . Why *what?*"

"Why'd you go?"

Foster shrugged hugely. "It's a free country. I . . . felt like it, that's all."

"How'd you like to fall down three flightsa stairs?"

Foster said, "So all right. So I blew town. So'd'a lotta other guys I could mention. No sense stickin' around havin' the bulls roust ya just 'cause some big shot got pushed."

Roche drank from the coffee cup, set it down, hitched his chair closer to the table, said, "Let's be getting down to cases here, Frankie. Before Jake Lingle's body was cold, two people in that tunnel picked you outta the mug books."

Foster curled a lip. "So they need fuckin' glasses, okay?"

"In that line-up this very day," Roche said, "four more made you. Six solid witnesses, Frankie. *And* this gun'a yours. We've got you, laddybuck."

Foster shifted in his chair, looked down at his hands, then up at Roche. He said, "I guess I wanta lawyer in on this."

"A lawyer," Roche said. "They cost money, Frankie. And who will it be footing the bill? Jack Zuta?"

Foster's expression slowly became no expression at all. He wet his lips, said, "That fuckin' pimp? Why him?"

"Least he could do," Roche said. "Seeing how he paid you to pull the trigger."

Officer Anthony S. Ruthy got off the El at the Stony Island stop, descended the stairs, and walked a block west to Blackstone. He walked slowly; directing traffic on Michigan Avenue in murderous heat took a lot out of a man.

Irene Ruthy opened the apartment door, tilted her cheek for a kiss, said, "You look ready to drop. Let me run you a hot bath, okay? Supper'll be ready in twenty minutes. Cold cuts and potato salad?"

Later, barefoot, wearing pajamas, Ruthy dozed in a lounge chair with the radio tuned to a segment of WMAQs mystery series *Unfinished Play*. A few minutes before ten, his wife prodded him awake, put a cold glass of beer in his hand, said, "I'm gonna run over and show Martha my new dress. Get you anything first?"

He finished the beer and a cigar while making up his mind, then got to his feet, turned off the radio and went into the bedroom to use the phone.

He dialed, gave the operator an extension number. After three rings a receiver went up and a voice said, "City Desk."

Ruthy said, "Dave Weber around?"

"Just came in," the voice said. "Hang on."

". . . This is Dave."

"Tony Ruthy," Ruthy said. "Got a hundred you can spare?"

Roche said, "Say by some miracle the size of Lazarus rising you do beat this rap and are back on the street. Juries what they are these days, sure, it could happen. But, Frankie, long as there's breath in your body you're poison to Zuta. Let him off the hook and inside a week I guarantee you're cold meat."

He drank the rest of his coffee, set the cup back on the tray. Below the tin reflector of an overhead light bulb a blue veil of cigarette smoke hung in the still air.

" 'Tis a deal you're being offered here, Frankie," Roche said. "Get up there in court, lay it all out for those twelve good men and true. Zuta fries, you do time as an accessory, and it's back on the street you'll be before your hair turns gray.

"But say no to me on this," Roche said, "and I bring Jack Zuta in here and make him the same offer. You think for one minute *he'll* turn it down? Burn to save the hide of some dime-a-dozen hood? Hah!"

He leaned forward, poked a finger against Foster's chest, said, "One way or another, Frankie, somebody's tender ass gets cooked. Is it gonna be Zuta's? Or yours?"

Foster said, "I got news for you, Roche: I don't scare wortha shit."

"I'll let you tell me that again," Roche said. "Say, ten minutes before they throw the switch." He glanced over at Wendt. "Let's be burying the man, Walter. As Eddie Ryan and well away from the nosy reporters."

174

When the door had closed, Roche leaned back in his chair. "Charlie?"

Rathbun said, "Given Officer Ruthy and the witnesses, plus the gun, we can probably get an indictment. But a conviction . . ." He spread his hands, shrugged, looked away.

"What is it troubles you, Charlie?" Roche said.

"The hair," Rathbun said. "The killer was blond, Pat; every witness keeps harping on the fact he was blond. You think the defense's not going to bring that out of any witness we put on the stand?"

"A wig," Roche said impatiently. "Either that or a dye job. Why else d'ya think he took his hat off after pulling the trigger, then stood there God knows how long, before he cut and run?"

Rathbun said, "Try saying in court it was a wig *or* a dye job, Pat, and defense objections would rattle your eardrums! And the bench would sustain. The State could only ask if, in the witnesses' *opinion*, the defendant's hair *might* have been a wig or dyed. Given a choice like that, what do you think a witness, reluctant to begin with, is likely to say?"

"A bridge," Roche said, "we'll be crossing once it's built."

That same night, John Hagan was in and out of seven North Side cabarets and speakeasies before ending up, at two in the morning, in the Club Southern, a Moran mob hangout at Broadway and Grace.

Maxie Eisen and Lou Alterie, seated at a rear table, their backs to the wall, welcomed him with hearty handshakes, effusive pats on the back and an offer of a drink. With the amenities out of the way, the three men settled down to a revue of gangland activities, past and present. Alterie spoke movingly of how he'd had highballs with Frank and Pete Gusenberg "right at that table over there!" the night before the Capones "turned a chopper loose on seven of the swellest guys in the world!"

Eventually the conversation got around to the Lingle rubout. Alterie's voice grew shrill, blaming the murder on "them fuckin' Capones!" Eisen shook his head: there was talk around that Jack Zuta figured in it somewhere, which was why he damned near got his ass blown off in that Loop shootout. Hagan casually mentioned hearing that an out-of-town shooter might have done the job on Lingle. That drew blank looks from both Alterie and Eisen, and talk drifted onto other subjects.

It lacked an hour till dawn when John Hagan, legs a bit rubbery after his tenth highball, left the Club Southern. A cab brought him to the Argyle Hotel, a few miles farther north.

The bleary-eyed clerk said, "Morning, Mister Hart," handed over the right key, and used the hotel's lone elevator to run him up to the fourth floor.

Hagan was able to strip off his shoes and pants before collapsing onto the bed. He turned on his side, muttered, "It's not gonna work," and was asleep.

Walter Wendt said, "That's all of 'em," and dropped six depositions on the desk in front of Roche.

Roche said, "All *right!*" He leafed through a couple of the neatly typed and bound instruments, said, " 'Tis a grand job the girls've done on such short notice, Walter. And you can tell them it's a bit extra they'll be finding in their next pay envelope. . . . Who's out there?"

Wendt said, "Joyner and Casey. Nevins'll be here any minute; he stopped off for breakfast. The rest are out on that Laflin Street brewery raid."

Roche brought out his watch, frowned at the time, said, "Not yet eight. Little early, I know. But I do want all six of these things signed and witnessed before—"

The phone rang. Roche pushed the papers aside, took up the receiver, said, "Roche here."

A voice said heavily, "Yeah, Mister Roche. This here's Lou Applegate. You know?"

A rush of premonition turned Roche's expression bleak. He said, "Glad you called, Mister Applegate. This statement you gave us is ready to be signed. Any minute now one of my men should be showing up out there with it."

The voice said, "Well, y'see, that's what I wanted to talk to you about, Mister Roche. This fella you had us look at yesterday?"

"What about him?"

The voice said, "Well, I got to talking it over with the missus, y'know? About him having black hair, while this fella I saw do the shooting, him being blond like I first told you, and all? Well, I gotta tell you this, Mister Roche: I realize now I had to be wrong about him. This man, yesterday? Not the right one."

Roche said coldly, "It's positive enough you were then. What's happened?"

The heavy voice took on an aggrieved note. "Who said anything about something happening? I got this reasonable doubt, that's all there is to it. Like you said yourself, if you got a reasonable—"

"Mister Applegate," Roche said. "Where is it you'll be in, say, an hour?"

"Well, far's I know," the voice said, "right here at home, I guess. But there's noth—"

Roche said, "I'll be there, Mister Applegate."

He replaced the receiver, took a slow deep breath, expelled it gustily, said, " 'Twould seem it's one less witness we have, Walter. Had to be expected, I suppose." He shrugged philosophically, said, "Could you be after sparing a bit of nicotine? For me jangled nerves, y'see."

Wendt said, "Long as you put it that way." He got out his pack of Sanos, shook one loose, and Roche reached for it.

The phone rang.

Slowly Roche withdrew his hand. The two men looked at each other, the same thought reflected in their eyes.

The phone rang again. Roche lifted the receiver, said, "Roche here."

The diaphragm rattled under the impact of a shrill voice. Roche said, "Hang on a minute, Mister Campbell." He covered the mouthpiece with a palm, said, "The newsstand downstairs, Walter. Get the morning editions of—"

He stopped short as Leonard Nevins, grim-faced, entered the office and silently plopped a freshly inked copy of the *Herald-Examiner*, face up, on the desk.

GANG GUNMAN NAMED LINGLE SLAYER
Witnesses Pick Frankie Foster,
North Side Mobster, As Killer

Roche, his expression stunned, looked up at Wendt and Nevins. The receiver made squawking sounds. Roche lifted it slowly, put it to his ear. He said, "I'll be calling you back, Mister Campbell," and hung up.

Nevins left. Then Charles Rathbun walked into the room, a folded newspaper under his arm. He saw the one open on the desk, said matter-of-factly, "It would appear you won't be needing this," dropped his copy into the wastebasket.

He swung out one of the two guest chairs, sat down, said, "I know it's small comfort to you, Pat, but these things have a way of getting out ahead of time. However, I don't think this is really all that . . . devastating."

Roche, tight-lipped, said, "Allow me to bring you up to date, Charlie. When that phone rings again, it'll be the third witness who'll no longer *be* a witness. Nor will it stop there." He thrust a forefinger at the headline. "Once they see the words 'North Side mobster,' we lose them all."

Humoring him, Rathbun said, "I can't say you're wrong, of course. But over the past few days I've talked to most of the witnesses at some length, found them to be honest, law-abiding citizens who—"

Roche's sharp gesture cut him off. He said, "Honest and law-abiding they are indeed. And *scared*, my friend. Give us their signed statements, put 'em before the bar and under oath—some might've stuck with us. But as it is . . ."

Abruptly he shoved back his chair, lunged to his feet, turned to the window, stood there, his back to the others. He said, " 'Tis solid evidence we have that Foster owned the gun. From that traffic cop, Ruthy: a positive make backed by his sworn and signed statement. Enough? We can't be positive. If there was one more string to our . . ."

He smacked a palm against his forehead. "And that we have! Zuta! I'd forgotten about Zuta!"

He wheeled sharply, slammed the flat of his hand against the desk top, said, "Jack Zuta. We find him, put him face to face with Foster, tighten the screws on *both* those sonsabitches."

Rathbun said, "Pat, there's some—"

Roche overrode him. "Foster might hold out on us; he's one tough egg. But not that pimp Zuta. Let him even *think* there's a chance he can wind up in the chair and I guarantee you the words'll come spilling out!"

Charles Rathbun put up a silencing hand. "Pat," he said quietly. "Will you listen to me a minute? It was on WGN not ten minutes ago. Zuta is dead."

The phone rang.

15

Waiting at the library checkout counter, Roche admired the huge room's veined marble walls, the colored stone mosaics, the insets of mother of pearl and favrile glass. A king's palace indeed; a shame not to have set foot in so much magnificence before this day.

From behind the counter, Peggy Norris said, "May I help you, sir?"

Roche said, "I'm Pat Roche, Miss Norris. Could you be sparing me a few minutes of your time?"

Her lips flattened with annoyance. "Why have you come here, Mister Roche? I said all I have to say on the telephone."

"Being busy at the time," Roche said, "much of it was lost on me, I'm sorry to admit. Could we talk in private somewhere?"

"I'm on duty, Mister Roche. Not free to come and go as I choose."

"'Tis not yet noon," Roche persisted. "Will you soon be having lunch?"

"Not for another half hour. But I have noth—"

"I'll be waiting," Roche said, and walked away.

At the foot of Madison Street, they turned east, crossed the avenue, entered Grant Park, and began following one of the winding paths.

He gave her a sidelong glance, liking the walk on her: head high, shoulders back. A grand figure, good legs—what he could see of 'em anyway, skirts being longer here lately. And going by the set of that chin, a stubborn lass; 'twould be no easy task changing her mind.

They found an unoccupied picnic table, sat down across from each other. Roche opened the paper bag, brought out sandwiches, two pint bottles of milk, straws and napkins.

He handed over a ham and cheese on rye, thrust straws into the bottles. He showed her a lopsided grin. "Confess it now: this beats eating in that cafeteria."

She forced a smile. "It *is* lovely."

She began unwrapping her sandwich, hesitated, put it down, said, "Mister Roche, I'm sure I'd be more . . . at ease if I had my say. First."

Roche said mildly, " 'Tis my full attention you have, Miss Norris."

"I want to repeat what I said earlier: I shall not be able to identify that man."

"Okay," Roche said. He stripped the paper away from his corned beef on rye, bit into it, chewed placidly.

Peggy Norris frowned, said, "I *would* like to explain why."

Roche put down the sandwich, sipped milk through his straw, put the bottle aside. He said, "Miss Norris. I know why. You read the morning paper. You found out Frank Foster's tied in with the North Side gang. Now you're scared to death his pals'll come looking for you with big black machine guns. So naturally you want out."

She stared at him defiantly. "Yes. I want out. And there's not a thing you can do to stop me."

Roche shrugged, said, "If that's the way you want it. Go ahead; have your lunch."

She was the first to look away. She said lamely, "You *do* have other witnesses."

"Not anymore," Roche said. "They read the same paper you did."

"I find that hard to believe," she said. "That policeman. Mister Ruthy. Doesn't he *have* to testify?"

Roche said, "Sure. He'll testify. But you see, lady, these days the cops in this town have a lousy reputation. Least where the public's concerned. So no jury's likely to believe this one. Not without witnesses like you to back him up."

Peggy Norris looked down at her hands. "I'm . . . sorry, Mister Roche."

Frustration brought a sudden rush of angry color to his face. "Damn it, woman, will you be after listening to me? We'll protect you. *I'll* protect you! Nobody'll get inside a mile'a you!"

Speaking with coldly contained precision, she said, "Thank you. But it so happens I live with my married sister. Can you protect her every time she goes to the store? Her husband's a car salesman. Do you expect to sit in the back seat holding a gun every time he demonstrates a car? They have two children. Will you go to school with them, eat with them, accompany them to the bathroom?"

He shook his head with weary impatience, said, "Come on, lady. Nobody's gonna harm your relatives. It's too many wild and woolly stories you've been listening to."

Peggy Norris's own Irish temper suddenly flared up. "And is it, now? Only last week it was in the papers where a bomb was thrown through a window, killing this seventy-year-old woman in her bedroom. Her son had seen a gangster shoot a man in a restaurant. Did somebody tell *him* nothing would happen to *his* relatives? My sister wants me to move out." Her voice caught in a sudden sob. "My own *sister!* How do you think that makes *me* feel?"

She snatched a handkerchief blindly from her purse, turned her back, blew her nose and dabbed at her eyes.

After a few moments, she blew her nose again, tucked the handkerchief away, turned to him. She said, "I really must get back, Mister Roche," and was rising to her feet when he said, "Is it Catholic you are, Miss Norris?"

She stared blankly at him. "Well—yes. Of course. But what does that have to do with it?"

Roche said, "Has everything to do with it, Miss Norris. From the day we left the cradle it's been drilled into us that mortal sin is made up of grievous matter, sufficient reflection, full consent of the will.

"Okay," Roche said. "Now you know damn well this matter is grievous, you know you've reflected a lot more than sufficiently, you know you've come to a decision with full consent of your will."

"Mister Roche. I'm not—"

He held up a hand. "Hear me out. When you confess this sin, no priest is gonna give you absolution till you agree to testify against Frankie Foster. Say no and you'll not be in a state of sanctifying grace. Get hit by a beer truck, you go straight to hell."

"You ... lying *bastard!*" The words were barely more than a strangled whisper. "That's the most ... contemptible—"

Grabbing her handbag, she jumped up, glared at him. "Now let me tell *you* something, Mister Roche. You're the one should see a priest! And don't you ever—*ever*—come near me again!"

By the time Roche was on his feet, Peggy Norris was gone. He started to call out to her, shrugged, sat down and reached for his sandwich.

He sat at his desk, a copy of the *Herald-Examiner* opened to the third page.

Most of it was taken up by pictures under a banner line reading DEATH OF A GANGLORD. Shots of Jack Zuta from police files, his body under a bloodstained sheet, the dance hall where he'd been gunned down, bullet holes in the piano, the desk clerk attempting to hide his face, the building exterior with a big black X marking the pavilion where the execution had taken place. And the paper had done what those hick cops couldn't do: dug up eyewitnesses, all of whom seemed to dwell at length on how this one guy stood over Zuta and blew a hole in his head. The coup de grace, as a reporter, showing off, called it.

He remembered what Bugs Moran had said after the massacre at that Clark Street garage. "Only Capone kills like that." Well, although Signor Caponi wasn't aware of it he'd about evened things up by removing that stupid pimp. Now Barney Bertsche'd take over Jack's territory and no harm done. Except that the problem Zuta had brought on by getting Lingle knocked off was still raising hell with the whole operation.

A knock at the door and Nuncio Cevico stepped in. He said, "Ecola Crimaldi's outside. With respect, he says he must speak with you at once."

"Does he say why?"

"No, Don Giuseppe. Only that you may find it of importance."

"Have him come in," Joe Aiello said.

Five years now he'd been away from the Windy City. Not a lot of changes; downtown looked about the same, but get out a ways and you see all these half-built apartment houses and office buildings nobody was working on. On top of that, a lot of streets needed fixing up and no sign of repair crews. What with the Depression and all, a lot of Bureau of Streets help must've been laid off. And the way he heard it, anybody that *did* manage to stay on the city payroll got paid with fancy pieces of paper called tax warrants. Oh sure, banks and the big department stores would take them off your hands. At a whopping discount!

A week ago he'd had that talk with Mister Rathbun and this fellow Roche. Most of the time since then he'd hung out with old pals and acquaintances tied in with the North Side mob. And had come up empty. West Side: same fucking thing. With all the out-of-town lamsters flocking to this burg, you'd think a few curly-haired blond guys would show up.

Now it was another day, four in the afternoon, and he was at one of the Bensinger billiard emporiums, shooting a little eight ball at a buck a game with a slim, undersized ex-con named Punky Walsh.

After his fourth loss in a row, Hagan racked his cue, said, "How about a beer?"

"Sounds good to me," Walsh said.

They picked up a couple of bottles and retreated to the rear of the large room. Except for a three-cushion match going on up front, they had the place pretty much to themselves.

Hagan gulped down some of his beer, rubbed a hand across his lips, and began the carefully worked-out and rehearsed story he'd been using during the past week.

"Punky," he said, "you're a guy gets around, so maybe you can give me a hand on something I been working on here lately. Could be a couple cees in it for you."

Walsh finished lighting a Lucky Strike, said, "Shoot."

Hagan said, "Strictly between the two of us, it's like this. Around four-five months back a very dear friend of mine from K.C. pulls a twenty-to-life bit in Leavenworth for knocking off a Fed while this warehouse raid was going on. The four guys in the place, my friend included, got away clean as a whistle.

"That shoulda ended it, right?" Hagan said. "Except here a week or two after, one of these four guys is nailed trying a bank stick-up. Well, damned if he don't up and beat the rap. How? By turning in my friend for killing that Fed!

"The sonofabitch walks," Hagan said. "Free as a fucking bird. His name? Who knows? One he used at that warehouse was Whitey Phillips. Probably comes up with a new one every time he changes his shirt. And no way am I gonna pry any info outta the Feds. Best I could come up with is he lit out for Chicago or maybe Detroit minute he hits the street.

"Now I'm not gonna get into why I'm looking for this prick," Hagan said. "You wanta take a guess, fine with me. But I by God want him found, and like I said, I'm ready to shell out a few bucks to that end. That's about it, Punky."

Walsh pinched out his cigarette, tossed the butt into a cuspidor, said, "I can nose around, sure. Long as it's not on the South Side. I don't get along too well, that parta town. Only first I gotta, ya know, have some idea what this bozo looks like."

"Way I hear it, kind of a pretty boy," Hagan said. "Not a faggot—I don't mean that. Light skin, wavy blond hair—or light brown it could be. Blue eyes, around six feet, twenty-five to twenty-eight, hundred fifty-sixty pounds, good build on him."

Walsh said, "Worth a couple-three cees to ya, huh?"

"For the right guy, cash on the line."

"Lemme see what I can do for ya," Punky Walsh said.

Seated at his desk, feet up and ankles crossed, Charles Rathbun said, "We went in with what we had: identification of Foster by that traffic cop and two witnesses at the scene, testimony tying ownership of the gun to him, the ballistics report, no supportable alibi. It turned out to be enough. I had Judge Trude's bailiff on the line just a few minutes ago. Foster's been indicted, no bail request was made, and as of the moment he's behind bars, with a trial date about to be set."

Roche said, "For such welcome news, 'tis a long face you're wearing there, Charlie."

Rathbun slammed his feet to the floor, leaned forward in his chair, said, " 'Welcome news,' my ass! When it comes to getting a conviction, we don't have a prayer. A few already shaky witnesses the defense'll make mincemeat of. No admissible motive. Foster's gun was used—sure. Only how do we go about proving it was in his possession at the time? The killer was blond, Foster's hair is black. And I can't count the times I've said this: juries—no matter what the evidence—simply will not convict a local mobster for murder."

Roche spread his hands, said, "You figure to give up on it, Charlie? Move to dismiss, maybe?"

Rathbun sank back, sighed heavily. "No, of course not. I could offer to consider some kind of deal, I suppose. But all that'd get me'd be the big horse laugh from the defense. And as for the colonel? My God, he'd hand me my head!"

Roche said, "Then let's keep our peckers up. Add, say, another ten men to the team and go right on with the raids. Maybe we oughta round up some'a the big shots for a change, charge *them* as vags. Make it so damned expensive and uncomfortable they'll hafta come up with what we need to put Foster away for good."

Rathbun made a tent of his fingers, looked down at them. He said quietly, "If it was Foster to begin with."

Roche said, "Dear Christ on the cross, Charlie! Don't start that again! I know you don't want to believe it, I know *why* you don't want to believe it. But like it or not, Charlie, Frankie Foster's the guy pulled that fucking trigger."

Raising his voice, the desk clerk at the Argyle Hotel said, "Oh, Mister Hart. There's a message for you."

John Hagan veered from his path to the elevator, came over to the desk and was handed a slip of paper. "The call came in only a few minutes ago, sir. Urgent, the gentleman said."

A Diversey exchange. Hagan entered the lobby phone booth, deposited a coin, dialed the number. Two rings, a click, a voice said, "Yeah?"

Hagan said, "It's me, Punky. Don't tell me you've come up with something already."

"Ya been in the Green Mill Gardens?" Walsh said.

"Not since I been back in town, no," Hagan said.

Walsh said, "Meet me there, eleven tonight," and hung up.

Angela Terrell said, "Well, hello there! How nice of you to call me!"

"It's been a while," Roche said.

"So it has."

An awkward pause. Roche said, "You knew we got Lingle's killer tucked away?"

"It was in the papers," Angela said. "Congratulations."

"Thank you."

Silence. Angela said, "For someone supposed to be sitting on top of the world you don't sound all that good."

" 'Tis nothing a healthy drink won't cure."

"Such as a snort or two of the fine Irish whiskey I just happen to have handy?"

"I guess you could be saying as much."

Suddenly they both were laughing. Angela said, "How soon can you be here?"

"A cab? Fifteen minutes."

"I'll set the latch," Angela said. "Case I'm still in the tub . . . I've missed you, Irish."

"The very words," Roche said, "from my own lips."

Smiling, Angela replaced the receiver, went to the hall door, released the lock, spent several minutes emptying ashtrays, wiping off the bar top, and rinsing glasses. She was about to enter the bedroom when the doorbell rang.

She hesitated, frowning, pulled the folds of her robe together, retied the belt, and went to the door. "Who is it?"

A cheerful voice said, "Delivery, ma'am."

She opened the door. A slender, olive-skinned young man stood there, his uniform cap at a jaunty angle and a package under one arm.

"Miss Terrell?"

Angela said, "Yes. But I wasn't—"

The young man said, "You'll need to sign for it, lady," and slipped past her.

In chambers, Cook County Criminal Court Judge Daniel Trude said, "I have a crowded calendar to contend with, gentlemen. If we can come to a mutually satisfactory trial date, I'll so enter it. Mister Levy?"

Defense Attorney Harold Levy said, "First opening you have, Your Honor, is fine with us. The earlier we go in, the sooner the jury can acquit Foster."

"Mister Rathbun?"

Charles Rathbun said, "If it please the court, the Prosecution is requesting sixty days to prepare our case."

Levy said, "Oh, Your Honor, this is beyond reason! Keeping my client locked up while Mister Rathbun grasps at straws is not only utterly unfair but a denial of the man's constitutional rights."

Rathbun said, "Keeping your client locked up was his idea. Why hasn't he requested bail?"

"Come off it, Charlie," Levy snapped. "You know damned well why not. He's got enemies outside hungry for a chance to bump him off. Reason he skipped town to begin with."

Rathbun said, "Bullshit. The reason he skip—"

Trude held up a silencing hand. "That's quite enough, gentlemen. However, I do agree that sixty days to prepare the state's case seems excessive." He took the court calendar from the desk top, skimmed through it, and said, "Monday, the thirteenth of October, ten A.M. Acceptable?"

She lay on her back, eyes half open, face twisted in a paroxysm of terror that came during the seconds before she died. Blood from severed carotid arteries formed a wide, still glistening stain in the carpet's heavy pile.

Roche sank to his knees beside her. Without conscious thought the Act of Contrition rose to his lips. "Oh my God, I am heartily sorry for having offended Thee. Please forgive this and all my other sins . . ."

Using the bedroom extension, he called Central Homicide and asked for Lieutenant Ian Duffield.

Not until then was he aware of the tears streaming down his cheeks.

Punky Walsh, fingers wrapped around a highball glass, was alone at a side table when Hagan walked into the Green Mill a few minutes past eleven. Ben Pollack's orchestra was on the stand, tuxedos and evening dresses filled the dance floor, and Al Kvale was crooning "Broadway Melody" into a microphone that hid most of his face.

Hagan took the chair across from Walsh, said, "How goes it, Punky?"

"Ya know what they charge a guy for a drink in this joint?" Walsh said. "Two bucks is what they charge ya. For one lousy jigger'a cut-to-hell Scotch and fizz water, two bucks. They don't know we got a Depression goin' on these days?"

"Bootleggers have to eat too," Hagan said. "What've you got for me, Punky?"

Walsh drank from his glass, set it down, swiveled his gaze around the large room. "'Kay. Take a gander that fella leanin' up against the wall over there. Near that side door?"

After checking out four false leads in the past five days, Hagan wasn't too hopeful. He peered through the blue layers of tobacco smoke drifting over the crowded tables. . . . Yeah. The guy sure *looked* blond enough. Under six feet by maybe two-three inches, weight hard to tell right off, and the face was a blur from this far away.

"Who's he supposed to be?" Hagan said.

"House man," Walsh said. "The bouncer. I heard somebody call him 'Lou,' but I wasn't goin' to start askin' questions. Ya know?"

Hagan got out his wallet, counted out five twenties, handed them over, said, "Another two, if it comes out he's the guy. Okay?"

Walsh drained his glass, left. Hagan caught the eye of a passing waiter, ordered a bourbon and water, got a cigarette burning. By the time the waiter was back, Hagan had his gambit.

"I'm supposed to look up a fellow works here," Hagan said. "Name's Lou."

"Only Lou around here I know of," the waiter said, "is Lou Bader. Bouncer."

Hagan said, "Kinda chunky? Black hair, what there is of it?"

"Not Lou Bader," the waiter said. "Blond hair and nobody'd call *him* chunky."

"No other Lou?"

"Not that I heard of," the waiter said. "And I been here three years now. The drink's a deuce."

Hagan paid him, added a dollar tip, said, "What time you close here?"

"Around four bells," the waiter said.

After picking a vantage point where he could keep an eye on both the front and side entrances to the Green Mill, John Hagan leaned against a light pole and settled down to wait.

He was on his third cigarette when, at 4:16, Leo Brothers, alias Lou Bader, wearing a gray tweed topcoat and gray fedora, came out, walked to the intersection of Broadway and Lawrence and boarded a southbound streetcar.

Hagan swung aboard as the car started to move. Neither man glanced at the other. Brothers dropped a nickel and two pennies into the coin box, took a transfer, entered the car and found a seat near the front. Hagan remained standing on the rear platform.

At Forty-seventh and South State they were among a group of six passengers transferring to an eastbound trolley. Both men got off at Lake Park. Brothers strode briskly south for two blocks along the wide avenue, stopped at the entrance to a large apartment building, opened one of the double doors, and went in.

At this hour the sidewalks were deserted. To the east, a heavily overcast sky showed the first signs of dawn. Hagan stepped out of the shadows, propped a hip against a car parked at the curb, lit a cigarette and eyed the building across from him. Red brick, fairly new, four floors with a green canvas canopy at the entry. A wooden sign read 1–1½–2 KITCHENETTE APT, FURNISHED, WEEK OR MONTH, INQUIRE WITHIN.

On looks alone the guy pretty much filled the bill. Maybe he'd never seen the inside of a prison cell, but fifteen years of rubbing elbows with lawbreakers told Hagan that Lou Bader was a member of the same fraternity. Of course it could turn out he hadn't been ten miles past the Chicago city limits in his life. That case Bader was of no use to him. But he knew damned well the man was bent.

He crossed the street, pushed back one of the heavy doors, and entered a deep narrow hallway. There were rows of mailboxes and bell buttons on both walls, at the far end a locked door. In the dim light from an overhead bulb he found the name L. BADER and the number 317.

Things were looking up. He yawned, lit a cigarette, and left the building.

An hour later John Hagan, back in his hotel room and still wearing a small self-satisfied smile, was asleep.

Lt. Ian Duffield, Homicide Division, said, "I went along with you on this, Pat. Kept you out of it, handed the papers the same story you handed me. Not that they believed a word of it. No more than I did, what little there was of it."

Roche said, "I gave you what I could, Ian. You know how it is."

"No," Duffield said, "I don't know how it is. That's the whole fucking point. But we've known each other for what—ten years now?—so, like I say, I went along with you."

They sat across from each other at a desk in a cramped office on the third floor of the city's central detective bureau. From behind a glass ventilator panel at the one window a cool damp breeze stirred the pages of a wall calendar extolling the virtues of Kolynos Dental Cream.

Duffield said, "Wasn't even two hours after the body gets to the morgue when I got this phone call. Brooklyn lawyer name of Balasari. 'I'm acting for Mister Julian Terrell,' he says in one'a these tight-ass voices. 'The father of the late Angela Terrell. Mister Terrell,' he says, 'has asked me to learn how soon he may claim the remains of his daughter.'

"I tell him," Duffield said, "there's the matter of positive identification by a family member, if at all possible, and a post-mortem to establish cause of death to get through first. Plus a coroner's inquest, although that can come afterwards. Could take, I tell him, three-four days. He says, 'I shall see to it that those details are expedited, sir,' and hangs up on me. You hear what I'm saying, Pat?"

"Every word, my friend," Roche said.

The lieutenant got to his feet, slammed down the window, returned to his chair. He said, "Then I get word how the Terrell girl's aunt shows up right after I talked to that lawyer and identified her. An hour—one *hour*—after that the autopsy is over with, a report filed, and the body picked up by Martin Brothers. Inside the *next* hour—now get this—she's cremated and that aunt of hers on the way to Brooklyn with the ashes. If it was her aunt to begin with. Which I kinda doubt, you wanta know the truth. Another thing: I still can't figure how word got to Brooklyn that fast.

"Now this is where it gets good," Duffield said. "I no sooner find *that* out when I get another call. Only this's from the guy at the top of the ladder around here. He says to me, 'Lieutenant, send up everything you have on that young woman killed over on Lake Shore Drive. As of now it's to be handled from this office and all inquiries referred to me.'

"A cover-up?" Duffield said. "The fix is in? Don't ask me, pal, I'm outta the picture. But just between us girls, who the fuck *was* this babe? And seeing as you're the fella breezed in and found her with her throat cut, what were you doing there in the first place? Stopped by to play a little hide the weenie?"

Roche forced a smile, stood up, went to the door. He said, "How the dear girl's father found out so quick, Ian, was that I made a phone call."

The door closed behind him.

One in the A.M. and Lou Bader was there. On the job, standing near the rear wall and talking to a young woman in a party dress and a little unsteady on her feet. Good crowd tonight: dance floor jammed, every table taken, hum of voices, the Pollack orchestra blaring out a heavily syncopated arrangement of "Nobody But You."

John Hagan finished his drink, butted his cigarette, moved past a swath of tables to the side door of the Green Mill Gardens and on out into Lawrence Avenue.

A Checker cab drew up at the corner to discharge a middle-aged man and an overweight woman wrapped in mink. Hagan buttoned his topcoat against the chill night air and stepped into the cab.

"Forty-sixth and Lake Park," John Hagan said.

Roche said, "When Margaret and I first moved to this town, it was constantly after me she was I should buy a nice automobile. Take rides in the countryside, she was forever saying. Get away from the dirt and the noise and the stink of the stockyards. Well, I kept putting it off, you see, till she finally gave up on the idea.

"Fact is," Roche said, " 'twas the thought of being behind the wheel of a senseless piece of moving machinery stopped me. And if the truth be known, I *like* the noise and the stink—within reason. And then getting around's easy enough; man can't walk more'n four blocks in any direction at all there's not a streetcar or the El or a foine seat on the bus. Sure and a bit longer it'll be taking to get where you're going. And pray tell, what's so bad about that?"

Wendt said, "Not a thing, Patrick. 'Specially when you have a swell Chevy coupe and an obliging fella to do the driving. At one-fifteen on a chilly morning, as it happens to be at this very moment."

The car stood at the curb outside Roche's apartment building, both men lounging in the front seat sharing Wendt's dwindling stock of Sanos. They sat there, lines of fatigue etching stubbled cheeks, eyes glassy, caught up in that semi-somnambulistic state where the mind wanders and the subconscious takes over.

Roche said, "Walter, ever take a look at Goose Island around this time'a night?"

"Why the billy blue hell," Wendt said, "would anybody wanta be anywhere *near* Goose Island this time'a night?"

Roche said, "Then's when it is they have the gas works over there goin' full blast. 'Tis something to see! They open up these big ovens and shovel in the coke and you'd be swearing 'twas the Devil's own playground there."

Wendt yawned hugely, said, "You wanta know the truth, Pat, I can hardly wait to miss it."

"Strange how this town can take hold of a man," Roche said. "Every land in all the world, every spoken tongue, and no more than a streetcar ride from where we sit at this minute. And each mile ridden, Walter, a college education in itself. Yet say as much to many a man lives here and sad to say, he'll not know what it is you're talking about.

"Six days each week," Roche said, "he follows the same path to his work and back again to his home. Come Sunday, granted he's a God-fearing man, he's at Mass in the morning, then straight to his parlor, the radio on and a newspaper in his hands. Not knowing and not caring what it's like five city blocks out of his way."

Wendt ground out his cigarette, bent to open the car door next to Roche, and said, "Patrick. Before you get on to something like maybe the evils of Prohibition, will you kindly pry your ass offa that seat, climb up the fucking stairs and go to bed?"

" 'Tis exactly what I'm about to do," Roche said.

Once the cab pulled away, John Hagan walked two blocks south on the east side of Lake Park before stopping among the shadows directly across from the apartment house.

A damp bone-chilling haze hung in the air, putting dim halos around street lamps. Slivers of light showed at the edges of drawn shades at one or two apartment windows facing the street. A rakish Auburn sports sedan sped by, trailing a woman's high-pitched laughter.

Hagan took a final deep drag on his cigarette, stepped on the glowing ember, walked across Lake Park and entered the apartment building hallway.

No one in sight, no sound. The stagnant odor of cigar smoke hung in the lifeless air.

Hagan went along the narrow hall until he reached the mailbox for 317. He was reluctant to ring the bell, but the possibility that Bader might have, say, a sleep-in girlfriend left him no choice.

He pressed the button, heard a strident buzz through the speaking tube, removed his finger, waited a few seconds, tried again. . . .

For a man of Hagan's shady talents, the inner-door lock posed no problem. He went through, passed the self-service elevator to a door marked STAIRS and on up the steps to the third floor.

Another narrow hallway, badly lit, smelling of rancid grease and something resembling shoe polish. Metal numbers, painted white, on the doors. He moved on, steps muffled by the worn carpeting, stopped outside 317, put an ear to the door, heard nothing. He tried the knob. Locked.

Twenty seconds later, the picklock back in his pocket, he was inside, his back to the closed door, waiting until his eyes adjusted to the darkness.

Two side windows, blinds drawn to the sills. Amorphous shapes slowly became a lounge chair, an upholstered couch, a floor lamp, a writing desk and its straight-backed chair, and little else. An archway led to a kitchen and breakfast nook; near that was an open door to what would be the bedroom.

Hagan tiptoed over, peered in. The window blind was up far enough for him to make out a tangle of sheets and blankets on the empty bed. He moved to the window, lowered the blind and turned on the bedside lamp.

The furnishings were second-hand schlock. Hagan crossed to the single dresser, made a thorough search of its three drawers, leaving everything exactly as he'd found it. He dipped into the pockets of the three bargain-basement suits hanging in the miniscule closet, pawed through the bathroom medicine chest.

Zero.

He turned off the light, raised the blind to its original position, returned to the living room and snapped on the floor lamp. Mismatched furniture from the same junk pile as that in the bedroom. He spent the next twenty minutes methodically hunting for clues to Lou Bader's identity and background.

Nothing. No album of snapshots, no letters from Mom or Pop or a friendly loan shark, no the-kid-keeps-asking-for-daddy note from an abandoned wife.

Hagan shrugged in defeat and was reaching for the floor-lamp switch when he spotted a small wicker wastebasket pushed far back under the kneehole of the writing desk. He bent, brought it out.

A crumpled white envelope, a sheet of typing paper, a gum wrapper, an empty condom tin. Hagan smoothed out the envelope. It showed, neatly typed, the name Louis Bader and the Lake Park address. But what riveted his interest were the words in the upper left-hand corner: "TriCity Transportation Union, 1108 East Bowker St., St. Louis, Missouri."

The St. Louis postmark was dated two days before. He got out a chewed pencil stub and a small notebook, copied the return address and company name on a fresh page, then examined the single sheet of typing paper. It had been folded lengthwise twice and both sides were blank. Why waste two cents mailing a thing like that? Answer: you don't. You fold it around something. Like a money order, maybe a check.

He recrumpled the envelope, dropped everything back into the wastebasket, placed it carefully under the desk and switched off the light.

At 10:17 that same morning, John Hagan boarded a train bound for St. Louis.

The voice on the phone had a stiff, coldly precise edge to it. "Let me speak to Patrick Roche."

"Not in right now," Wendt said. "Who wants him?"

"My name," the voice said, "is Ness. Eliot Ness. With the Prohibition Bureau, Department of Justice."

"Oh sure," Wendt said. "I'm Walter Wendt, Mister Ness. Maybe I can help you."

The conversation that followed ended four minutes later when Eliot Ness slammed down the receiver.

Homicide Lieutenant Ian Duffield said, "Few things I've dug up you might wanta hear about, Pat. On this frienda yours, got her throat cut?"

"Seems to me," Roche said, "I heard somewhere you'd been pulled off it, the case."

They were at a secluded table near the rear wall of Barney's Steak House on West Randolph. It was well after one in the afternoon and the lunch crowd had pretty much thinned out.

"You heard right," Duffield said. "But y'see I have this bump of curiosity, I guess you'd call it. Anyhow, I've been doing a little . . . well, let's say snooping around the edges when nobody's looking. And I'd like your word you'll keep all what I'm telling you under your hat, okay?"

"'Tis my solemn promise you have, Ian," Roche said.

"Well, a couple things," Duffield said. "First place, this wasn't a burglary. Leather case full of damned expensive jewelry on the lady's dressing table. Right out in the open, untouched. And no signs of forced entry, so she must've let the guy in herself.

"Now there's people in and out of that building all day long," Duffield said. "Workmen, guests, delivery guys, the tenants themselves. So you see what I'd be up against here, even if I didn't have my hands tied."

Duffield forked the last morsel of his steak into his mouth and chewed briefly before pushing the plate aside. He drank from his coffee cup, set it down.

"Now here's where it gets real interesting, Pat," Lieutenant Duffield said. "Regular doorman out there's this kid named Jerry Kafka. Well, turns out it was his day off, the girl got killed. Only he don't show up for work the next day. Fact he don't show up since. Skipped out, no notice to his boss, nothing. Lives with his mother, she hasn't seen him, don't know where he is. I'd'a put a want out on him except I'm off the case.

"Something else funny I run into," Duffield said. "Bootlegger name'a Crimaldi services that same building. Ecola Crimaldi—one'a

Joe Aiello's boys. Maybe you've run across him? Crimaldi? Had him in year or so back on a dago got shot over on Milton."

Roche said, "Doesn't ring a bell, the name."

"What I'm getting at," Duffield said, "booze deliveries to that apartment house stopped right after for a few days. Might've been on account of the cops around asking questions. Then they started deliveries again, only this time it's a different ginzo bringing in the stuff."

He finished his coffee, signaled the waiter for a refill, offered Roche a cigarette, took one for himself, and lighted both with a beat-up Zippo. Outside, a mild drizzle had turned into a steady downpour and pedestrians hurried past holding newspapers over their heads.

"Wanta know how it looks to me, Pat?" Duffield said. "Like a mob killing is how. Some way or other, the Terrell girl gets tied in with somebody in the Aiello gang. You find out about it, put the screws to her for information you can use to knock over Aiello's joints because of the Lingle kill. Aiello figures out where the leak's coming from, and the young lady ends up with her throat cut."

Duffield leaned back in his chair, brushed cigarette ash from his shirt front, said, "'Course you can tell me I'm all wrong on this. Hell, I might even believe you. Either way, I just want you to know it's strictly between the both of us, okay?"

Roche said, "I'll be leveling with you, Ian. The lass had nothing to do with any of the Aiello bums. Jake Lingle's girl, she was. Till the day he died. I did see her a time or two, hoping it was a little light she might throw on why he was killed there.

"From what you say," Roche said, "'twould seem it got out she was close to him, that I was calling on her and who I was. Probably this doorman; 'twas him led me to her in the first place."

Lieutenant Duffield said, "Why don't we have a little more coffee, wait for this rain to let up? 'Fore we have to get out in it."

Wendt said, "Looks like we got a big-shot member of the U.S. of A. government mad at us, Patrick."

Roche shook water off his hat, hung it and his raincoat on a wall hook, said, "And who would that be, Walter?"

"Mister Eliot Ness is the name," Wendt said. "That big warehouse'a

Capone's on Archer and Wallace we took apart last night? Well, Mister Ness phoned a while ago, raising hell. Way he tells it, his boys raided the joint early this morning. Along with a couple reporters and a *Daily News* photographer. Real disappointed finding all that whiskey gone. Had a great deal to say, Mister Ness did, about how we were interfering with Department of Justice operations and that he wanted a stop put to it unless we got a go-ahead from him first."

"A dedicated man, Ness," Roche said. "Takes his job to heart there. And what did *you* say?"

"That we had a job to do," Wendt said, "that we were doing it, and the hell with him."

Roche laughed, said, "C'mon, Walter, you didn't actually say as much."

"Close enough," Wendt said. "Anyway, he hung up without a pleasant goodbye."

"A bit too fond of the publicity, Eliot," Roche said. "Likes his picture in the papers and so on. I'll be giving him a call, day or so. Smooth his ruffled feathers, as the saying goes."

Captain Ross Lowry, Twelfth Precinct, St. Louis Police Department, shook Hagan's hand warmly, said, "Good to see ya, John! How long's it been?"

"Least a couple'a years," Hagan said. "I hafta admit you look like life agrees with you these days."

"Can't complain," Lowry said. He closed his office door, jerked a thumb at a chair alongside the desk, said, "Go ahead, rest your butt."

They sat down. Lowry picked a cigar stub off the ashtray, puffed it back to life, said, "What brings you to these parts?"

Hagan said, "Know anything about a local outfit called TriCity Transportation Union?"

Captain Lowry raised an eyebrow. "TriCity, yeah. On the east side'a town. Bowker Street. What about it?"

"They on the legit, Ross?"

"Let me answer that this way," Lowry said. "Buster Wortman's behind it. Last year or so a lotta east side guys outta work start using their cars as cheap-fare cabs. Haul three-four fares at a time, two bits apiece. Well, Buster sets up this so-called union of his, begins putting the squeeze on these guys. Join up or get your head busted."

Hagan said, "Tell you why I'm asking, Ross. Begin with, I'm back in the agency business, just me so far but I expect to expand, you know? Anyway, I got this client. Fellow owns one of the biggest used-car operations in K.C. Month or two back, a salesman of his emptied out the office safe, heisted a 'twenty-nine Chandler Royal Eight right off the lot and lit out for parts unknown.

"Well, my client took it personal, Ross," Hagan said. "'Don't give a shit what it costs me,' he tells me, 'I want that sonofabitch found, yanked back here and sent up.' Matter of pride's the way he feels about it."

Lowry said, "You think he's in town?"

"I turned up this broad he was banging," Hagan said. "Made her sore, way he ran out on her, and she finally tells me about him getting checks in the mail from some union. In St. Louis. 'Three Cities' was as close she could come to it. Only union here anywhere near that in the phone book is this TriCity outfit."

"Give me the name," Lowry said.

"Louis Bader," Hagan said. "My guess it'll be an alias."

Captain Lowry ground out his cigar in the ashtray, said, "Sit still a minute," and left the office. Hagan found a two-month-old copy of *Captain Billy's Whizbang* on top of a bank of filing cabinets.

Five minutes later Lowry returned with a manila folder, sat down, opened it, took out half a dozen report forms complete with mug shots. He unclipped the photos, dropped them on the desk in front of his visitor, said, "Some of Buster Wortman's boys tied in with Tri-City. Go ahead, try your luck."

Hagan stopped at number four. Louis Bader. But neatly typed below the two exposures was the name Leo V. Brothers.

From the *Chicago Post*, Oct. 23, 1930:

The body of Gerald Kafka, 24, an employee of a fashionable Lake Shore Drive address, was recovered yesterday off Montrose Beach. Kafka, reported missing nine days earlier, had been bound, gagged and shot twice through the head. Although the victim had no known criminal record, the slaying appeared to be a gangland execution, and police are investigating that angle.

One thing you could say for the phone booths on the Palmer House mezzanine, they had class. Each like a small room almost, carpet on the floor, overhead light, a little bench to sit on while you made your call. Close the door and nobody outside heard a word. A grand hotel, the Palmer House. What with the swell restaurants like the Empire Room there, and in the barber shop downstairs all those silver dollars stuck in the floor.

He stacked a supply of coins on the ledge below the phone, got out the slip of paper with the right number on it, reached for the receiver . . . and drew back his hand.

No question, this would cost the man his life. Take that into the confessional and you damned well knew what the penance would be. Yet hold it back and, unshriven, you're likely to end up with your arse on the points of Satan's pitchfork. A sobering thought, that.

Or you could think of yourself as the good Lord's instrument of justice and be after passing up Father Mahaffey entirely.

He picked up the receiver and placed a person-to-person call to Anthony Balasari, attorney-at-law, Brooklyn, New York.

John Torrio said, "Don Giuliano Torenello came to see me a few days ago. Maybe you know the name?"

"Sure," Capone said. "Took over the Brooklyn Mafia couple years back. About the time Frankie Yale got hisself shot to pieces, right?"

They were seated on the bench of a redwood picnic table at a deserted camp site near the banks of the Fox River some forty miles west of Chicago. The sky was heavily overcast, the temperature in the low forties. Two cars—Capone's heavily armored sedan and a black Chrysler limousine—were drawn up a short distance away where four bodyguards, in form-fitting overcoats and gray fedoras, were lounging.

Torrio said, "The Don's only daughter, Angelina, had been living in Chicago. You may remember her, Alphonse, ten years or so ago you met the train she came in on and found her a place to live."

"Well . . . sorta," Capone said. "Good-looking babe but kinda snotty, I remember right."

Torrio said, "She was murdered last week, Alphonse. In her own apartment, her throat cut. Surprised you didn't read about it in the papers."

"Who reads the papers anymore?" Capone said. "Fulla guys jumping outta windas, banks closing up, a lotta poor slobs peddling apples on the street. I even quit listening to the radio, you know? Besides, I don't have to tell you I got my own problems."

Torrio said, "It seems Angelina was carrying on with a man that got himself killed here a few months back. The same man, Alphonse, whose death brought on these problems of yours."

Capone stared at him, slack-jawed. "Wait just one fucking minute here, J. T. You talking about Lingle? *Jake* Lingle?"

"No question," John Torrio said. "Some cop found out about the two of them, told her he'd keep it quiet if she'd spill what Lingle'd told her about the rackets. Least, that's the way it looks."

"Who's this cop?"

Torrio said, "That, the Don doesn't know. But he *did* learn that she was killed on the direct order of Giuseppe Aiello." He leaned back, folded his hands across his slight paunch, said, "And that, my dear friend, is why I'm here in Chicago after all these years."

Capone brushed cigar ash from the lapels of his camel-hair overcoat, drew up its collar against the chill air, said, "Okay, J. T. Anything you want, you got."

Torrio said, "Like I told you, Don Giuliano came to see me. He asks that I seek your permission to send some of his men into Chicago to avenge his daughter's death. But he knows of the difficulties you're having and doesn't wish to add to them by any act on his part."

"Now that's damned nice of him, J. T.," Capone said. "Me, I was in his place, I'd just up and go in, do the job and the hell with whose toes get stepped on."

Torrio smiled, shrugged. "These Sicilians have their ways of doing things, Alphonse. As I found out long ago, no one truly understands Sicilians, least of all the Italians."

Capone dropped the cigar butt, ground it out with the heel of his shoe. He said, "Tell Torenello not to bother sending his boys out here. Joe Aiello's been a pain in the ass for too long as it is. Between what this Irish prick Roche's been doing to me and the way business is, I been thinking for weeks now on taking over the North Side. So you go right ahead, J. T., let the Don know I'll have some news for him. Real soon."

FALL GUY

Frank Foster did not kill Alfred Lingle.

—Charles Rathbun,
1930

16

At 2:17 P.M., John Hagan said, "That's him, Rocky. Coming out now. Hold up till he passes us."

Leo Brothers, wearing a three-piece blue serge suit, a dark gray fedora, and a light gray topcoat, paused under the building canopy to light a cigarette, then began walking north toward the streetcar line at Forty-seventh. The day was clear, with a slight breeze off the lake, and except for a middle-aged woman wheeling a baby carriage, the sidewalk was empty.

Brothers was a few steps past the green Dodge sedan parked at the curb when its two front doors swung open and Hagan and Rocco DiGarmo got out, moved smoothly up behind him.

"How they treating you, Leo?" Hagan said.

Brothers took another step, stopped, turned, showed the two men a blank expression, said, "You talking to me?"

"Who else?" Hagan said.

Brothers said, "Looks like you got the wrong man, mister. My name's Louis Bader."

"Sure it is," Hagan said. He put his right hand in the pocket of his topcoat, stepped closer to Brothers and jabbed the muzzle of a handgun against his spine. "But in St. Louis it's Leo Brothers. So let's take a nice ride, okay? Frisk him, Rocky."

Rocco grinned, showing a missing incisor, and patted him down. Brothers, hands held at chest level, said, "You guys coppers?"

"Don't talk dirty," John Hagan said.

The two-story brick building stood on the west side of Cicero Avenue between an Italian restaurant and a grocery. Lettered across the wide window, its Venetian blind lowered, were the words:

CICERO STATE TRUST & SAVINGS BANK
"Growing with the Community"
Nicholas Reznick, President   Assets over $2,000,000

Taped to the inner side of the front door's glass panel was a placard:

THIS BANK CLOSED
TILL FURTHER NOTICE
by order
ILLINOIS STATE BANKING COMM.
SPRINGFIELD, ILL.

Inside, John Hagan and Leo Brothers sat side by side on a slatted bench near the empty teller cages, sitting in the silence like two strangers in a dentist's waiting room. Hagan, his expression placid, puffed on a cigarette; Brothers, puzzled and worried, gnawed at a hangnail.

Hagan took a last puff of his Murad, exhaled smoke into the room's dead bone-chilling air. He pinched out the coal, dropped the stub on the carpeting. Brothers gave him a quick, nervous glance. Sounding plaintive, he said, "Look, mister. Loosen up a little, will ya? I gotta right to know why you hauled me down—"

At the bank's rear wall a key grated in a door marked EMERGENCY EXIT ONLY. It swung slowly back and Frankie Rio, right hand buried in a pocket of his topcoat, slipped in. After a single sweeping glance at the room, he stepped aside and Al Capone entered.

While Rio closed and locked the door, Capone strode over to the two men on the bench. Ignoring Hagan, he stopped in front of Brothers, looked him full in the face. Brothers endured the cold, probing stare for a few seconds, then wet his lips and looked down at his hands.

Abruptly Capone turned, went through the swing gate of a railing guarding a row of private offices. He opened a door marked MR. REZ-NICK, crooked a finger at Hagan and disappeared inside.

Hagan followed him into the darkened office, closed the door. Capone was raising the shades at the two windows. He came back to an executive-sized desk that took up most of the center of the room, drew out the leather-backed swivel chair, wiped the seat with his handkerchief, and sat down. After mopping dust from a section of the desk's glass top, he dropped the handkerchief into a wastebasket, said, "Sit down, John."

Hagan drew a chair up to the desk. Frowning, Capone leaned back, pointed a thumb at the door, said, "You trying to tell me *he* looks like Frankie Foster?"

Hagan said, "You'd be surprised, Mister Capone, how close he comes to matching what the witnesses said. Built a lot like him, real close to the age you wanted, and that hair of his is the real McCoy—not some wig or a dye job.

"On top of that," Hagan said, "he's from outta town. St. Louis. No connection with any'a the Chicago mobs I could come up with. And you wanted a guy that's hot? Well, Mister Capone, this guy's burning up! Warrant out for him down there. For knocking off some young fella drove a cab."

"What good's all that," Capone said, "if the face's wrong? That's what people look at—the face."

Hagan said, "Believe me, Mister Capone, when I tell you there's not all that much of a difference. And the way I hear it, these people you're talking about, these witnesses, had a good look at this Foster fella and pretty much said it wasn't him they saw plug Lingle. On topa that, Mister Capone, you hafta keep in mind it's been quite a while now since then. The shooting, I mean."

Capone sat fingering his chin thoughtfully. Finally he said, "How much've you told him?"

"Just that you needed a job done and how maybe I could swing it his way."

Capone nodded, said, "Get him in here."

Hagan stood up, opened the door, put his head out, said, "Leo."

Brothers stepped in, hat in hand, hesitated uncertainly, then approached the desk. Hagan said, "Leo Brothers, Mister Capone."

The thought of offering his hand never entered Brothers's head. He said, "Real pleased to make your acquaintance, sir."

"Sit down, Leo," Capone said mildly.

Taking Hagan's chair, Brothers settled back, dropped his hat next to him on the floor. He crossed his legs, forced his expression into relaxed lines, waited. Capone brought a box of Melachrinos from his overcoat, lighted one, blew out the match. He said, "This cab driver. Why'd you kill him?"

Brothers said, "Had to do with a union down there, Mister Capone. Not so much the fella himself wouldn't join up, you understand. But he was giving us trouble by trying to keep anybody else from signing on. I can't begin to tell you how many times he was told to lay off. Guy just wouldn't listen."

"So you put a bullet in him. When was this?"

"Year ago last August," Brothers said.

Capone said, "John here tells me you're working at the Green Mill. Kind of risky, wouldn't you say? Out in the open, a want hanging over you. St. Louis must've sent out readers. Some cop up here makes you, back you go."

Brothers said, "Well, matter of fact, Mister Capone, that warrant out on me? A frienda mine down there put the kibosh on it. Means I'm pretty much in the clear right now. Long's my name don't pop up, anyway."

"This friend," Capone said. "Buster Wortman?"

Brothers said, "Well, yes sir. Mister Wortman's helping us organize this union I spoke of."

Capone took in a lungful of smoke, exhaled, made a face, tossed the cigarette into the wastebasket. He drew himself closer to the desk, said, "This last June. Around the tentha the month. You in town back then?"

Brothers thought for a moment, shook his head. "Well, no sir. Matter of fact I wasn't. I got into this . . . situation, see, and had to blow town for a few weeks. Got me a job with this bootlegger outside'a Muncie, Indiana. Fella by the name of Schoenburg."

Seated on the office couch, Hagan said, "That'd be Alex Schoenburg, Mister Capone. I know of him."

Capone said, "You call yourself Bader when you were in Muncie?"

Brothers shook his head. "No sir. Lewis Blake."

Capone straightened, stretched his arms high, yawned. He said, "I have to admit it, Leo, you impress me as being a stand-up guy. Why I've been asking all these questions is to find out if you're the right man to handle a job for me. A big job. Now let me tell you what it is."

The tension that had gripped Leo Brothers from the moment he'd been forced into Hagan's car at gunpoint suddenly evaporated. "Yes *sir*, Mister Capone. Whatever it is, you can count on me. A hundred percent."

"Good," Capone said. "You're going to the pen, Leo. For killing Jake Lingle."

Mrs. Milano said, "It wasn't for the Depression, you'd not find an empty apartment in the whole neighborhood. But I guess I don't have to tell you, Mrs.—"

"Whitney," the blonde in the red dress said.

"—what's going on these days," Mrs. Milano said. "Well, all I can say is the sooner they get that man Hoover out of the White House, the sooner decent people can go back to work."

She stopped at the door to a second-floor apartment, used a key from her apron pocket to unlock it, and the two women went into a small living room. It was bare of furnishings, the window shades drawn. Indentations in the threadbare carpeting marked where the last tenant's furniture had stood.

"Two bedrooms, a full bath, lots of closet space," Mrs. Milano said. "We get thirty dollars a month for it, pay for your own gas and lights. Go right ahead and take a good look around for yourself, Mrs. Woodley."

"Whitney," the blonde in the red dress said. She walked over to one of the living room's two windows, raised the blind, looked down onto Kolmar Avenue. A few cars along both curbs, bare-limbed trees lining the narrow parkways between sidewalks and the street. Directly across from her stood a three-story yellow brick apartment house, the number 205 visible above the door. Between 205 and the building on the left was a small courtyard turfed with yellowing grass.

The blonde in the red dress let the shade drop back into place. She said, "We'll take it. My husband'll move our things in this weekend. If that's okay with you."

"Two months in advance," Mrs. Milano said. "Come on downstairs and I'll give you the keys and your receipt."

Mr. Pellegrini said, "Nice young couple, cutest kid y'ever seen, Mrs. Avers—and I hadda put 'em out in the street. Lost his job, couldn't pay the rent, what am I s'posed to do? I got my own bills to pay."

The blonde in the red dress stepped over to one of the bedroom windows, raised the blind, and looked down at the small courtyard of yellowing grass three floors below. She said, "It's swell, Mr. Pellegrini. We'll be moving in by the end of the week."

"Two months, seventy dollars," Pellegrini said. "In cash, seein' how fast the banks can close up on you these days."

Leo Brothers, openly incredulous, said, "I don't get you, Mister Capone. That reporter you're talking about here, they got the fella, I thought. It was all over the papers. Frank somebody."

"They can't make it stick," Capone said. "No jury in this town'll ever send him up. But somebody's got to take the rap, so I'm giving 'em you."

Worry was beginning to crawl back into Brothers's expression. He said, "For the life of me, Mister Capone, I don't see how you can do it. From what I hear, people, a lot of people, seen it happen. So they got no reason to finger some guy they never—"

"And there's where you're wrong, Leo," Capone said. "Foster'd be halfway to the pen right now if the papers hadn't spilled the beans about him being one of the Moran-Aiello gang. But it got out and it scared those witnesses. You can't blame 'em; nobody wants a busted head or their house blown up.

"But let me tell you something," Capone, said. "Those people feel bad." He thumped his chest. "Right in here. They wanta think they're good honest citizens. They want their families to think it— their friends. Give 'em a chance to finger some outta-town punk like you—somebody it's safe to finger—and they're gonna talk themselves into believing *he's* the guy. Case you don't know it, that's human nature."

Brothers rubbed his hands together nervously. He said, "Jeez, I dunno, Mister Capone. Sure sounds like you're fixin' to get me electrocuted or something."

"That's stupid, Leo," Capone said. "I been buying off judges and juries halfa my life. I guarantee you, worst you'll end up with is one-to-fourteen years. Behave yourself, you're out in ten, maybe even eight."

" 'Less they let me off altogether," Brothers said.

Capone shook his head. "Not a chance. I can't afford to let that happen."

Brothers said, "Ten years. That's an awful big bite out of a fella's life, Mister Capone."

"I have to agree with you there, Leo," Capone said. "But thinka the jolt you could end up with for killing that cab driver. And I'll have that taken care of.

"Understand, it's not I'm asking you to do this for nothing," Capone said. "Minute you finish doing your time and come out, you're on easy street the resta your life. That you got my word on."

Pasquale Prestocomo said, "You sure you want to do this, Joe? I mean, look, why leave town? Nobody knows you're inside'a twenty miles of here. And you're welcome to stay long as you want to."

"Hell, I know that, Patsy," Joe Aiello said. "You and Marie—the best! But in my line you learn to . . . well, you learn to smell trouble before it catches up with you." He smiled. "That is, if you expect to go on breathing."

He glanced at his watch, said, "Where's that damned cab? I got a train to catch and I'm already running late."

Prestocomo said, "You'll make it. Traffic's light this time of night."

"I'll wait out front," Aiello said. As they shook hands, a horn gave three short sounds from the street. Prestocomo drew open the foyer door, Aiello picked up his suitcase, said, "*Addio*, Pasquale," and walked out into Kolmar Avenue.

A Checker taxi was at the curb. Aiello started toward it . . . and from a darkened second-floor window directly across the street a machine-gun opened fire.

The taxi took off, tires screeching. Aiello, hit several times, staggered, dropped the suitcase. The building corner loomed a few steps to his left. Crouching, he stumbled toward it as a burst of slugs tore into the bricks inches above his head. And then he was out of range, reeling toward the safety of a doorway beyond a small courtyard.

From a bedroom window three floors above the grass-covered area, a second machine gun, this one held by Danny Stanton, put thirty-seven bullets into the body of Giuseppe Aiello.

Charles Rathbun said, "I do apologize for waking your family and getting you out of bed at such an ungodly hour. But I knew you'd want to hear immediately what John's come up with."

Not taking his eyes off John Hagan, Roche said, "Calm down, Charlie, take a seat. Before it's a heart attack you'll be having."

Hagan and Rathbun took chairs at the porcelain-topped table in the brightly lighted kitchen. Roche, in pajamas, robe, and slippers, found a glass, filled it with milk, closed the refrigerator door. He said, "Would you have a smoke you could spare, Mister Hagan?"

"Sure do," Hagan said, and got out his pack of Murads. Roche took one, accepted a light. He drank from the glass, set it on the counter and propped a hip against the sink. Down the hall a bedroom door slammed shut.

"All right, Charlie," Roche said, "let's hear it."

Adding dramatic emphasis to each word, Rathbun said, "Pat, Frank Foster did not kill Alfred Lingle!"

"That so?" Roche said. "How'd you figure *that* out?"

Sounding annoyed, Rathbun said, "I must say you don't seem at all surprised. And here all along you were so . . . insistent Foster was our man."

"Oh, it's surprised I am," Roche said. "What I'd like now are the whys and wherefores."

Rathbun gestured to Hagan, said, "Go ahead, John. Tell the man."

Hagan said, "Like I think I told you when we had that first meet, Mister Roche, I'd bumped into this fella in K.C. a while back. Guy outta Chicago and tight with the Moran people? Said the word around was an outta-town redhot put that bullet in Lingle?"

Roche took a saucer from a pantry shelf, dropped cigarette ash into it, said, "Get on with it."

Hagan took a deep breath, let it out, said, "Anyway, after I talked to you two gentlemen that night, I took a stab at looking up some of the North Side fellas I knew back before I moved to Kansas City. Did a little drinking with them, got into a few games'a pool, poker, you know.

"Anyhow," Hagan said, "these men know me as a stand-up person, somebody they don't have to be leery about talking in front of. Well, here about a week or so back, this fella and I were sitting around lapping up the booze in a speakeasy out around Halsted and Addison, when the Lingle subject came up and how the law was trying to pin the job on this Foster.

"Well, this fella kinda laughed about it," Hagan said. 'Coppers are way off base,' he said to me. 'From what I hear, man they want comes from outta town. Still here, too. Got a job in some nightclub around Broadway and Wilson.' "

"This man did the talking," Roche said. "He have a name?"

Hagan said, "All due respect, Mister Roche, that part I'm leaving out. I give you the name, you go after him on this, I'm up to my lower lip in shit. And it's all hearsay to begin with."

Roche grunted, flicked cigarette ash into the saucer, drank from the milk glass, said, "What else?"

"Well," Hagan said, "I start making the rounds of night spots along Wilson and up and down Broadway. Nothing. Then here one night I walk into the Green Mill Gardens. Broadway and Lawrence, as I'm sure you know. And there by God he is. . . . Mind if I smoke a cigarette, Mister Roche?"

"Long as you watch your ashes," Roche said.

Hagan set fire to one of his Murads, dropped the match into the saucer, said, "Had to be him, this fella I saw. Dead ringer for how the papers said the Lingle shooter looks. Right build on him, about five-nine, blond hair and all. Had to be him, Mister Roche, no two ways about it.

"Goes by the name Louis Bader," Hagan said. "Club bouncer. Now I didn't want to maybe spook the gentleman by asking about him where he works. So I did a little quiet digging on my own, found out he was from St. Louis and took a run down there.

"Now this is the part," Hagan said, "I think you'll find worth hearing about, Mister Roche. Bader's real name is Leo Vincent Brothers and as of right now there's a St. Louis murder rap hanging over him."

Rathbun was smiling smugly. He said, "There you have it, Pat. Now you see why I kept insisting all along Foster wasn't our man."

Roche said, "So far what we've heard here's not worth a nun's fart. Add it up. Some North Side grifter finds out this Bader . . . Brothers—whatever the name is—is wanted for murder in St. Louis. And whatta you know—he's got blond hair! So this grifter tacks on a little here, a little there, and comes up with a juicy piece of gossip: 'Tis Brothers that killed Lingle.

"What gets left out," Roche said, "is that Foster's gun was used, that Foster blew town right after the shooting, that Foster had no alibi for the time the trigger was pulled, that Foster was working for Jack Zuta—who it just so happens wanted Lingle dead—that Foster was fingered by six witnesses. So if you'll excuse me, I'll be after getting back to bed."

Rathbun slapped his hand against the tabletop, said, "God almighty, Pat, what do you want to do—stay on this thing the rest of your life? For your information, the colonel's getting damned impatient over the way this case is dragging out—and you certainly can't blame him."

Roche said, "Let me understand you, Charlie. Send *somebody* up? *Any*body? Just to keep the colonel happy?"

Lunging to his feet, Rathbun said, "You son of a bitch! I resent that!"

Roche's expression did not change. He said, "And resent it you should, Charlie. Granting it's not true."

The flood of angry color slowly faded from Rathbun's face. He said, "I suggest we bring this Brothers in, put him in a line-up, give the witnesses a shot at him, then take it from there. All I ask is that you keep an open mind."

"Okay," Roche said. "An open mind you want, an open mind you'll get. But don't let your hopes soar too high." His gaze swung to John Hagan. "Because, Charlie, this stink we're smelling in here? 'Tis not from me bare feet."

McHugh said, "Hey! George! Got a minute?"

George Moran, helping his wife from a cab at the Madison Street entrance to Union Station, turned sharply as several men descended on him. Recognizing them as reporters, he relaxed visibly, forced a smile, said, "Didn't expect to run into any'a you boys. What's on your mind?"

McPhaul said, "Any objections to letting us in on where you and Mrs. Moran are headed?"

The cab driver set two suitcases on the sidewalk. Moran thrust a bill into his hand, waved him off as a redcap came over to collect the bags.

"New Orleans," Moran said. "Little vacation trip. Nice and warm down there this time'a year I understand."

Pasley said, "Too bad you won't be taking in Joe Aiello's funeral. You and him being business partners and all."

Some of the friendliness in Moran's expression faded. He said,

"Listen, fellas, you're gonna have to excuse me. We got this train to catch, see."

McHugh said, "One last thing, George. Let's say for the sake of argument you decide to make it a good long vacation. That case, what's going to keep Al Capone from stepping in, taking over those North Side interests of yours?"

Moran said, "Now you listen to me, big shot. Right now I don't give a shit if that greaseball takes over the whole fucking country. Go put *that* in your goddamn paper!"

Leo Brothers finished shaving and was drying his face when the buzzer sounded from the downstairs lobby. He left the bathroom, went to the intercom, held down the button, said, "Yeah?"

A male voice came through the tube. "Mister Louis Bader?"

"Who wants to know?"

"Post office. There's this letter for you."

"So put it in the box, why don'tcha?"

"You're gonna have to sign for it. Registered mail. Look, you're too busy or somethin', you can pick it up anytime tomorrow at the sub-station on—"

"Who's it from?"

"Listen, mister, you wanta come down here and sign for this thing or not?"

"Just tell me where it's *from*, that's all."

A windy sigh floated up the tube. "St. Louis. TriCity Union. Okay?"

"Be right there," Brothers said. He grabbed his shirt from a chair back, slipped it on, went to the door, opened it.

From behind a leveled .38, Walter Wendt said, "You're under arrest."

"Lemme talk to the City Desk."

"One moment, sir."

". . . City Desk; Burke."

"Gotta hot tip for you, Mister Burke."

"Who's this?"

"Forget that. 'Bout an hour ago Pat Roche's boys picked up a St. Louis shooter name'a Lou Bader. Only his real moniker's Leo Brothers, see?"

"What is it they've got on him? This Brothers."

"Now I ain't shittin' ya on this, Mister Burke. They're sayin' he's the one *really* knocked off Jake Lingle."

17

Walter Wendt said, "We're out here at the Graemere Hotel, Pat. Suite seven-eleven. Fred's gone on in to pick up Tony Ruthy. Oughta be here any minute now."

"No reporters around?" Roche asked.

"None I spotted."

"Brothers tell you anything?"

"Just keeps wanting to know why we picked him up," Wendt said. "And getting no answers."

"That's the ticket," Roche said. "Soon's I manage to get holda Charlie, we'll be there. Seven-eleven, you said?"

"Yeah. Name on the register's O'Brien."

"Good Irish name," Roche said and hung up.

Wendt replaced the receiver. The door buzzer sounded. Wendt said, "Who is it?" a muffled voice said, "Fred," and Wendt admitted Joyner and Anthony Ruthy, the latter wearing his police uniform.

Speaking in a low voice, Wendt said, "My name's Walter Wendt, officer. State's attorney's office. Man we want you to see's in the next room. Walk in there, take a good solid look at him, don't say a word, then turn around and come back in here. Will you do that for me, sir?"

Ruthy shrugged, said, "Don't know why not. Who's he supposed to be?"

"That," Wendt said, "is what we're hoping you can tell us." He nodded at the closed door to the adjoining room. "Any time you're ready."

Ruthy dropped his uniform cap on the coffee table, went to the bedroom door, opened it, and passed through.

Leo Brothers stood at the one window, looking down onto Homan Avenue seven floors below. John Greer, on the bed, his back propped against the headboard, was reading a newspaper. As Ruthy entered, Greer put aside the paper, said, "Hey, Lou. You got company."

Brothers turned. Ruthy moved to within a few feet of him, stared him squarely in the face. Nobody spoke, neither man moved. Nothing changed in Brothers's expression. . . .

Wendt and Joyner looked up sharply as Anthony Ruthy emerged from the bedroom. He closed the door, came over to retrieve his cap, said, "Okay, so I took a look at the guy. Now what?"

Walter Wendt said, "All right if I call you Tony?"

Ruthy shrugged, said, "Fine with me."

Wendt said, "That fellow in there, Tony. Have you seen him before? Now I'd like you to think about it before you answer one way or the other."

"What's to think about?" Ruthy said. "Gee, I'd like to help you fellas. But I hafta tell you I never seen that guy before in my life."

Wendt gestured in surrender, said, "If you didn't, you didn't. Thanks for your time."

Joyner said, "Let's go, Tony."

Shortly after five that evening Roche and Rathbun arrived at the suite. Wendt gave them a word-by-word account of the traffic officer's earlier statement.

Rathbun pounded a fist against his thigh in frustration. "I say the man's covering up. What else can he do? He was so positive in naming Foster the killer at that arraignment that now he *can't* back down. You know where that leaves us? We go ahead, charge Brothers. We put Ruthy on the stand, he refuses to identify Brothers. What happens? Brothers walks.

"So, we *don't* put him on the stand," Rathbun said. "That case, you can be damned sure the defense will. Result? Ruthy sticks to his story, Brothers walks."

Roche said, "'Tis a bit ahead of ourselves we're getting here, Charlie. 'Less we first come up with witnesses who'll pick him out of a line-up, there won't *be* a trial."

"That, we can get into later," Rathbun said. He pointed at the closed bedroom door. "But for now I suggest we go in there, sit Mister Bader—or Brothers, whatever he calls himself—down and see if we can't sweat some answers out of him."

Rachael Schoenburg said, "Alex. I heard a car door slam. Out front."

Her husband stood up, reached for the radio volume knob, turned it down, said, "Dwight Peabody, I guess. He said somethin' about stoppin' in after supper for a couple quartsa rye."

Footsteps sounded on the porch and knuckles rapped sharply at the door. Schoenburg went over, snapped on the porch light, parted the white dimity curtains, peered out. Under the bulb's faint yellow rays he made out the figures of two men in dark overcoats, collars turned up, the brims of fedoras pulled low.

Schoenburg felt a stirring of alarm. He said, "Get in the kitchen, Rachael."

The second knock rattled the door's oval glass inset. Schoenburg turned the bolt, opened up.

Danny Stanton said, "You Alex Schoenburg?"

"Reckon so," Schoenburg said.

Willie Heeney said, "How's about us comin' in, okay?"

"I don't know you fellas," Schoenburg said. "Whatta you want?"

"Just to talk to you, Mister Schoenburg," Stanton said. "Nothing to worry about."

Heeney said, "C'mon, will ya? It's colder'n a fuckin' iceberg out here."

Schoenburg let the two men in, closed the door. Gloves came off, overcoats were unbuttoned, scarves unwound and stuffed into pockets. Schoenburg said, "Offer you fellas a drink?"

Heeney rubbed his hands together briskly, said, "Now you're talkin'! Little bourbon, huh?"

"Same for me," Stanton said.

Alex Schoenburg opened a walnut sideboard, took out glasses and a bottle, poured two liberal shots, handed them over. His two visitors found chairs, sampled their drinks as their host sat down across from them.

Stanton put down his glass, reached into the inner pocket of his overcoat, brought out a square of cardboard, leaned over, handed it to Schoenburg and said, "Tell me about this guy, Alex."

Two mug shots of Leo Brothers, front and profile, from police files. Nothing to indicate the city. Schoenburg looked up slowly, his expression blank. He said, "You the law?"

"Bad guess," Stanton said.

"Name's Blake," Schoenburg said. "Lewis Blake. Nice young fella. Worked for me a while. Last summer, that was."

"Hauling wet goods, I hear," Stanton said.

Schoenburg made a meaningless gesture, said nothing. Stanton plucked the card from his fingers, tucked it away, said, "Here's how it goes, Alex. Anybody should happen to come around askin' about this guy, he never worked for you, you never saw him, never even heard of him. That goes for your wife, your kids, your pals, even the fucking preacher in your church. His picture shows up in the papers, you don't know it from a pig's ass."

The two men stood up. Scarves were replaced, coats rebuttoned, gloves drawn on. Schoenburg opened the door.

About to follow Heeney out, Stanton paused, patted Schoenburg gently on the shoulder, said, "Don't make no mistakes, Alex. Or we're gonna hafta come back here and drink some more'a your lousy bourbon."

"Sure wouldn't want that to happen," Alex Schoenburg said.

Roche said, "Let's get back to last spring, Leo. You had this job at the Green Mill Gardens till when?"

"About maybe the enda April, I'd have to say," Brothers said. Mister Voiler at the club could tell you better on that."

"Why'd you leave?"

"Little problem come up."

"At the Gardens?"

"No, no. Everything was copacetic there."

"Then what was it?"

"Well, I got this guy sore at me for some reason. Fella in big with the North Side mob. So I hadda duck out, you see."

"Then you *did* leave town."

"No sir, I didn't. That part we already been through, Mister Roche."

Rathbun, seated nearby, stirred impatiently, said, "I'd like to cut in here, Pat. If you don't mind?"

Roche shrugged, leaned back, said, "Help yourself, Charlie."

"Leo," Rathbun said, "I want you to look me straight in the eye. . . . Now you're asking us to believe that after your alleged disagreement with this unnamed mobster, you holed up with a friend somewhere on the West Side. Correct?"

"Yes sir."

"And that you decline to furnish the name of this friend inasmuch as he was wanted—and is still wanted—by the Chicago police?"

"Yes sir, Mister Rathbun. One thing I'm not's a stoolie."

"Now," Rathbun said, "directing your attention to June ninth of this year, where to the best of your knowledge were you between the hours of twelve noon and two P.M.?"

Brothers showed him a puzzled scowl. "I don't get you, Mister Rathbun. What's all this—what's *any*'a this—got to do with me being wanted in St. Louis?"

"Do you decline to answer that question?"

Brothers said, "Hey, c'mon. Ninth of June? You're talking about . . . five months back, for godsake. I coulda been anywhere 'round town."

"Including the Loop area?"

"Maybe. I don't know."

Rathbun said, "Leo. Sometime tomorrow morning you'll be placed in a line-up. A number of witnesses to a murder that took place in Chicago will be present. We have every reason to believe that most, if not all, of those witnesses will identify you as the man who, on June nine of this year, shot to death Alfred J. Lingle."

"Mister Rathbun," Leo Brothers said calmly, "you're nuts."

Leaving Brothers in the custody of Wendt and John Greer for the night, Roche and Rathbun stopped off at the hotel's restaurant for an early dinner.

Speaking around a mouthful of steak sandwich, Roche said, "I tell you the man was expecting it, Charlie. Never turned a hair. Looked you right in the eye, he did, and easy as you please, said, 'You're nuts.'"

"Come on, Pat," Rathbun said. "He knew damned well all along we were wise to him. You'd have got the same reaction if I'd accused him of bumping off . . . Mickey Mouse."

Roche said, "And as the whole town knows, 'tis Frankie Foster behind the bars waiting to be tried. As well he should be. So don't let it surprise you if nobody at the Brothers's line-up tomorrow fingers your fella."

"He's our man, Pat," Rathbun said. "I know it. I know it because I feel it." He tapped his chest. "Right in here. And when we're finished with that line-up, *you'll* know it!"

Crossing the the hotel lobby, Rathbun stopped to speak to the bell captain. A burly individual in tan coveralls said, "How they treatin' yuh there, Benny?" to the man at the newsstand, dumped a bound bundle of papers on the ledge, and vanished.

Roche drifted over, waited for Benny to cut the twine, dropped a nickel on the counter, and took one of the papers, its ink still damp.

A familiar face stared back at him. A headline blared, NEW SUSPECT HELD IN LINGLE SLAYING.

From behind him, Charles Rathbun said, "Ready when you are, Pat."

Roche turned. Angry blood had suffused his face. He thrust the paper at Rathbun, said thickly, "They got it all. His name, his record, the fact he's not connected with any Chicago mob."

Rathbun said, "Jesus, Pat. How could this've . . ."

"Who gives a shit *how?*" Roche said. " 'Tis my congratulations you have, Charlie. Seems you just got yourself a conviction."

18

Windrows of soot-crusted snow from the previous week's storm lined the parkway in front of 7423 Rogers Avenue: two floors of red brick, trimmed in forest green. A gaunt cottonwood at the southern end thrust its bare branches at a gray March sky.

Assistant State's Attorney C. Wayland Brooks, in his late thirties, was a tall, cold-eyed man with an athletic build and strong features topped off with a thick shock of prematurely graying hair. He was seated at a Florentine desk in his second-floor study and talking with Roche and Rathbun in tan leather chairs across from him.

Brooks said, "Now that Brothers's lawyers have run out of ways to stall prosecution, trial will definitely start the sixteenth. Incidentally, Sabath will be on the bench. Instead of Judge Finnegan."

Rathbun said, "I'd say we're better off with Sabath. A bit too fond of the bottle, I grant you, but he does have a tendency to lean toward the state."

"We won't need any extra edge," Brooks said. "Not on this one. Eight solid witnesses, positive identifications right down the line."

He rose, went to a dark wood liquor cabinet between the room's two windows, lifted the top, brought out a cut-glass decanter, said, "I trust you're both bourbon drinkers. As the bootleggers say, this stuff's right off the boat."

He set three glasses on the desk top, poured from the carafe. Lifting a glass, he said, "A toast, gentlemen: Confusion to our colleagues at the other table."

They drank. Refills were declined. Brooks said, "You seem a bit on the quiet side, Pat. Is something bothering you?"

Roche said, " 'Tis me—*my* feeling it's a bit early to be patting ourselves on the back here."

"Do you foresee any particular problem?" Brooks said.

"One for sure," Roche said. "This cop. Ruthy. He gets up there, says positively Leo Brothers *wasn't* the fella he chased up Randolph Street that day . . . well, the jury's gonna start having some heavy doubts."

Brooks said, "I was about to get into that very thing, Pat."

He extracted a manila folder from a sizable stack on the desk, took out three pages of typescript stapled together. He said, "Late yesterday afternoon, Officer Ruthy came to my office. Entirely of his own volition. The man was deeply disturbed. He confessed he'd been holding something back, something he'd been ashamed to admit before, but which he now felt obligated to reveal."

Brooks turned to the second page of the report, eyed it briefly, looked up, saw Roche's slowly hardening expression.

"Six years ago," Brooks said, "a patrol car Ruthy was riding in was struck by an ambulance. Ruthy sustained a brain injury. Since then he has suffered recurring dizzy spells, complicated by—and these are his own words—'crazy visions.' Naturally I—"

Roche said, "So they got to him."

Brooks stiffened. Before he could speak, Rathbun said wearily, "For the love of God, Pat, *now* what?"

Ignoring him, eyeing Brooks levelly, Roche said, "Do I hafta spell it out to you, Wayland? You're no amateur in this business. Yet you can sit there and tell us a police officer on active full-time duty—the one man whose testimony could get Brothers off—suddenly walks in, says he's been crazy for years. And you let him get away with it?"

Brooks said, "Are you suggesting I'd be a party to—"

Overriding him, Roche said, "You're not even in the fucking ballgame. Ruthy's either been paid off or he's had the fear of God put in him."

Rathbun leaned back, threw up his hands, said, "I don't believe this!"

"And why would you?" Roche said. "Seeing how you're so damned anxious to send somebody up and be a hero to Colonel Mc-Corm—"

Purpling with rage, Rathbun came halfway out of his chair, said, "Shut up! Don't *ever* let me hear—"

Brooks slammed a fist against the desk top. "That's enough! Both of you!"

In the sudden quiet, Rathbun sank back, looked down at his trembling hands. Brooks said, "We're all on the same side, gentlemen. Let's try to keep that in mind. . . . Pat, my own reaction to Ruthy's story was much the same as yours. Immediately after he left my office, I sent for a copy of his medical history from police files."

Roche said, "I got one last November, Wayland. 'Twas a mild concussion the man had. Two weeks' sick leave, back on full duty. That ended it."

"You talk to his personal physician?"

"After six *years!*"

Brooks said, "Well, *I* did. Some months after the accident Ruthy began having periodic hallucinatory episodes during moments of unusual activity or mental stress."

Roche shook his head in grudging respect, said, "The son of a bitch. He just don't miss a trick, the man."

Brooks said, "The man? *What* man? Who the hell are you talking about?"

"Who it is I'm talking about," Roche said, "is a wop name of Alphonse Capone, and now it all begins to add up. When he found out we couldn't take Foster to trial on what we had in the way of dependable witnesses, he knew damned well we'd go right on raiding mob joints, costing him and Aiello maybe a couple'a million a week.

"So," Roche said, "when the Big Fella found out we hadn't a chance in hell of putting Foster away, he brings in John Hagan to find a patsy for us. Has to be an outta-town hood, made to order for a jury afraid to nail a local shooter. And whatta you know—we fell for it."

"This is absurd!" Rathbun said. "You make Capone sound like—like some kind of Machiavellian genius."

"*Another* goombah," Roche said. "Must run in the family. Here's a man head of a business brings in, so I'm told, least a hundred twenty million a year. Two or three hundred people on the payroll—not counting politicians, judges, and not even the Almighty knows how many cops. A man who's got a city of three million souls by the throat. Sound like a genius to you? Does to me."

Roche said, "Here's a little something extra you can chew on. Brothers's got three lawyers lined up. Two of 'em—Bob Cantwell and Tyrrell Krum—are heavy hitters and get fees to match. Number three's Louie Piquett; he's been slipping Al Capone legal advice for years. Now 'tis a question I have for you fellas. Who would you say is paying for all this high-priced talent? Leo Brothers? The man don't have a pot to piss in. Or maybe 'tis the Women's Christian Temperance Union he's counting on to foot the bill."

He got to his feet, scooped up his overcoat and hat and was halfway to the door when Rathbun said, "Pat."

Roche turned. "Yeah?"

Rathbun said, "If Brothers *is* innocent, that's one thing. But if he's not, if he gets off because of some bullheaded move on your part, it could ruin you."

Their eyes met, held. Roche said, "What it is you're really saying, Charlie, is that it could ruin you."

The door closed behind him.

THE TRIAL

This is the most gigantic frame-up since the crucifixion of Christ!

—*Louis Piquett, 1931*
Defense attorney

19

DAY ONE

The Court clerk intoned, "All rise. Hear ye, hear ye, this court now is in session, the honorable Justice Joseph Sabath presiding."

Judge Sabath, a stocky, heavyset man in his late fifties, fully robed, settled into his chair behind the elevated bench. He adjusted his pince-nez, smoothed his thinning gray hair, rapped his gavel once, and the spectators resumed their seats.

The court clerk said, "People of the state of Illinois versus Leo V. Brothers, defendant, called herewith and being charged with first degree murder."

Judge Sabath said, "Let the record show that the defendant is in court, that the jury is present, and that counsel for both the state and the defense are likewise present. . . . Mister Brooks?"

C. Wayland Brooks half-stood, said, "Ready for the People, your honor," and sank back.

"Mister Piquett?"

"The defense is ready, Judge," Louis Piquett said.

Sabath said, "Has the defendant been furnished with a copy of the indictment?"

"Yes, Your Honor," Piquett said.

"The clerk will read the indictment."

Clearing his throat, the clerk began reading aloud from a typewritten page: "The aforesaid indictment charges that Leo V. Brothers, othewise called Louis Bader, did, on the ninth day of June, A.D. 1930, in the county of Cook and state of Illinois, with a certain revolver, unlawfully, feloniously and of his malice aforethought, by shooting, kill and murder one Alfred J. Lingle."

The clerk put aside the paper and sat down. A rustle of stirring bodies, then a woman near the rear began to sob uncontrollably and rushed out the door.

A single rap of the gavel quieted the room. Judge Sabath looked at Leo Brothers, seated between Piquett and Tyrrell Krum at the defense table, and said, "You have heard the indictment, Mister Brothers. How do you plead, sir? Guilty or not guilty as charged?"

Not rising, Piquett said negligently, "The defendant, Leo V. Brothers, pleads not guilty, Your Honor."

"Very well," Sabath said. He bent forward slightly, peered at Brooks. "Your opening statement, Mister Brooks?"

"Thank you, Your Honor." Brooks got to his feet, left the table, and walked slowly over to the railing of the jury box. Slowly, deliberately, he scanned the faces of the twelve seated men.

"Gentlemen of the jury," he said, "Alfred J. Lingle died June ninth, 1930, at or about one P.M. He died in a Michigan Avenue underpass, face down in the filth of cigarette and cigar butts, gum wrappers, and so on. His death came as the result of a bullet fired from behind and into the back of his head by a cowardly assassin.

"The manner of this assassination," Brooks said, "marks it undeniably as a gangland execution. We—each and every one of us—are all too familiar with such murders in this city. Well over six hundred—*six hundred!*—in the last ten years alone. I say to you it is time the people of our city let the underworld know in no uncertain terms that our patience is here and now exhausted, that we do not propose to allow the murderer of Alfred J. Lingle to add still another such unsolved slaying to that list."

While waiting for that last sentence to take full effect, Brooks returned to the counsel table for a drink of water, then came back to take a position in front of the jury.

Brooks said, "Indicative of the contempt these gangland assassins have for our citizens is the fact that the defendant in this case gunned down Alfred Lingle in full view of a score of passersby, confident that none would have the courage to identify him if caught. Well, let me tell you this, gentlemen of the jury: he could not have been more mistaken! The state will call eight—*eight!*—witnesses to the stand, each of them prepared to state unequivocally that the man they saw shoot and kill Alfred Lingle was the defendant Leo Vincent Brothers. . . . I thank you."

In the hushed silence Wayland Brooks turned away, strode briskly to his place at the counsel table, sat down. Judge Sabath glanced up at the wall clock, said, "Since it seems we're approaching the lunch hour, this court stands adjourned till two o'clock this afternoon."

Tyrrell Krum, holding a tray loaded with a coffee cup, a slice of apple pie, and a plate of beef stew, said, "I hate to see a man eat alone, Wayland."

Brooks looked up from his chair at a corner table in the criminal courts' crowded cafeteria, smiled, said, "Sit down, Tyrrell. But only if you swear I won't end up with indigestion."

Krum set out his food, got rid of the tray, took the chair across from Brooks, said, "I was surprised not to see Holman in court this morning."

"John had a couple loose ends to clear up," Brooks said. "He'll be with me this afternoon."

For a few minutes both men ate in silence. Finally Krum put down his cup, said, "Nice tight opening statement you made, Wayland. Especially that bit about Lingle dying in a pile of cigar and cigarette butts. You could see the jury cringe from clear across the room."

"It came to me around three this morning," Brooks said. "I always seem to have this trouble falling asleep the night before a trial opens. After that—like a baby."

"Never fazes me," Krum said. Grinning, he added, "But of course I only defend the innocent."

"So I've noticed," Brooks said.

"Speaking of innocent," Krum said, "brings to mind my client. Innocent—but nervous as a virgin at a pimps' picnic. Scared to death he'll get railroaded right into the hot seat. All that rhetoric of yours about how it's time to put a stop to letting gangland killers get off? Kind of got to him. That and this bullshit about having eight witnesses ready to finger him."

"So?"

"Like I said," Krum continued, "the man is scared stupid. Stupid enough to want to settle for a fourteen-year sentence, no matter how hard we try to dissuade him."

"No dice, Tyrrell," Brooks said. "We want—and expect to get—a death sentence. We might—just might, you understand—entertain life without possibility of parole."

Krum said, "All you've got is eyewitnesses, Wayland. You can't establish motive, there's no record of his owning or even having possession of that gun, you have no admissible evidence of a criminal record. In short, my friend, there's not a snowball's chance in hell of your winning this one."

"Then why are we having this conversation?"

Krum shrugged, said, "Just killing time, I guess."

Glancing at his watch, Wayland Brooks said, "Five till two." He stood, picked up his hat. "Can't afford to keep His Honor waiting, now can we?"

Judge Joseph Sabath said, "Does the defense wish to make its opening statement at this time?"

Tyrrell Krum got to his feet, said, "We do, Your Honor." He circled the table, faced the jury, said, "Gentlemen of the jury, we now reach the point where shortly the defendant, Leo Vincent Brothers, is going to have his say on the charge of murder the state has filed against him.

"Mister Brooks, learned counsel for the prosecution, has mentioned something like five or six witnesses as ready to testify they

236

saw Leo Brothers on Randolph Street on the day and at the time Alfred Lingle was killed, that he was running up some tunnel steps and across the street and into some alley. Well, the defense wants to say that we, too, have five or six witnesses who saw that man run away and that these witnesses stand ready to testify he was not Leo Brothers.

"Now," Krum said, "we are going to show, by evidence, exactly the kind of man Leo Vincent Brothers is, that he did not shoot Alfred Lingle, that he knew nothing about it, wasn't there, in fact was many miles away. We will show you, prove to you, that during the time Leo Brothers lived in Chicago he never did anything to reflect on him, that he was an ordinary fellow living an ordinary life.

"We are going to show you gentlemen," Krum said, "by our evidence, that the murder charge against Leo Brothers is purely and simply a frame-up—a frame-up engineered by certain men ambitious to succeed in the prosecution of Leo Brothers; that the frame-up is for the sole purpose of satisfying a high-placed, prominent figure in this city and that somebody *present in this courtroom* will be handsomely rewarded for pinning the murder of Alfred Lingle on Leo Vincent Brothers."

DAY THREE

Wayland Brooks said, "The state calls Warren Williams."

Williams came to the stand, raised his hand while the court clerk administered the oath, then took the witness chair as Brooks came over to him.

"Mister Williams," Brooks said, "will you please tell us where you were on or about one P.M. on Monday, June ninth of last year?"

Williams leaned back in the chair, crossed his legs, said, "Sure. I was standing at the southwest corner of Michigan and Randolph Street."

"Just standing there, is that right?"

"Yes sir. I was waiting for this guy to get back from lunch, see. So I could call him up on the phone. About maybe a job."

"You were unemployed at the time?"

"At the time, yes sir."

"Now," Brooks said, "while you were standing there, at the corner of Michigan and Randolph, did you hear and see anything at all unusual?"

"Yes sir, I sure did."

"And what was it you saw and heard?"

"Well, I was leaning against this lamppost there when I hear this muffled report. About half a minute later I saw this man, this fella, come running out of this tunnel across the street from me. The east side of the street."

"Then what, if anything, did this man you mention do next?"

"Well, he come zigzagging across Michigan, running between the traffic, and just before he got to where I was standing, a car nearly run him down. He jumped back and his face jerks up and I get a real good look at him."

"A real good look," Brooks repeated with slow emphasis. "And what, if anything, did this man then do?"

"He got to in front of the library and ran to the north side of Randolph and begun running west on Randolph. And all the time he kept looking back like he wanted to find out if somebody was following—"

Louis Piquett, at the defense table, bounded to his feet. "Oh, Your Honor! Objection! The witness can't possibly—"

"Calm down, Mister Piquett," Sabath said mildly. "Your objection is sustained. . . . You may proceed, Mister Brooks."

Brooks said, "Getting back to this fleeing man, Mister Williams. Did you observe anyone follow him down Randolph Street?"

"Yes sir. A policeman and a couple other fellows."

"And the man they were following—have you seen him since that day?"

"Yes sir."

"Is he presently in this courtroom?"

"Yes sir."

"Would you please point him out for us?"

"Yes sir. He's the man sitting over there to the left of Mister Piquett."

Brooks said, "Let the record show that the witness has indicated the defendant, Leo Brothers. . . . Now, Mister Williams, you have seen other suspects in this case, is that correct?"

"Yes sir."

"Have you ever, through a sworn statement, identified any of those suspects until you identified Mister Brothers?"

"No sir."

"And all you have testified to here today took place in the city of Chicago, Cook County, Illinois?"

"Yes sir."

"Thank you, Mister Williams," Brooks said and turned away.

Judge Sabath said, "Will the defense cross-examine?"

Piquett said, "Yes, Your Honor." He left his chair, strode over to confront the man on the stand. "Mister Williams. When did you first become aware that a reward would be paid for the arrest and conviction of the man who killed Jake Lingle?"

"Well, I can't say for sure exactly when."

"But you did know about it?"

"Yes sir. From what I read in the newspapers. Around fifty or sixty thousand dollars from what the *Examiner* and the *Tribune* and the *American* said."

"And for your testimoney here today, were you promised a share of that reward if the defendant was convicted?"

"No sir, I was not."

"Do you feel you would be entitled to a share of that money?"

"No sir. Positively not. It was my duty to tell what it was I saw."

Piquett said, "Very admirable of you, Mister Williams. Now this man you saw running. Did he have a hat on?"

"Not on, no sir. He was just holding it in his hand."

"Why do you think he was carrying it, instead of wearing it?"

Brooks said, "Objection, your honor. The question calls for an opinion."

Judge Sabath nodded. "Sustained. Continue, Mister Piquett."

Piquett said, "You testified moments ago that you viewed other suspects in this case. Reminding you, sir, that you are under oath, did you at any time previous to veiwing Mister Brothers identify one of those other suspects as the man you saw running across Michigan Avenue?"

"Not that I made a sworn statement on, no sir."

Piquett said, "Let's not quibble, Mister Williams. Did you or did you not point out another man to the authorities as the man you saw?"

"Yes sir, I did. But I—"

"You have answered the question, sir. That will be all." Piquett turned, went back to his chair.

Sabath said, "Redirect, Mister Brooks?"

"Thank you, Your Honor." Without leaving his seat, Brooks said, "Mister Williams. Referring to the suspect you first identified, what caused you to change your mind about his being the right man?"

"Well, sir," Williams said, "I wasn't all that sure to begin with. The guy was built a lot like Brothers, over there, but when I thought about it after, I realized the face wasn't right and the hair was the wrong color—black instead of blond. So, when a cop named Roche asked me to sign a statement, I naturally had to say no to him."

DAY FIVE

Judge Joseph Sabath waited until quiet settled over the crowded courtroom, then said, "Your next witness, Mister Brooks?"

"The state," Brooks said, "calls Patrick Campbell to the stand."

Campbell came forward, swore to tell the truth, the whole truth, and nothing but the truth, and took the witness chair. He sat stiffly erect, jaw set, arms folded tightly across his chest.

Brooks said, "And what is your address and occupation, Mister Campbell?"

The witness said, "I am a plumber in business for myself and I live with my mother at seven-five-one-four Cornell."

"Calling your attention," Brooks said, "to the date June ninth,

1930, at or about one-thirty on that afternoon. Please tell the court where you were at that time and date."

"I was near the subway of Michigan and Randolph."

"This was in the city of Chicago?"

"Yes sir, it was."

"And what, if anything, did you see and hear at that time and place?"

"I had just come out of the subway when I hear this shot from someplace behind me. Anyway, it sounded to me like a shot. Tell you the truth, I didn't pay all that much attention to it, just kept on going across Michigan there. Anyway, just as this fella was about to run right by me from behind, I hear somebody holler, 'Stop that man.'"

"Did you get a good look at this man running right by you?"

"Yes sir, I certainly did."

"Go on, please."

"Well, this fella that was running, I started to run right in back of him, you see, right up Randolph Street as far as the alley between Michigan and Wabash there. Me and this cop and this other fella lost him when this man ducked into Wabash Avenue."

"And you say you got a good look at this man you chased?"

"Yes sir."

"And you would have no trouble recognizing him if you were to see him again?"

"No trouble at all, Mister Brooks."

"Is the man you saw that day, the man you chased up Randolph Street, in this courtroom at the present time?"

"Yes sir."

"Please rise and point him out to the jury."

Campbell got to his feet, leveled a forefinger. "That's him, sitting right there between them two lawyers."

"Indicating the defendant, Leo Vincent Brothers." Turning away, Brooks said, "Your witness, Mister Krum."

"Just a few questions, Mister Campbell," Krum said. "You are aware of the sizable reward offered for the arrest and conviction of Lingle's killer, are you not?"

"I read about it. In the papers."

"Around sixty thousand dollars, isn't that right?"

"Somewhere about that, I guess it is."

"Wouldn't mind getting your hands on some of it, would you?"

Brooks said, "Your Honor. This is not proper cross."

"I will allow it," Sabath said. "Within limits."

"Wouldn't mind at all, would you, sir?" Krum said.

"A man can always use money; sure."

"And were you promised a slice of the pie if Mister Brothers gets sent up?"

"No sir, I was not."

"You're all that positive?"

Brooks interrupted. "Objection. Question asked and answered."

"Sustained. Get on with it, Mister Krum."

Krum said, "Between the time you say you saw Mister Brothers on Michigan Avenue and your appearance here today, did you see him anywhere else?"

"Well, yes sir. I did."

"How did that happen?"

"Well, around January, I think it was—somewhere around in then I'd have to say it was."

"And *where* did this happen?"

"Well, at this hotel. A Mister Roche took me there, to a room there where several men were standing around."

"Were any of them known to you by sight?"

"Just this one guy. Him I recognized."

"When you say you recognized him, was this before or after Mister Roche directed your attention to him, pointed him out as the man who might have shot Alfred Lingle?"

"Nobody pointed him out. Minute I walked in and seen those men, I spotted the guy I chased up Randolph Street. And that's him, setting right over there right now," Campbell said.

Wayland Brooks said, "Thank you, Mister Davidson," and went back to his chair.

Judge Sabath said, "Does the defense intend to cross-examine the witness?"

Louis Piquett rose, said, "Thank you, Your Honor," walked over to the stand, said, "Mister Davidson. May I ask how old you are, sir?"

"I'm a little past twenty-five."

"A driver for the Yellow Cab Company, you say?"

"Yes sir."

"You are the sixth witness to testify for the People in this trial. Were you aware of that, sir?"

"No sir, I wasn't."

"Now let me ask you, were you present in this courtroom while any one of those six witnesses was testifying?"

"No sir."

"Have you at any time read or had quoted to you such testimony?"

"No sir. I don't even know if it was in the newspapers."

"Then would it surprise you, Mister Davidson, to learn that, except for minor departures, your testimony was almost word for word identical to that of those other witnesses?"

Brooks stood, said, "What is this, Your Honor? Is counsel summing up here? I move to strike all that as both improper and grossly prejudicial."

Sabath said, "So ordered. The jury will disregard Mister Piquett's question and its implications."

"Exception," Piquett snapped.

"Noted. Now let's get on with it, Counselor."

"Yes sir. . . . Now, Mister Davidson, you *have* heard about or read about the reward offered for the arrest and conviction of whoever killed Alfred Lingle?"

"It was in all the papers."

"Then you knew about it?"

"Yes sir."

"How much, if any, of that reward were you promised for your testimony here today?"

"Not a single dime. It never even came up."

"You're asking us to believe, Mister Davidson, that on all the occasions you were with investigators and attorneys for the state, none of them so much as mentioned the reward?"

Wayland Brooks broke in sharply. "Objection. Already asked and answered."

"Sustained," Judge Sabath said.

"Your Honor," Piquett said. "The defense is attempting to—"

"I've ruled on the objection," Sabath said. "You may have an exception. Continue."

Piquett sighed, spread his hands in surrender, turned away. "I have no more questions for this witness."

"Redirect, Mister Brooks?"

"No, Your Honor."

"You may step down, Mister Davidson."

Judge Sabath said, "At your request, Mister Brooks, the jury is for the time being out of the courtroom. However, I want counsel for both sides to understand what transpires during the jury's absence will go into the record."

Wayland Brooks said, "Before the People call the next witness, Your Honor, I would like to make a statement concerning him. For the record."

"Go right ahead."

Brooks said, "The witness I'm referring to, Your Honor, is Police Officer Anthony Ruthy. As recounted by witnesses already heard, Ruthy figured heavily in what transpired at the time Lingle was murdered.

"The State," Brooks said, "has recently learned that some years back Officer Ruthy sustained a brain injury during an accident, that because of the incident we believe him to be mentally unbalanced during moments of stress, that he was in that state of mind at the time he identified one Frank Foster as Lingle's killer during Foster's arraignment on that same charge some months back. For these reasons the State is reluctant to call Ruthy as its witness in this present case."

At the defense table, Cantwell hastily scribbled a few words on a slip of paper and passed it to Tyrrell Krum.

Judge Sabath said, "Does the defense wish to comment?"

Krum glanced at the scrawled message. It read, *Get us the hell out of here!* He pocketed the note, got slowly to his feet, said, "This is all news to us, Your Honor. We request an adjournment for time to discuss it."

Sabath reached for his gavel, sounded it once. "Court stands adjourned till two P.M."

"Well, Counselor," Sabath said. "May we now get on with the trial?"

Krum said, "Your Honor, Ruthy's testimony is of primary importance to the defense. Regardless of what the State intends to do, we expect to subpoena him as our witness."

"In that case," Brooks said sharply, "we will contend that he is an unreliable witness and ask that the court call him as the *court's* witness. So that, if necessary, *both* sides can cross-examine him."

Sabath adjusted his pince-nez, lifted an eyebrow at Krum. "Well, Counselor?"

Krum said, "The defense must object, Your Honor. It is vital to the interests of our client that we be able to use normal legal procedure to question Ruthy."

Sabath said, "Mister Brooks's suggestion that Ruthy become the Court's witness seems the sensible way out of this dilemma and still follow established precedent. Your objection is overruled. Now, let's have the jury back in here."

Judge Sabath said, "How long have you been on the police force, Mister Ruthy?"

"Since 1922, Your Honor. But I've been off duty now and then because of this sickness in my head."

"Were you on duty at Michigan Avenue and Randolph Street at or about one-thirty P.M. on June ninth of last year?"

"Yes sir, I was."

"Do you recall anything unusual as happening at that time and place on that day?"

"Well, I had this vision, Judge."

Sabath motioned for Brooks to come forward, said, "You may cross-examine, Counselor."

"Officer Ruthy," Brooks began, "will you tell this court and the gentlemen of the jury about the vision you speak of?"

"I will be glad to," Ruthy said, "if they will understand my vision. There was a policeman right in front of me. Then he was gone and this man was running right toward me and he was nearly hit by this automobile. I paid no more attention to that. I still had this vision in front of me. Somebody hollered, 'Get him,' and I turned around and ran. The man ahead of me was running and the vision also.

"He went up the alley," Ruthy said. "And so did this vision. Then the man and the vision, both, were gone and I don't know where. So I went back and down into the tunnel to the trains, you see. Gee whiz, I didn't know what about that then. There was a man lying there. On his stomach. And there was a hat lying there, and a little gun."

Wayland Brooks said, "Would the bailiff bring this witness a glass of water, please?"

Ruthy, red-faced and sweating, his hand trembling, took the glass, gulped down the contents. Waiting till the officer had regained composure, Brooks said, "Would you mind telling the jury, Officer, if you have had other . . . difficulties with your, ah, head?"

"Well, I still have plenty of them," Ruthy said. "I do not know just how to express myself. I get them . . . I will make it from the good Lord down. They come in front of me, just like Abe Lincoln. I never seen Abe Lincoln in my life, he just comes. Last Sunday night I had a black dog over my face, plain. And not so long ago I had a vision. It seemed to be terrible, the years to come, for people to raise children, white people in general, to think they will be ruled by the yellow race. I cannot help it, I am telling you that is just what comes."

Brooks said, "Thank you, Officer," and returned to his place at the table.

Sabath said, "Will the defense cross-examine?"

Piquett started to rise. Krum caught him by the sleeve, said softly, "Watch it, for chrissake. The whole jury's about ready to bust out crying."

Positioning himself between Ruthy and the jury, Piquett said solicitously, "Do you feel up to answering a few more questions, Officer Ruthy? I'll try to be brief."

"I am trying to help," Ruthy said.

"I know that, sir. . . . Now, was it during your visionary moments when you identified Frankie Foster as the man who you chased that day, the man who gunned down Alfred Lingle? Or was it Abraham Lincoln?"

"Abraham Lincoln?" Ruthy said. "It wasn't Abe Lincoln."

"In fact," Piquett said, "it wasn't a vision at all, was it? Wasn't it actually Frank Foster you chased up Randolph Street on June ninth?"

"It was this vision," Ruthy said. "It came running up from the tunnel and across the street."

"When you were in court a few months ago, at the time Frank Foster was arraigned, while you were testifying there, did you talk about these visions you claim to have?"

"No sir. I guess I didn't."

"Would you mind repeating that answer, sir? Raise your voice, please, so that the jury can be sure to hear you."

Ruthy said, "I guess I didn't tell about the visions then."

Piquett gave the jury a meaningful look, then stepped away. "That will be all, Officer."

Sabath said, "Mister Brooks? Have you other questions for this witness?"

"No, Your Honor."

Sabath said, "You may step down, Mister Ruthy."

Wayland Brooks said, "That concludes our case, Your Honor. The People rest."

Piquett said, "May I have a moment, Your Honor? To confer with my associate?"

"Make it brief, please."

Piquett returned to the defense table, held a whispered conversation with Cantwell, then said, "If Your Honor please, at this time the defense has a motion. Without the jury present."

"Very well."

Once the jury had filed out, Sabath said, "Let's hear the motion, Counselor."

Piquett said, "It goes to a directed verdict, Your Honor. Nothing has been shown that the defendant fired the shot. The nearest the prosecution can tie in the gun was the fact that a witness says he *concludes* the defendant dropped a gun. Also, there is no motive shown; in fact the prosecution's entire case rests solely on eyewitness identification. In light of all this, the defense moves that the court instruct the jury to bring in a verdict of 'Not guilty.'"

Sabath said, "Do you desire to answer, Mister Brooks?"

"Move to deny, Your Honor."

"The motion," Sabath said, "is denied."

Piquett's shoulders lifted in a faint shrug. "Objection."

"Overruled. You may take an exception."

"Yes. We take an exception."

"Noted. Let's have the jury in and go on."

20

DAY TWELVE

Lawrence O'Malley said, "Yes sir, I seen the man that done the shooting. I was inside of six feet of him at the most."

Turning toward the defense table, Piquett said, "Mister Brothers. Will you stand up, please?"

Brothers got to his feet, gave the man in the witness chair a tentative smile. Piquett said, "Take a good look at this man, Mister O'Malley, and tell the jury if he is the one you saw, from a distance of less than six feet, shoot Alfred Lingle."

"No sir, he sure ain't," O'Malley said. "Nothing like him. Guy I saw do the shooting looked more like a wop."

Brothers sat down. Piquett said, "Your witness."

Wayland Brooks said, "When was it, Mister O'Malley, that you first notified the authorities you'd seen Lingle shot?"

O'Malley said, "When I first saw the picture of this fella I just looked at—Brothers—in the *Tribune* as being arrested for the killing."

"Do you regard yourself as a public-spirited citizen?"

"Yes sir. I sure do."

"Then as a public-spirited citizen, why did you let seven

2 4 9

months—*seven months,* Mister O'Malley—pass before going to the police with your story?"

O'Malley glared at him, said, "The reason is I own my own home and was working, making big money at the time, and I did not want to have my home bothered if it was a gangster, and I did not want to have my job interfered with. I was making more money than I could if I fooled around with any public officers."

"So much for public spirit, eh, Mister O'Malley?"

Piquett bounded from his chair, screamed, "Oh, Your Honor, I pro—"

"Withdraw the question," Brooks said, smiling. "I've finished with this witness."

Robert Cantwell said, "How close were you to him?"

"Not over five feet," Richard Sewell said. "I saw his full face and profile."

"Now that you have taken a good close look at the defendant, can you tell us if he is the man you saw?"

"He definitely is not the man I saw."

"Thank you," Cantwell said and turned away.

Without leaving his chair, Brooks said, "You heard this shot, you saw a man run from the tunnel, you saw the attempt to catch him. Is all that correct, Mister Sewell?"

"It is, yes sir."

"And what, if anything, did you do immediately after that?"

"I got on a bus and went home."

"How long afterward did you notify the police of what you saw that day?"

"Well, I can't say exactly."

"Days? Weeks? Months?"

"A couple of months, I suppose it was."

"Wouldn't four months be more like it?"

"Well . . ."

"You may step down, Mister Sewell."

Piquett said, "The man seated between Mister Cantwell and Mister Krum at the defense table. Is he the man you saw shoot Alfred Lingle on the day in question?"

"Absolutely not," Richard Dimvale said. "Wrong size and wrong color hair."

"Your witness, Mister Brooks."

Brooks said, "A few moments ago you stated that the killer had black hair, isn't that right, Mister Dimvale?"

"Yes sir."

Brooks returned to the table, picked up a sheet of paper, came back to the man on the stand, said, "Yet at the detective bureau that same afternoon did you not sign this statement declaring the killer's hair was blond?"

"Well, yes sir, I expect I did. But I must have been a bit overexcited at the time."

"That's all, Mister Dimvale."

The witness left the stand. Judge Sabath looked at his notes, then glanced over at the defendant's three attorneys. "Well, gentlemen?"

Tyrrell Krum rose slowly to his feet. Nothing showed in his expression. "Your Honor, the defense rests."

DAY THIRTEEN

After lighting his fifth Camel of the last hour from the butt of the fourth, Leo Brothers went back to pacing the holding-cell floor.

Right off the bat he shoulda said, "Look, I don't like this idea doing time for something I never done in the first place. So count me out, okay?"

Sure, he could've said that. And ended up in a ditch or the bottom of the fucking lake. You don't say no to Al Capone and live to tell about it. Or maybe a ditch or the lake'd be better'n waiting till they got around to frying your ass in that fireless cooker down there in Joliet.

Because that was damn well where it looked like he was headed. You could see it by the way that jury wouldn't even *look* at him, for chrissake. He remembered hearing somewhere that was a bad sign. Who wants to look at a guy you're going to burn? Even his own lawyers. They didn't have to tell him. You could see it in their face.

Fourteen years, the Big Fella said. Out in eight and we take good care of you the rest of your life. Yeah? What if he was shitting you? Nobody could be all that sure what a jury's going to do. They come back and say burn old Leo. What then? You start yelling how you're innocent? That old Scarface set you up? They'd laugh in your stupid face!

A key turned in the barred door. "They're waiting for you downstairs, pal," the guard said.

"Tony Ruthy broke their backs," Brooks said. "Juries expect a police officer to side with the prosecution, so his testimony usually gets no special credence. But let him get on the stand and, as in this case, say it *wasn't* Brothers he'd chased . . . we'd be the ones wearing long faces instead of Krum and Piquett."

"I'd like to share your confidence, Wayland," Charles Rathbun said. "But I regret to say that I still have my doubts. We haven't been able to pin the gun to Brothers. And motive hasn't been established."

"Those are loose ends we can tie up in our summation," John Holman said.

"And tied up they will be," Brooks said. "Gentlemen, let me crawl out on a limb right here and now. The jury won't need more than . . . all right, eight hours. Ten at the most. And the verdict we'll get? Guilty. The sentence? Death!"

Knuckles rapped twice at the conference room's closed door.

Wayland Brooks picked up the .38-caliber Colt revolver, held it aloft, said, "The murder weapon, gentlemen of the jury. Who can say how many hands—criminal hands—it has passed through since leaving the Von Frantzius gun shop nearly three years ago? How can we know? How can anyone know? Criminals don't keep such incriminating records.

"But I can tell you where this gun ended up," Brooks said. "On that tunnel floor, discarded there by Leo Brothers. Tossed aside by this hired killer after cold-bloodedly and with malice aforethought shooting Alfred Lingle to death."

Replacing the gun with the other exhibits, Brooks said, "Let us now consider the motive behind Alfred Lingle's murder. Gentlemen, what is the motive for *any* gangland killing? The elimination of a business rival? Revenge for a double cross? Retaliation for some earlier gangland murder? It is entirely likely that Leo Brothers never laid eyes on Jake Lingle till he was pointed out as the designated target. For that is gangland's way."

Brooks thrust a finger at the defendant, said, "Gentlemen of the jury, there is no penalty too severe for the coward who pulled that trigger. For his crime the People ask that Leo Brothers be found guilty of murder in the first degree and that he be put to death in the manner prescribed by the laws of this great state. . . . I thank you."

During his three-hour summation to the jury, Louis Piquett, for the defense, made reference to the Last Supper, the American flag, the "bumping off" of Julius Caesar, the depressed state of the economy, the Eighteenth Amendment, the Republican Party, and the defendant's white-haired mother.

"The great question here," he thundered, "is who killed Jake Lingle and why. Why have you not been informed of the motives behind the prosecution of this young man? Is it a prosecution by the state's attorney? Or is it a prosecution fostered by the all-powerful *Chicago Tribune*?

"You know as well as I do," Piquett said, "that the State has been unable to show motive in this case. After eight months of investigation by that master psychologist and detective, Pat Roche, they haven't found the motive behind Lingle's murder.

"I repeat: who killed Jake Lingle and why? Gentlemen of the jury, I say to you that this is the most gigantic frame-up since the crucifixion of Christ!"

DAY FIFTEEN

Judge Joseph Sabath said, "Mister Crotzer, has the jury reached a verdict?"

The foreman got to his feet. "We have, Your Honor."

"And how say you?"

Reading aloud from the sheet of paper he was holding, Herman W. Crotzer said, "We, the jury, find the defendant, Leo V. Brothers, otherwise called Louis V. Bader, guilty of murder in manner and form as charged in the indictment, and we fix his punishment at imprisonment in the penitentiary for the term of fourteen years."

"Shit!" muttered C. Wayland Brooks.

"Okay," juror number three said, "you guys want a statement, I'll give ya a statement. Right off, nine of us wanted to send this cocksucker—excuse me—up for life. Two even wanted to stick his ass in the electric chair. Maybe Lingle *wasn't* exactly on the up-and-up, but from what I hear he was a pretty decent sorta fella. Good-looking wife and a couple real cute kids, ya know? A cinch he wasn't no gangster like this Leo Brothers.

"Anyway," juror number three said, "there's this one guy, he wanted to let Brothers off altogether. Can you feature that? The rest of us was finally ready to settle for life, no parole. But ya think this one fella I mentioned—streetcar conductor name of Hagelman, I think it is—would give in? Not a chance! You was to ask me, I'd say somebody paid him off! But don't put that in your papers, okay?

"Well," juror number three said, "after twenty-seven hours, for godsake, this conductor, or whatever, said he'd go for fourteen years—take it or leave it. What the hell could we do? Spend the rest of our life in that stinking room?"

AFTERMATH

The good people of Chicago have every reason
to celebrate. For this is the day the mobs
died!

—*Charles Rathbun*
April 3, 1931

21

Alphonse Capone said, "Hey, John! About time you got here. Pull up a chair. Frank, pour the man a drink!"

"A highball'd hit the spot," John Hagan said. "Scotch." He sat down across from Capone, leaned back, crossed his legs, said, "I assume you've already heard the news?"

Capone laughed. "'Heard the news,' my ass! I *make* the news in this town, my friend."

Frank Rio came over, handed Hagan a Scotch and soda. Hagan drank deeply, set the glass on the edge of the desk. He said, "I must admit, Mister Capone, I never thought you'd actually pull it off."

"Too bad they're not all this easy," Capone said. "Take this income-tax rap I got coming up. That one's gonna cost me some real dough to fix. But at least I finally'll get Roche and them fucking raidsa his offa my back."

He opened the desk's center drawer, took out an envelope, tossed it over to Hagan, said, "For one hell of a job, John. Go ahead, count it. It's not enough, say so."

John Hagan turned back the flap and took out a sheaf of bank notes. He leafed through them, looked up, said, "Twenty-*five* thousand, Mister Capone? I understood you to say—"

"Call the extra five a bonus," Capone said. "One thing I'm not is a piker. Tack on that reward money the papers owe you for turning in Brothers, and you got yourself—what? Around seventy-five grand? Just don't let 'em Jew you out of it, is all."

Hagan said, "Looks like I'm going to have a problem there. This lawyer—Rathbun? Talked to him on the phone only a couple hours ago."

"So?"

Hagan said, "Well, going by what the colonel told him, looks like the *Tribune*'ll pay me their twenty-five. But word's already around the rest of them may end up reneging on me.

"Not," Hagan said, "that they're going to come right out and say so, but the way I get it, they don't believe Leo Brothers did the job on Lingle at all."

Wayland Brooks said, "From what I hear, Louie Piquett's talking appeal."

"Man doesn't have a leg to stand on," Rathbun said. He picked a glass of champagne from the tray of a passing waiter. "Not that it'll keep him from taking it all the way to the Supreme Court of the sovereign state of Illinois. Hates to lose, does our Mister Piquett. Even when he gets off lucky."

At nine o'clock that same evening, the state's attorney's branch office on the fifth floor at 77 West Washington Street was crowded with staff members, newsmen, political figures, along with assorted well-wishers and hangers-on of both sexes. Temporary bars dispensed a variety of liquors, hor d'oeuvres were varied and plentiful, and a radio near the switchboard was bringing in the music of Duke Ellington's band from the Edgewater Beach Hotel.

Patrick Roche, alone in his office, heels on the desk top and holding a glass of uncut King's Ransom, looked up as a *Daily News* reporter wandered in with a drink of his own. He set a plate of canapés on the desk, said, "Dig in, Pat," and sank into a chair.

Roche lowered his feet, picked out a couple of cheese-loaded crackers, used his drink to wash them down.

The reporter said, "You look tired, Pat. Kind of used up, huh?

Working on one case damn near a year? Oughta take yourself some time off. A nice vacation."

" 'Tis a thought that's crossed my mind, the vacation," Roche said. "Maybe even make it a permanent one, far's working for the state goes."

"The hell you say! What all of a sudden brought this on?"

"Nothing I want to get into."

"All right if I print it?"

Roche yawned, shrugged, sampled his drink, said, "Call me first of the week and I'll let you know. One way or the other."

"But let's say you do pull out. What next?"

Roche said, "Well, Walter and me . . . You know Walter. Walter Wendt?"

"Come on, Pat," the reporter said. "Walter? Known the guy for I don't know how long it's been."

"Anyway," Roche said, " 'tis an idea we've been kicking around now the last couple months. Go into business. Open our own agency. Private detectives."

"The hell you say! Wendt anywhere around?"

"He begged off for tonight. Something about coming down with a cold, the man."

In the outer office, metal rapped sharply against a glass and the voice of Charles Rathbun rose above the crowd sounds. "Ladies and gentlemen. May I have your attention, please?"

Voices stilled and the room gradually quieted. "I'll call you, Pat," the reporter said and went out, leaving his drink on the desk. Pat found another cracker, this one coated with anchovy paste, and stayed where he was.

Raising his voice, Rathbun said, "I want to express my appreciation to each and every one for coming here tonight. As you know, during the past ten months or so, the members of our relatively small organization have put aside all personal interests to join in what I can only refer to as a crusade—a crusade for justice, a crusade to restore the honor and good name of our city.

"We had been given a job to do," Rathbun said. "A job which in light of past investigations of a like nature, seemed almost impossible to carry out successfully. Today, with the conviction and sentencing of Leo Brothers that job is finished.

"But far more has been accomplished," Rathbun said, "than the answer to who killed Alfred Lingle. For the first time in the history of organized crime in Chicago, a gangland killing has resulted in a conviction. No longer can its gunmen be sure of immunity from the law. No longer can its crime lords maintain their power by wholesale threats, violence, and murder.

"In short, ladies and gentlemen," Rathbun said, "this is the day the mobs died!"

A burst of applause followed that last ringing statement. Roche had heard enough. Rising, he tossed down the rest of the drink, got into his topcoat, clapped on his hat and left the suite.

A reporter with the City News Bureau followed him out, walked with him to the elevators. Once Roche had accepted the offer of a cigarette and a light, the newsman said, "For what was supposed to be the trial of the century, this one was sure a letdown. Like watching your neighbor water the lawn."

Roche said, "And what was it you were after expecting? Another Leopold and Loeb, this case? Maybe like in the movies, somebody jumps up in court there and confesses at the last minute?"

"Well, Jesus, Pat. This guy was up for murder. You'd think they'd at least—"

"Sure enough, he was," Roche said. "Except both sides knew going in, the man was cooked. Hell, even the jury knew it, you could see it on their faces that first day. Wayland Brooks? He sleepwalked through the whole trial, didn't break a sweat. And what kind of a defense is it that takes one day—*one day!*—to put on, supposed to keep a client outta the chair. On a speeding ticket they'd'a done better!

"I don't know," Roche said, "what went on in that jury room. But when they came back in and said fourteen-to-life, I thought Brooks *and* Piquett would shit their pants on the spot. To them both, it was seeing a dead man rise up from his coffin. A man who should never'a been in that courtroom to begin with."

The elevator door rolled open. Roche said, " 'Tis long past my bedtime, Larry. Goodnight to you." And he turned away.

The Bureau man caught him by the sleeve. "Wait a minute! What d'ya mean, he shouldn't've been in the courtroom to begin with? Brothers?"

"All right, Larry," Roche said. "Here's me last words on the subject. One'a these days the truth's bound to come out. I only hope to Christ I'm still around when it does."

The elevator door clanged shut behind him.

FOR THE RECORD

Patrick T. Roche—After resigning as chief investigator for the Cook County State's Attorney, Roche and Walter Wendt formed Patrick Roche Services, a private detective agency. In 1934, Roche ran unsuccessfully as the Republican candidate for the office of Cook County Sheriff. In 1945, he was placed in charge of the municipal fingerprint and identification bureau. Roche died of natural causes on July 11, 1955.

Walter Wendt—At the time of his death of natural causes on February 16, 1962, Wendt managed two South Side bowling lanes. He was seventy-five.

Charles F. Rathbun—While a resident of Augusta, Georgia, and after a long and distinguished career as an attorney, Rathbun died of natural causes in November 1955.

Colonel Robert Rutherford McCormick—Died April 1, 1955, of natural causes.

C. Wayland Brooks—In 1940, backed by the *Chicago Tribune*, Brooks became a United States Senator, serving in that capacity from 1940 to 1949. He died of natural causes on January 11, 1957.

Alphonse Capone— On October 24, 1931, Capone was sentenced to prison for eleven years for income tax evasion. Between that date and November 16, 1939, he served out his time in federal penitentiaries. On January 25, 1947, his mind and body ravaged by syphilis, Alphonse Capone died of bronchial pneumonia at his Palm Island estate off the coast of Florida. He was forty-eight.

Leo Vincent Brothers— In 1936, former Chicago mayor William Hale Thompson told the Illinois Parole Board that Brothers had been "convicted on framed-up evidence." After his release from the Illinois state prison on June 10, 1940, Brothers was returned to St. Louis, tried and acquitted of the 1929 murder of a cab driver. Shortly afterward he was given partnerships in mob-operated taxicab and loan companies in St. Louis. On September 18, 1950, Brothers was shot down at his suburban home by an unidentified gunman and died of his wounds three months later.

Frankie Foster (Ferdinand Bruna)— Three months after the Brothers conviction, the indictment against Foster for the Lingle murder was dropped. He left Chicago soon afterward and for years was employed by Nevada gaming casinos. He died of natural causes in Los Angeles on April 22, 1967.

John Hagan— Although the *Chicago Tribune* paid Hagan a $25,000 reward for information leading to the conviction of Lingle's putative killer, other Chicago newspapers reneged on paying their share, privately stating that they did not believe Brothers was guilty. Hagan later bought a farm near Unionville, Missouri, sold it a few years later, and moved to Collinsville, Missouri. After the death of his wife, he remarried and moved to Newport, Virginia. On July 11, 1954, Hagan died of natural causes. He was sixty-one.

George "Bugs" Moran— After abdicating as Chicago's North Side ganglord, Moran's criminal career declined steadily. In 1957, while serving a sentence in Leavenworth for bank robbery, he died of natural causes and was buried in the prison cemetery. He was sixty-four.

Police Officer Anthony Ruthy— On April 28, 1931, three weeks after the close of the Brothers trial and while on duty at his Michigan Avenue post, Ruthy was shot dead by "person or persons unknown."

Danny Stanton— After Al Capone disappeared from the Chicago scene, Stanton was eased completely out of the organization. On May 5, 1943, he was shot dead during a barroom brawl on Chicago's South Side. The killer pleaded self-defense and was released.